NIGHT WITCH

Also by *New York Times* bestselling author Jaymin Eve

WEATHERSTONE COLLEGE
Spellcaster

SHADOW BEAST SHIFTERS
Rejected
Reclaimed
Reborn
Deserted
Compelled
Glamoured

SHIFTER CITY FATED MATES
A Curse of Fate
A Twist of Luck
A Claim of Fortune
A Bond of Trust

FALLEN FAE GODS
Gilded Wings
Crimson Skies

SUPERNATURAL ACADEMY
Year One
Year Two
Year Three

NIGHT WITCH

JAYMIN EVE

MIRA

Recycling programs
for this product may
not exist in your area.

ISBN-13: 978-1-335-00117-7

Night Witch

MIRA
22 Adelaide St. West, 41st Floor
Toronto, Ontario M5H 4E3, Canada
MIRABooks.com

HarperCollins Publishers
Macken House, 39/40 Mayor Street Upper,
Dublin 1, D01 C9W8, Ireland
www.HarperCollins.com

Printed in Lithuania

To those who fight their monsters in the dark.

You are not alone.

We fight together.

NIGHT WITCH

CHAPTER 1

Music pumped around me. It was Eighties Night, and as Whitney Houston's "I Wanna Dance with Somebody" blasted through the rink, I skated past a lilac-haired chick with heavy eyeliner, hip checking her in the side and sending her flying. "Bitch," she screeched, tumbling into the wall, but I didn't look back. She'd been gunning for me all night; I just got the first decent hit in.

Roller Derby was therapeutic, and I was all about keeping my temper in check these days. This was the perfect solution to working off my frustrations.

When the event was over, and I'd been hit more than once myself, I dragged my sorry, exhausted ass off the floor and up to the booth where I'd left my sneakers. Switching out of my skates, I hobbled over to my cubby to stash them, then made my way to the counter to finish my shift. But before I got there, a shout grabbed my attention.

"Paisley Hallistar, you are fucking brutal."

Spinning with a shriek, I threw myself at Sara Collier, one of my best friends from Weatherstone College. I wrapped my arms around her, and she made happy noises as we rocked back and forth and hugged through "Like a Prayer" by Madonna.

My eyes were damp when I pulled away to look her over.

Dressed in her skinny jeans, a tight red sweater, and red heels, she looked gorgeous. "You actually made it." Swiping at my cheeks to catch any escaped tears, I was surprised to find a smile on my face. A real smile. For the first time in a month.

"Of course I did. You needed me, girl, and now that I'm back from Romania, you've got me for as long as it takes."

"Haley?" I asked, checking in on our other bestie, Haley Michaels, who'd been trying to make this trip as well.

The three of us had been separated since the end of the school year, during which I'd had everything I knew about myself and my life torn apart.

Sara shook her head, and a fraction of my excitement faded. "Her dad's injury is worse than they thought. She's going to stay and help out for a few more days. But she'll meet us in the city for your dad's trial."

Haley's dad had broken his right leg, left arm, and a few ribs at his job on the docks. A cable had snapped, sending heavy boxes tumbling down around him. They didn't have money for healers, so he was going to have to go about it the human way, which meant a fairly extensive recovery process.

"I'll send another care package," I said, lifting my long hair off my sweaty neck in search of a cool breeze. Winter might be approaching, but this room was always packed and stifling during derby nights.

"I'll go halves," Sara said, before she grabbed my hand again. "I'm so excited to finally be here. *Sleepover at Paisley's.* After you tell me all the news, of course."

Technically, I was still on shift, but my boss wouldn't care with the night winding down, so I dragged Sara over to the chairs in the corner and we collapsed together. "I have so much to tell you," I said as we faced each other. "I've been scared to text details because this is crazy shit."

Sara didn't look surprised—I might have been cagey in

texts and calls, but she knew the basics from last year and what I'd managed to convey in cryptic messages. "I've got the rest of winter break, so spill everything."

Taking a deep breath, I attempted to organize my thoughts before deciding there was no making sense of what had happened. Lowering my voice to a sliver above a whisper, I said, "I'm the one who created the monsters."

Might as well hit her with the biggie and hope her first instinct wasn't to punch—or hex—me. Or worse, report me to the High Council of Magic.

I trusted my friends, but after Belle—the fourth of our friendship group, and the one I was trying my best not to think about—spilled my secrets to her father last year, it was hard to not have doubts. Even if I was fairly sure that particular friend had *innocently* dropped my ass in the fire.

To Sara's credit, she didn't freak out. Her eyes widened, and her lips parted, but she remained silent.

"I didn't know," I hurried to add. "It's to do with my affinity, and what I think is a recessive gene that allows me to touch previously off-limit planes of existence. I don't know if it means I'm just a beefed-up necromancer or what, but there's a difference in my magic."

A magic I still knew very little about and that wasn't under my control.

Sara's eyes grew even wider, until she resembled an anime character. "It killed someone," she blurted as the color drained from her pretty features.

I closed my eyes, forcing panic and disgust back inside the box where I'd been shoving them for weeks. Knowing I was directly to blame for the death of a student had given me a new set of nightmares to add to the old ones, making me wake up screaming more than once.

"I'm trying to figure out how to live with that," I said

when I could face her again. My emotions were locked down hard because I couldn't lose it. *Not ever again.* "I don't know what to do once the monsters are here. I can't get angry or upset, because it could trigger another event, and I'm not sure I can even go back to Weatherstone next year."

That had Sara jerking upright and grabbing my arm, and to my surprise, she showed no hesitance or fear in touching me. "You have to come back! How else will you learn to control it unless you're at the best magic school in the country?"

"I don't think Weatherstone can help me. If this is the recessive gene, it was wiped out centuries ago." Though clearly some of us had slipped through the cracks. Like Gran.

"Start at the beginning," Sara said, still holding me. "Tell me everything."

Fuck. This was not going to be a short conversation, but with Kate Bush's "Running Up That Hill" blaring as the perfect background track, I decided I couldn't keep trying to navigate this alone. My parents had promised to tell me everything they knew, but it turned out, outside of the book they'd given me and the letters from Gran, they didn't know much. My affinity had taken all of us by surprise.

The two biggest changes were Gran's letters providing a potion that would suppress the magic and the loss of my crystals. All forms of crystal amplified my powers, which was a big *no* at the moment.

Oh, and Mom had also made me promise never to talk about my abilities to anyone. Not to my siblings. Not to my friends.

I'd tried to keep my promise, but I was breaking apart in ways that I feared I couldn't come back from. I had to talk to someone about it, and Sara hadn't run screaming . . .

"Logan and I got into a fight . . . that night on All Hallows' Eve . . . right after you left me in the graveyard. It was about Dad, and the suspension from school, and he basically implied that Belle was the one who got Dad into trouble by spilling everything to Elder Monroe."

Sara didn't look shocked by this either. "I've been thinking this over and drew the same conclusion about Belle's new relationship with her dad being half of our trouble. In a bid to get him to love her, she revealed everything. She wouldn't expect he'd use that information to try to hurt her friend."

"Yep, and considering I've barely heard from her . . . She doesn't answer my calls, and her return texts are so short that they might as well be a fucking thumbs-up emoji."

"Me and Haley too." Sara's face fell. "She's cut us all off."

"Or her dad cut her off from us."

We exchanged a dark stare, but there was nothing we could do to help Belle at the moment. I'd be seeing her father in the city in a few days, when Dad's trial got underway.

I'd hopefully get some answers then.

"Okay, so you had a fight . . ." Sara prodded me along.

"Right, we had a fight, and I was so pissed off. He riled me up until I wanted to punch him in the fucking junk."

Sara gave a shrugging nod. "I bet that's not all you want to do with his junk. It's impressive junk. You don't damage the goods unless you've used them first."

It felt weird to laugh, but she wasn't completely wrong. "Keep it in your pants, witch. Logan is most likely an evil bastard, no matter how sexy he looks."

Sara didn't appear convinced.

I continued. "When we fought, the blanket suppressing Weatherstone was gone, and with the All Hallows' energy beating down on me, my own power was swirling like crazy. Then the monsters started to appear. I was jabbing my finger at Logan, and with each one, another creature showed up." My voice shook as I recalled the moment I realized it had been me all along. "I couldn't really deny my involvement after that."

"We felt the energy," she told me, her voice softening. "Everyone in the whole school did. When we couldn't find you in the graveyard, we freaked the fuck out and raced for the headmaster, only to find him on the phone with your dad, who said he'd stopped by to grab you early. Not that we fucking believed him, but we couldn't do much until we called you the next day."

When Sara and Haley called, I'd barely managed more than a couple of awkward sentences, since I couldn't reveal any secrets over the phone. Mom had made me promise—she might not have answers, but she did have new rules. She'd lose her shit if she knew I was spilling all of this to Sara.

"Do you think I'm a monster too?" One of my greatest fears was that by the time the dust settled on everyone learning who I was, I'd be completely alone. "Now that you know the truth?"

Sara's face crumpled and a tear escaped as she threw herself forward, hugging me as tightly as she could. "Paisley Hallistar," she rasped against my shoulder. "I should smack you. I would never think you were a monster." She pulled away and I stared into the depths of her dark eyes. "Magic is volatile, and you're dealing with a recessive gene of energy that was wiped out years ago. This is not your fault. You're one of the best witches I've ever known, and you risked your life to try to kill that monster."

The irony of battling a monster that I'd conjured wasn't lost on me, and my mind drifted to the book. *The Reapers of Purgatory* was the only book I'd found that contained information about my affinity. *Night witch.*

Night witches were said to exist in the shadows and consume the darkness. We were vilified as demon-witches by the very council who had wiped *every one of us they could find* from existence. In the book, we were also referred to as *reapers*, but it wasn't clear why.

The book itself wasn't particularly long, but it detailed a maternally-passed-on affinity that was so terrifying to the magical community that in the late 1800s they tested every witch and destroyed the ones who were reapers. Then they cast a spell to wipe them from the memories of every other magical being.

But a few survived.

A few like my gran, who smuggled these books with them so they could let their daughters know what to expect. Only select witches inherited the gene. Neither of my sisters had or my mom—but I did. Mom had come for me that night after reading the letters Gran left her, letters she'd ignored for decades, only to feel the pull to read them that night. She'd felt my explosion of magic as well, the way a mother had a sixth sense when their children were in danger.

Gran had stepped in.

I knew it with every part of the magical essence inside me.

Are you a reaper? I'd asked Mom the next morning, and she shook her head.

I'm not a reaper, she'd whispered, face wreathed in anguish. It was clear she'd slept as little as me. *I know you're wondering if one of these monsters destroyed Logan's mom, and I wish I could tell you it wasn't, but I truly don't know what happened that day.*

I couldn't get more information out of her, and now we were silent strangers in a house filled with tension.

"So, what's the plan?" Sara asked as she leaned back in the uncomfortable vinyl chairs, which creaked every time one of us shifted. "How are you going to learn about your magic if you can't use it? Have you heard from Logan? He's clearly kept your secret, since the council isn't smashing your door down. He might be a good one to help us."

Logan Kingston. The spellcaster who was one of the most powerful warlocks in the world. His deep rumbling voice was never far from my mind . . .

Paisley belongs to me. You know that, and I'll kill anyone that takes her from me.

I'd asked Mom what he meant by that statement he'd made in the graveyard, and she'd waved me off. *He's acted as if he's had a claim on you since you were born. You should stay away from him. The last thing you need is to get attached to Rafael's son.*

It was excellent advice, and *there was no fucking way I was taking it.* My fascination with Logan wasn't going anywhere. If anything, it was stronger than ever. He owed me answers. I would not rest until I had them.

"Not a single word," I said with a huff. "Bastard claimed me and then ghosted."

It was Logan's modus operandi, so why it pissed me off so much was anyone's guess. To be fair, though, he had said he'd give Mom one month before he came for me. A timeline that ended tonight.

As Eighties Night started to wrap up, the lights grew brighter and it was time to start packing up. That part they wouldn't let me skip. "Let me clean up and clock out so we can get out of here. Mom said it was fine for you to take the spare room. Fair warning, it's no bigger than a closet."

Sara waved me off. "I'd sleep on the floor if it meant hanging with you, girl. Do your job. I'll wait here."

The relief at having my friend back, and the fact she hadn't run screaming from me when I confessed that I was responsible for the monsters who'd roamed Weatherstone last year, put extra pep in my step. I rushed through the last of the closing duties, zeroed out the cash register, and waved to James, my manager, as I walked out the door with Sara.

"Come on," I said, heading for my Jeep Wrangler. Well, Mom's Jeep that she let me borrow for work. My phone buzzed in my pocket as I pulled out of the rink's lot and headed for home, but I ignored it and asked Sara about her time in Romania.

"I have forty-two cousins," she said with a snort. "It was fucking chaos, even though I enjoyed catching up with them all. My Romanian is rusty though. They kept laughing at my accent."

By the time we got home, it was after midnight, and I was wrecked. Sara got settled in the guest room downstairs, and it was only when I crawled into bed after a quick shower that I remembered the buzz of my phone earlier.

Hoping like Hel it was Belle, I swiped the screen and tiredly squinted at the message.

Unknown number: Nice skating tonight, Precious.

Every iota of sleepiness fled my body as I tightened my hold on my phone, staring at the screen. Had Logan been at the rink tonight?

CHAPTER 2

After two sleeping pills and two hours of tossing and turning to get to sleep, I still woke stupidly early the next morning. As I rolled over with a yawn, my gaze rested on the phone sitting on my bedside table, and I was reminded of that late-night text. Swiping to check it was still there, I found myself hesitating over the reply before my annoyance at the spellcaster kicked in and I wrote back:

Paisley: How the fuck did you get my number?

Stalkcaster: I've had your number
since you first got a phone.

Wait, what?

Paisley: You've had my number since I was sixteen?

I'd actually been fifteen when I got my first phone, which there was no way he knew.

Stalkcaster: Fifteen, Precious. Don't lie to me, sweetheart.

Fucking Hel.

I'd saved his contact as "Stalkcaster" as a joke, but apparently my assumption that stalking *was* his favorite pastime was spot-on. Scary, *creepy* bastard.

Paisley: Okay, not creepy at all. But seriously, what do you want, Logan? Are you going to tell me about what happened in the graveyard . . . or maybe what happened when we were kids?

He read my message, and I waited for his reply, but when nothing came through, I threw the phone to the side. *Calm, Paisley. Calm the fuck down.*

My magic swirled, and I quickly counted the days since I'd had my last suppression potion. *Four.* I was definitely due for another dose, so shrugging on my robe, I slipped my phone in my pocket and headed downstairs.

Mom was in the kitchen, her smile guarded when I stepped into the sunny room. Everything gleamed, the cabinets shiny and white, and the scent of mint and lavender from her cleaning spell was as familiar as the witch herself. "Morning," I said huskily, desperate for coffee. "Sara not awake yet?"

"Not yet, honey," she said, and I closed my eyes as she ruffled my hair. It almost felt like old times, but then she was gone, choosing not to linger.

Grabbing a mug, I filled it with coffee, cream, and sugar, and tried not to wish it were a Weatherstone breakfast cart coffee. I'd kill for one of their sandwiches as well.

Taking my mug into the living room, I found my oldest brother, Trevor, in conversation with Dad. Trevor eyed me for a beat, before turning away to pretend I didn't exist.

This had become my norm since the end of my first year at Weatherstone.

When my parents refused to tell my brothers and sisters about my affinity, and they'd forced me to do the same, my siblings felt betrayed. We didn't keep secrets, and they always had my back. They didn't understand why this situation was different, and to see the censure in their eyes broke me. I'd never felt lonelier in my life.

If Mom hadn't scared me by pointing out that everyone in our family would be under scrutiny from the council, I'd have spilled everything weeks ago. It was only my siblings' safety that held my tongue.

Sara, hopefully, wasn't as closely connected and wouldn't be monitored. It'd been a weak moment to spill my secret last night, and I could only hope there'd be no fallout from it.

Wandering to the back porch, I descended the stairs into the garden and made my way out the side gate. I'd taken to walking out here, near Simon and Morris's enclosure. The twins' familiars weren't super friendly with me these days, but I felt closer to my sisters by being here.

Sara's voice drifted out through the open hallway window as she greeted my family, and I dismissed a brief worry that I should have stayed to make sure she was comfortable. Sara was not only confident, but she'd also met all my family before and always made herself at home wherever she was.

Lifting my head, I sent out a prayer to Selene that Sara wouldn't be in any danger from my desperate confessions last night. I mean, she wasn't a Hallistar and couldn't have anything to do with this fucked-up recessive gene.

Outside the gate, I headed deeper into the forest in search of solace and peace. My phone buzzed, and I forced myself not to check it like a desperate, needy witch. Logan Kingston was as destructive to me as the power I held inside myself. But there was no suppression potion that would work against him.

When I was surrounded by trees, I stopped and breathed in the damp scent of decaying matter—pine and cedar from the trees, and an earthiness that reminded me of magic. Of herbs and spells and Weatherstone.

I missed that stupid place. Or maybe I missed the *before* my life was torn to fucking pieces.

As my energy settled, I let nature hold my pain in her palm and give me a brief moment of reprieve.

My phone buzzed again, destroying my moment, and I couldn't ignore it any longer.

Stalkcaster: I'll tell you what bonds us, Paisley Hallistar.

Stalkcaster: And it will change everything.

There was a figurative explosion of flutters in my chest, and it was almost too much sensation to handle. Short, shallow breaths rocked me, and I barely held back a strangled yelp when a hand landed on my shoulder. I spun to find Sara, bleary-eyed and in a robe as well, shivering in the chilly forest air.

We hadn't had any snow yet this season, but it wouldn't be long if that icy breeze was any indication.

"Pais, you okay?" she asked, glancing into the dark undergrowth beyond, as if searching for a threat. I felt swirls of her air affinity move around us, warming the space. "What happened?"

Not sure what to tell her about Logan, because he was confusing as fuck and never followed any rules, I linked my arm through hers. "I'm all good. Just jumping at shadows. We should get inside."

She looked back once, then fell in step beside me. "After last night, I think we're past secrets, friend."

She was right. "Logan messaged me." She gasped and I quickly added, "I got it last night after you went to bed." Technically true, since I didn't read it until afterward.

"What did he say?"

Swallowing roughly, unsure how I felt, I mumbled, "That he was going to tell me what bonds us, and that it'll change everything."

Sara pulled me even closer. "I'm both terrified and turned on for you. It's a confusing combination."

I nudged her with a snort, before sobering. "Yeah, that pretty much sums it up."

We walked for a few seconds in silence and I found myself needing to warn her. "I know this goes without saying, but please don't talk to anyone about what I told you last night. My siblings don't even know because it's a dangerous situation. They're too closely related, but as my friend, I want you to be careful. I couldn't live with myself if anything happened to you."

Her delicate features took on a fierce glow. "Girl, you know I'll never speak a word of it. I'm here for you, and I will follow your lead." Her hug was just as fierce as her expression. "Love you, Pais."

"Love you too." I sniffled against her shoulder.

She jerked away. "Now, can we get back to the hottest fucking warlock in existence messaging you last night?"

"Hot but possibly evil," I reminded her.

Her rasp of laughter was comforting. "Come on, you know he's not evil. You can't possibly believe that after everything that happened. He saved your life multiple times, and you make sweet fucking magic together." Her eyes twinkled at the double entendre, since Logan and I had both made magic and slept together. "Change isn't always a bad thing, Pais. You two can't keep existing in this love-hate bubble. It's destructive, and you deserve better."

I soaked up her optimism, needing the bolster to my own. "You're right," I agreed, "we can't continue the way we were. But I have no idea if we can exist without animosity, thanks to our rather horrific family history. Will the truth set us free, or destroy us completely?"

She shrugged. "Either way, you have no choice but to take the leap." She tugged me toward the back porch. "Now come on, your mom was almost done with breakfast when I left, and I'm starving."

I followed her into the house, my nose twitching at the scent of bacon and pancakes.

My favorites.

Just like every other day of winter break.

My relationship with my parents might have been strained, but they showed their love in other ways. "I've got another shift today," I told Sara as we entered the kitchen. "You want to hang out at work?"

"Fuck yes. I'm here for you, babe. Your third sister, even if it's by choice and not blood."

My blood sisters, Jenna and Alice, were spending a lot of time with their new coven, Blessed Souls of Spokane, and barely came home to sleep. It made it easier to keep my secret, but also harder because I missed them so much. This was the change I'd been terrified of when they graduated from Weatherstone, and it hurt as much as I'd expected.

Needing a top-up before breakfast, I dragged Sara to the coffeepot, and she moaned when I handed her a cup. Black with sugar, as was her preference. "You are a goddess," she sighed.

Night witch, I mentally corrected.

Practically the same thing.

After I refilled my cup as well, we headed for the dining room, where Mom had already set the table and was ferrying food into the center. Along with the pancakes and bacon, she had fruit salad and yogurt. My other favorites.

I tried not to break down and bawl in front of everyone. Our family was strained, but we weren't broken. We'd loved each other through hard times before, and I had all the faith we'd come out the other side.

"Sara, we're so happy you could stay for the break," Mom said, giving her one of her genuine smiles.

"Me too, Mrs. Hallistar," she replied happily. "Thank you so much for extending the invitation to stay with Pais."

Mom shushed her. "You're always welcome. Have a seat, breakfast is almost ready."

Sara took the seat beside me, and I found myself staring at Jensen and Trevor, who were sprawled on the opposite side of the table. Trevor's expression was cool—even as his rage simmered just below the surface.

"Heard from Belle?" he asked politely.

Squinting at him, I shook my head. "Not really."

Sara snorted an unamused laugh. "Yeah, she's been hitting us with one-word replies at best."

The fires of Trevor's elemental energy burned bright in his eyes. "You don't think that's fucking strange? Shouldn't you give a shit and maybe check in on her?"

"Trevor!" Mom shot over her best motherly glare. "If you can't be polite, you can leave this room."

Trevor cursed again and shoved his chair back. "Yeah, probably a good fucking idea. I'd rather eat anywhere but here."

Jensen watched it all impassively and was the only one still treating me somewhat normally, even if he was reserved. He shot me a sympathetic smile, before tucking into his pancakes smothered in honey.

As the front door slammed and Trevor's car roared to life outside, my eyes burned, and I stared down at my plate. Breakfast had lost its appeal, but as Dad strolled in and took his seat at the end of the table, I forced myself to stay put.

With Dad's trial only days away, I needed these last moments of normalcy.

CHAPTER 3

After that awkward breakfast, Sara and I escaped to get dressed and head for the skate rink again. "Can you skate?" I asked her, when we pulled into the parking lot.

"Nope," she said, with emphasis. "If you put wheels on my feet, I will die."

I rolled my eyes. "Dramatic much? You'll be fine. I'll give you some lessons when I get a break."

Her expression indicated she'd rather visit a gynecologist healer than learn to skate, but she didn't argue as we got out of the Jeep and I locked the doors.

The rink had been open for a few hours already, but it was quiet through the week and wouldn't pick up until this evening. After I dropped my bag off in the cubby and introduced Sara to my manager, James, I deposited her on the couch. "I have a break in a couple of hours," I told her. "You good until then? Order food and drinks, and it's on me."

"Yes, I'm good, witch. Fuck off and do your job."

Ah, the love.

We were in the human world, but her use of the word *witch* wouldn't cause any issues. Humans would just assume it was a substitute for *bitch*, and in a way, it was.

James eyed me closely as I hurried behind the counter and grabbed a cloth, ready to wipe down the benches. "You okay, Hallistar?" he asked, the bright blue of his eyes deepening as he watched me.

His parents owned this place, and he'd been the manager for the last two years. He was twenty-five and the most relaxed human I'd ever met. He didn't sweat the small shit and let me skate as much as I needed to get out of my own head. It didn't hurt that he was hot, even if he wasn't my type. Tall, blond, blue-eyed, and tanned. He looked like a Californian surfer, except he hated swimming and would rather snowboard.

"All good," I shot back, with a sassy wink. "Just ready to wipe some tables."

He was propped against the counter, arms crossed over his broad chest as he drawled, "Yeah, you've always been my most enthusiastic cleaner."

Whoops. Yeah, cleaning wasn't my strong suit. Magic took care of it at home, so I was rather lazy in that department.

"Work in progress," I said with a shrug.

His smirk turned into a nice laugh. "Your progress is fine. Now get that cute ass to work."

He was a flirt, and I didn't even blink twice when he mentioned my ass. He'd never made any sort of move on me, and I figured by now that this was just how our friendship rolled.

A customer came up to rent skates and he turned away to serve them. As I got to work on a sticky table, my phone buzzed, and I immediately pulled it from my back pocket to read the message:

Stalkcaster: James Bronson wants to die.

My heart fucking stopped. The phone slipped from my fingers, and it was only the threadbare red carpet that stopped it from smashing. With panicked heartbeats filling my ears, I turned and glanced across the rink, but I couldn't see Logan anywhere.

"Paisley." I jerked when a strong hand wrapped around my wrist, only to find James's concerned face in front of me. "Sweetheart, are you okay?"

Shit. Fuck. Shit and fuck.

He held my phone, and I snatched it back to stop him reading the message. But he caught my wrist again and scanned the screen still lit up in my hand.

"What is this about?" he murmured, and I yanked on his hold, silently demanding he release me. "Do you have a jealous boyfriend waiting in the wings, Paisley?" He lifted his head and searched the room just as I'd done.

I shook my head, violently. "No! He's just an asshole. Ignore him. His bark is worse than his bite." *Absolute fucking lie.* Logan could wipe James out of existence with a flick of his energy.

Thankfully, when I tugged on my hand again, James released me and my phone. "Are you in trouble, Paisley?" His normally lighthearted expression was serious. "Do you need my help? Because I'm here for whatever you need."

My phone buzzed, and we both looked at it.

Stalkcaster: He has ten seconds, Precious.

I could practically feel Logan's fury and magic radiating around us.

I took a step away from James, and then another. "I'm totally fine," I assured him, needing him to believe me. "We should get to work." I waved to where two girls were waiting at the counter. Tiffany and Gertie came in here at least twice a week to flirt with James.

James examined me closely, and it was clear that he thought I was hiding from an abusive ex. Or something equally as nefarious.

Turning away from him, and hoping he'd take a hint and leave me alone, I quickly searched the room once more, but there was no sign of Logan. I shot back a quick text.

Paisley: Back the Hel off, fuckwit. James is my friend and that's all. Even if he wasn't, you don't get to dictate any part of my life. We screwed once. Stop being creepy.

I shoved my phone back in my pocket and got to work.

The next couple of hours passed quickly. James kept an annoyingly close eye on me, even as I took a break to give Sara some lessons. It turned out she was completely correct when she said if I put her on wheels she was going to die.

"You're not normally clumsy," I said with a burst of laughter as I grabbed her to stop a face-plant for the twentieth time. "What's happening here?"

She couldn't keep her balance, no matter how I tried to guide her. Eventually we gave up and ate nachos and drank soda for thirty minutes before I was hauled back to work by James.

My phone buzzed more than once during my shift, but I resolutely ignored it.

By the time Candace arrived to relieve me, I was exhausted, mostly from the tension of expecting Logan to show his face. Despite the messages indicating he was watching, he never made an actual appearance.

"Ready to go?" I slumped on the couch next to Sara.

She threw back the last of her wine—she'd finished a

bottle to calm her nerves after skate lessons—and jumped to her feet. "Go where? Can we go dancing? I need to burn off some of my powe—energy." She glanced around, but no humans were paying us any attention.

As a fully bloomed witch, I understood the fire in her blood.

The suppression potion, which I'd taken just before we left home, tempered my magic, but the fires burning deep inside were as strong as ever. "You need to get laid."

I received the full force of her puppy dog eyes. "Please, Paisley. Please, please."

It was only ten, so we had plenty of time to head out for the night. "You're cute when you beg," I said with a sigh. "Okay, let's swing by home so I can get changed. Then we'll catch an Uber."

Sara let out a shriek, drawing attention our way.

She didn't care.

"Let's go, witch. I'm so ready. It was a *long* few weeks in Romania."

I understood better than I wished I did.

My dry patch was a desert at this point. Might as well burn in the heat.

The Witching Hour was a club in downtown Spokane, and while it was open to humans, it was owned by a witch. No one knew which witch—*hah!*—but she catered to our kind. If you knew what to ask for.

"Come on, pleaseeee," Sara was begging *again*, and I caved *again*.

"Okay, one wine. ONE! I'm still hungover from the last time I drank witch wine."

Not to mention it ended up being one of the worst nights of my life, with Dad losing his job. One way or another, his trial would bring it all to an end, but I'd never forget waking up half-dead and learning what happened.

We weren't old enough to purchase the wine legally, but Sara had been chatting up a warlock at the bar, and he was more than happy to provide us with drinks in exchange for my bestie's ass in his hands as they danced in the middle of a floor filled with writhing bodies.

She was in her signature red, a short bodycon dress that hugged every curve. Her dark hair was curled down her back, and she wore five-inch heels to elevate her tiny stature.

Sipping my drink, I enjoyed the slide of warmth into my center as I watched the dance floor. The beat was dark and heavy, and with each sip of witch wine, the need to move filled me. My black dress was as tight and revealing as Sara's, leaving my long legs on display. I wore heeled boots that shot me just over six feet tall.

I'd decided to let loose tonight. Sara had curled my golden-brown hair and lined my eyes in smoky shadows. My magic was suppressed, there were no monsters—I was topped up on potion—and I could ignore my problems for a few hours.

Throwing back the wine, I set the glass on the table and headed for the dance floor. My phone, tucked in my black chain shoulder bag, buzzed against my side, and I felt it all the way through my blood.

I was still ignoring his messages.

There was a mix of human and magical folk dancing, and for once I didn't gravitate toward those with power. I just moved. The beat grew more intense, and with the heat of wine in my veins, I lifted my arms and swayed.

Losing myself.

Here, I wasn't a demon-witch responsible for deaths.

I wasn't worried about having my head removed due to a recessive gene.

I was a just a witch shaking her ass.

Firm hands landed on my hips, and as the scent of mint and evergreen washed over me, I released a long breath. I knew he'd come for me eventually, and now that he was here, the part of me that had been adrift since All Hallows' finally settled.

Letting myself lean against him, the beat and energy filled us as we moved. Logan's hard body pressed against my back, and his right hand slid possessively across my stomach, pulling me closer. Not a word was spoken, but our magic swirled with us, gliding over my skin until I was needy and breathless. We drew attention . . . or one of us did.

The six and a half feet of gorgeous warlock, no doubt, but I didn't care.

I'd been craving this moment since that first message . . . Actually, since the moment he told Mom that I belonged to him and he'd give her a month.

I'd been subconsciously counting down.

The connection between us was slightly dulled by the suppression potion, but my magic would always find Logan.

It would recognize its match, even in a crowd of a million.

Logan spun me to face him, and despite the heels, I still had to tilt my head back to meet the ice of his light green eyes. That mossy ring at the center drew me closer, and our movement slowed as electricity crackled in the air, and Logan leaned down.

I forgot how to breathe, anticipating what he'd do next. "Precious," he rumbled, a barely leashed ferality in my name. "You're so fucking gorgeous."

Those words sent a shiver down my spine, and I had to ask, "Where have you been? Why are you here now?"

His gaze remained firmly on my face as he took me in

like he'd missed every part of me. "I kept my word and left you alone for a month. But I can't stay away any longer."

My stomach flipped, and I couldn't deny the pull that I'd always felt between us. It was stronger than ever, and when his lips pressed against mine, I lost track of existence and the crowd faded around us. The music muted, as if we'd slipped underwater and were sinking away from the world.

As Logan demanded entrance, his tongue swiped across mine while his hands slid lower and wrapped around the bare skin of my thighs. He yanked me higher until our faces were even, and on instinct, my legs enclosed his waist. I hadn't had a chance to really see what he wore, but I could feel denim brush my thighs, and the added friction had me arching against the spellcaster.

Our kiss deepened as I slid my hands into his thick dark hair, yanking him closer in a desperate, drugging way. The flex of his fingers against my bare skin had moans spilling from my lips. "Come home with me tonight, Precious," he breathed.

Goddess. "Will I be safe?"

He pulled back enough to shoot me a smile, and it was in no way reassuring. "Define *safe?*"

"Are you going to murder me tonight?"

That darkly angled smile grew. "Not tonight, *sweetheart.*"

I narrowed my eyes, sensing he'd used that particular pet name more than a few times thanks to James. Logan Kingston was a straight-up psychopath, so why the Hel was I so turned on?

"Wait here," I said, wiggling until he released me back to my feet. "Don't fucking move."

His eyes narrowed, and I already knew he wasn't a fan of being told what to do. Which was tough luck tonight.

I felt his hard gaze on me as I turned away to search for Sara, knowing I couldn't leave without her.

Every instinct might have me wanting to climb that spellcaster like a fucking tree, but my friends would always come first.

CHAPTER 4

Sara was more than a little consumed with her drinks-buying warlock, and I had to tap her on the arm three times before she stopped trying to devour him.

"I'm thinking about taking off," I said, staring into her flushed face. The warlock waited just behind her, pushing back strands of his dirty-blond hair. He wasn't as tall or built as Logan, but he was still a big guy. "Ready to head out now?"

She shifted her gaze to him and shook her head. Lust all but dripped from her. "I think I'll stay out for a few hours. Don't wait up for me."

I hesitated and turned to the warlock. "What's your fucking name?"

To his credit, he didn't snap back, just smiled as if I were amusing. "Alaric Holder. I'm part of your parents' coven."

He was? I'd never seen him in my life.

"Nice, Alaric. I'll know where to find you to murder your ass if you hurt her. We clear?"

His amusement didn't go anywhere. "Crystal clear. She's safe with me."

Words didn't mean shit. "I'm going to need your phone number and to see some identification."

He didn't even hesitate as he pulled his phone from his pocket and produced a picture of his Blessed Souls admission certificate, along with rattling off his number, which I added to my phone.

"I'll be fine," Sara said with a chuckle, "but I love you for caring . . ."

She trailed off as her eyes went wide, focused behind me.

A blast of energy slid over my skin, and heat caressed my spine as I let out a sigh. "Thought I told you to keep your ass over there."

Logan's hand glided over my shoulder and wrapped possessively around the base of my throat. His hold didn't hurt, but it was firm as he tilted my head back until I stared up into his face. "Looked like you needed my help," he drawled.

This fucker was playing with me, because the situation was clearly well in hand.

"Logan Kingston . . ." Alaric dragged Sara closer and sidled himself in front of her—he was awfully protective for a warlock who'd met her not even an hour ago. "What are you doing here in Spokane?"

Was this asshole really that famous?

Logan didn't remove his gaze from mine. "This is where my mate is, elemental. Where she is, is where I am." He released me, and I felt oxygen flood my lungs, even though he hadn't been holding me tight enough to restrict airflow.

"Mate!" Sara squeaked again, trying to nudge around Alaric.

Mate? What in the Hel?

The magical community rarely used that archaic term these days, preferring *husband* and *wife*, in the way of humans. Our ceremonies were done differently, but within the parameters of getting a marriage license.

But before we acclimated, we had mates.

Mates and mate bonds.

"What are you talki—"

He gripped my hips, spun me to face him, and lifted me over his shoulder like I weighed nothing. One of his big hands wrapped around my ass to keep me from flashing the entire club. "She'll see you tomorrow, Sara," he said, striding off, my bag dangling down his back too. The crowd parted for him, recognizing the predator in their midst.

I heard Sara call after me. "You okay?"

"Yep," I shouted back, having no idea if that was true.

Logan was about as safe as stumbling into a pack of wolves and hoping they wouldn't eat you alive. But he'd told me that he'd explain our past, and with him throwing out the word *mate*, I needed those answers more than ever.

Outside, icy air hit my exposed skin, and I slapped at his shoulder. "Put me down, Logan. I can fucking walk."

To my surprise, he set me on my feet, keeping hold of my hips until I was steady on my heeled boots. Thank the goddess I hadn't had more than one witch wine; I needed my wits about me around Logan.

"Thank you," I said, watching him to find his expression revealed nothing.

His eyes though . . .

They fucking burned.

Scorched me to the pavement and my hands trembled as I tucked them against my sides. Logan shrugged off his long wool coat and draped it over my shoulders.

Most of the time I'd known this spellcaster, he'd been putting me in his clothes . . . surrounding me in his warmth and scent.

I fucking hated it.

I fucking loved it.

"Where are you taking me?" I asked. "And why, for the love of Selene, did you just refer to me as your mate?"

He held out a hand. "Do you trust me, Paisley?"

"Not even a little."

The burn of his eyes increased. "Good."

I took his hand anyway because I needed answers.

He led me into a small alleyway near the club. It looked deserted, and I gasped when Logan opened a portal right there *in the fucking human world* with no prior arrangements.

"Are you allowed to do that?" I said sharply, looking around for witnesses.

Logan shrugged. "Define *allowed*."

He loved to use that line, and I didn't bother to reply. Clearly Logan was above such trivialities as the law or the High Council of Magic, and I honestly didn't care tonight. Between the wine, his energy, and my own powers, I had much larger worries.

Our hands remained linked, but Logan didn't force me into his portal. He gave me the choice to go with him or not, and I wondered what would happen if I just spun on one booted heel and left this alley. Left the spellcaster who was as dangerous as he was destructive.

His expression remained cocky, as if he expected me to run, which had me stiffening my resolve. Straightening my spine, I stepped into the unknown. We traveled through the magic together and Logan's hold on me never wavered.

On the other side, I found myself staring up at a set of wrought iron gates that rivaled Weatherstone's. These didn't have glittery gold accents but were solid black, with just a large *K* in the center. Swirls of lavender-scented air moved around us, and it was warmer than back in Spokane.

"This isn't your dad's place, right?" I scrutinized the shadows for Rafael Kingston.

Logan's laugh was low and strangely soothing. "I'd never bring you near him, Precious. You most definitely wouldn't be safe, and the last year of keeping you alive would have been for nothing." He had kept me alive, and I still had no clue why.

When Logan approached, the gates opened. The scenery beyond remained shrouded in darkness, which he could have easily lit up with magic but didn't. A shiver traced down my spine at how alone I was with a spellcaster who I desired but didn't trust.

Still, if Logan wanted me dead, he could have killed me hundreds of times at Weatherstone. He'd promised me that I'd be safe tonight, and I believed him.

We were silent as we walked up a wide driveway. "We're in Michigan," Logan said, surprising me by freely revealing information. "This was where Mom grew up."

The mention of his mom twisted my heart until my chest ached. The knowledge of my power and how she died wouldn't stop bugging me. Mom might not be a night witch, but she'd been there the day Logan's mom died. Her best friend *had* been killed by a shadowy creature, and I couldn't help but think it was still somehow all connected to me.

"Is it your dad's house now?" I asked, forcing those worrisome thoughts away.

Logan shook his head. "No, she left everything to me. A full property portfolio at six years old."

My steps slowed, and he slowed with me as I tried to comprehend how much he'd lost at such a young age. "I'm sorry you had to go through that, Logan. I wish you didn't have to grow up without your mom."

His expression was somber as he lifted his free hand and brushed it across my cheek. "She wasn't the only one I lost," he murmured, shaking his head. "You were beautiful as a child, Paisley. I can remember the first time you raced across the park and tackle-hugged me. I mean, I'm sure you did it before that, but I don't remember those times. I remember you at four, fierce, and so loyal. You defended me against my dad."

"I did?" Flickers of memories, there but out of reach. "Was your dad an asshole even back then?"

His lips tugged into a brief smile. "In a manner. He wasn't as hard as he is today, but he's always expected a lot of me. You didn't like when someone bossed your Logie around."

I snorted. "Fuck. That's kind of cute, actually."

Even in the low light of the moon, I could see the twinkle in Logan's eyes. "Better than 'Stalkcaster.'"

Heat infused my cheeks, and I hoped the darkness hid my flushed face. "How do you know that? You really are a stalker."

He didn't even try to deny it. "When it comes to you, Paisley Hallistar, I have no fucking limits."

With that, he tugged me toward his house once more. The driveway was paved in a gorgeous gray mottled stone that reflected the moonlight. When the house came into view, it was as impressive as Weatherstone. Huge, it sprawled over what looked like an acre of land, and went up three stories. I expected it would be Gothic in style, but instead it screamed country Hamptons, with wraparound porches, light gray weatherboard walls, white shutters, earthy stone accents, and pillars leading up the front steps.

"It's beautiful," I breathed.

Logan pulled me closer to his side, his warmth seeping into me. "Mom was a country girl. She wanted me to experience this as well, countering Dad, who enjoyed penthouses and glass cages. This is my sanctuary. A sanctuary I've never shared with anyone."

I glanced up at him, my lashes obscuring him briefly as I blinked through my confusion. "No one? Like ever?"

We'd reached the three steps leading up to the front porch, which held rocking chairs and a suspended swing lounge attached to the white rafters above. "Only Noah and Tobias. There's no one else I trust enough with this location."

I knew Noah, his giant friend who spoke very little but scared many with his mere presence. Tobias was a new one, though, and it reminded me that despite the odd familiarity I felt around him and our shared history, there was a lot I didn't know about this warlock. Everything, really.

"Why would you trust me enough to bring me here?" I whispered, my throat unexpectedly tighter. "Why would you call me mate when we were all but enemies at school?"

None of this made any sense to me.

Logan had blown hot and cold constantly during my freshman year, but now he was here, acting as if we were connected on a cosmic level.

"Last year I was playing a role," he said with a shrug. "One designed to keep you safe from Rafael until I knew the best way to thwart his plans. But now that your powers are revealed, I'm fairly sure it's too late for concealment."

Rafael, the fucking thorn in my family's side.

Logan moved closer to me. "I also can't stay away from you any longer. You're here because it's time for you to understand that what's mine is yours, Paisley. That's how mate bonds work."

As I opened my mouth to demand more answers about this alleged *mate bond,* he added, "You'll learn everything in time, but just trust that we are more than you see. You must *feel* it to truly understand."

With that, he tugged on my hand and I was stunned enough to silently follow him onto the porch, where the scent of cedar wrapped around me.

The front door opened without his touch, as if the entire house was keyed to Logan's energy.

"I'm going to give you this address," he said as we crossed the threshold, "so you know you can always run here. Even if everything goes to shit. Even if I'm not here to protect you."

My heart dropped at the very thought, and my throat was instantly thick with emotions.

Fuck, I couldn't fall for Logan, and I could never rely on him either.

"You run here, Paisley," he finished seriously, "and not even my dad will find you."

With that ominous statement, light filled the house, illuminating the stunning interior. To our right, wide-planked timber floors, shiny and mahogany, led into a sitting room with cream walls and large bay windows to showcase what would no doubt be a magnificent view.

We didn't enter that room, though, ending up in a huge kitchen with cheery yellow walls, off-white cabinets, and speckled granite counters. "Are you hungry?" he asked, releasing my hand. There was a slow slide as our fingers separated, and I shivered at the loss of his power mingling with mine. It was warm enough in here that I didn't need his heavy coat, and when I shrugged it off and held it out to him, his heated gaze ran over my skimpy dress.

"Thanks for the loan," I said as he draped it over one of the pretty white stools at the kitchen island. I ditched my bag as well and left it on the same stool.

"Anytime, Precious. Now sit," he said briskly. "I'll make us food."

I all but collapsed onto another stool, and Logan, with an infuriatingly delicious smirk, strode around the island while he rolled up the sleeves of his white dress shirt. A shock of bronze skin and colored tattoos stood out against the stark white, and I tried not to drool over the sexy spell-caster.

I'd never had a chance to simply observe Logan, not like this. Relaxed and without the hard mask he'd always worn at Weatherstone. He was comfortable in this house, and there was a softer cast to the powerful warlock.

"Do you like pasta?" he asked, startling me from my thoughts.

"I love pasta," I said quickly, hoping he hadn't noticed me examining him like I'd have to identify him in a lineup later. "Do you need any help?"

He shook his head. "Sit and talk to me while I cook. Let me look after you tonight."

Goddess of all that was holy.

I almost combusted in my chair.

An angry and sarcastic Logan was sexy.

An attentive and caring Logan was absolutely devastating.

I was completely and totally screwed.

CHAPTER 5

I'd thought about Logan a lot over the past year. I knew he was a powerful spellcaster, and a snarling asshole who on occasion showed a soft and caring side.

But I'd never expected him to know how to cook.

I'd learned to cook from my mom, who could turn five ingredients into a masterpiece, provided she had her basket of herbs and spices. Logan didn't have a mom, and his family was clearly wealthy with the means to employ a chef, so when he bustled around setting pasta to boil, cooking chicken, and adding sauce and pesto to bring the dish to life, I was frankly a touch baffled.

And turned on.

He'd made the pesto from a fresh batch of basil, pine nuts, olive oil, and garlic, for fuck's sake.

"Is there anything you're not good at? Other than humility?"

He chuckled, seemingly taking no offense. "Confidence comes from knowing you're the best. I won't hide that part of myself. When everyone knows your strengths, they mind their manners."

He didn't even need to flex his power to command respect; it came from the aura he presented to the world. Others instinctively recognized the apex predator in their midst.

"So, your favorite shows are K-dramas and anime," he said as he stirred the cream base of his sauce, thickening it with cornstarch. "Your favorite food is salmon sushi, which I already knew because you eat half the tray at Weatherstone each meal. And you're an absolute coffee addict. Even if you do fill it with cream and sugar."

"*Addict* is a little harsh," I said, groaning as he dropped a basket of fresh bread rolls and churned butter before me. My stomach rumbled as I buttered a piece and bit into the bread, which was crispy on the outside and soft in the middle. "Rich people have better bread," I noted around another huffy groan.

Logan watched me intently, his hand stilling on the spoon in the sauce. "I went to the local markets today before I tracked you down. I wanted to make sure you had the best."

That level of care and consideration was enough to have strong waves of want and need erupting within me. I'd always craved the same soul-deep love my parents had, and on occasion Logan gave me a glimpse of what life with him could be like.

A life I desperately wanted.

"What's your favorite food?" I asked, attempting to bring myself back to reality.

Logan fucking Kingston was not the soulmate I could bring home to my family. He might have used the word *mate*, but it had to be some sort of game. Playing with my emotions before he went in for the kill.

"Pizza. Any sort of pizza, provided the base is crispy and wood-fired."

Rich-person pizza as well. "And your favorite movies? Let me guess . . . action?"

"Yep. I don't mind anime as well. If there's a lot of fight scenes." He added the cooked chicken to his sauce, along with fresh spinach and sundried tomatoes. "What's your favorite music?" He was the one asking questions now. "Do you listen to any particular genre?"

I pulled off another piece of bread and scooped butter onto it. "I enjoy country and pop. Dance if I'm out in the clubs. Eighties if it's Roller Derby. You?"

He'd had multiple guitars in his dorm at Weatherstone, so I had to assume he was a music lover too.

Logan took a second to answer, draining the pasta first, before he returned to the stove, mixing it all together. "Rock and heavy metal. I've been in a band with Noah and Tobias for a few years. It started as a way for us to have a break from life and responsibilities, and somehow we've picked up quite the underground following."

I blinked at him, trying to wrap my mind around this piece of information. "You have an actual band?" I was suddenly desperate to see this rock star side of him. "That's amazing. I'd love to see you perform one day."

"I think I can arrange that," he said as he gave me a soft smile, and I was hit with a sudden urge to jump over the island between us.

Before I could follow through on that intrusive but not altogether unpleasant thought, Logan placed a bowl of pasta in front of me. A second dish landed on the spot to my right, and then he poured us both a glass of red wine from a bottle he'd had breathing for about ten minutes.

I took a sip of the tart but delicious merlot, watching as he quickly and competently slid a bowl of parmesan cheese between us, along with napkins and cutlery. "Usually, I'd set us up in the dining area," he said as he finally sat down beside me, close enough that I could feel his magic and heat along my skin. "But I've always enjoyed eating in here. It's just . . . warmer."

"I love this kitchen," I said, my guard falling in the face of Logan's openness. "It's right out of my dream house."

He brushed his thumb across my cheek. "It's your house too, so it's good that you love it." His words were casual, but the meaning behind them . . . This was connected to his mate bond comments, and I needed those answers. Now.

"What the heck are you talking about?"

My fork was in my hand, but I hadn't had a chance to taste the dish yet as I stared at him. Logan twisted his fork in the pasta and lifted a bite to my lips. "Eat, Precious," he said, meeting my gaze. "You've lost weight since All Hallows'. Now, I personally don't care what you weigh. You're perfect no matter what. But I do care if you're not taking care of your health."

Without thought, I opened my mouth and accepted the bite. A wash of cream, pesto, garlic, and spice coated my tongue and I moaned softly. "Holy goddess. This is incredible, Logan."

He smiled, looking genuinely happy. He nudged my bowl toward me, and I decided a few more minutes wouldn't hurt to wait for answers.

We ate in companionable silence, and it wasn't until my bowl was almost finished and I was taking a sip of wine that Logan spoke: "Why is your power muted?"

I jerked, spilling a few drops of red across the counter. "You can tell it's muted?"

He shot me a look that said, *I'm a spellcaster, of course I can.*

"Mom gave me a potion to suppress my power. She's growing these ancient herbs, and she had these letters from my gran, who was *like me*, and there was a spell in there. It's been working."

Logan's expression didn't give a lot away, but I felt his energy grow stronger. "What else did she tell you? Have you made any ground in trying to figure out your power and how to control it?"

A derisive laugh escaped. "Control it? Not a chance. The advice was to hide my power for the rest of my life."

Now he was definitely pissed off. "That'll never work long term. You're too powerful, Pais. You cannot let this magic control you. You must do the controlling."

Easy for him to say. His affinity wasn't outlawed and punishable by death.

"She gave me a book with information." I had no idea why I was spilling all of my secrets to Logan when he told me nothing, but it appeared I couldn't help myself. "I'm not sure I'll ever control my power. It said that this reaper energy should be used with others in our affinity. That's why it was so hard for me to unlock my magic at school. It also indicated that the energy I'd felt freshman year, when I thought I was being followed, was my own power reaching through the planes of existence. I can touch almost all of them."

Logan was watching me closely, but he wasn't saying anything, which left me feeling out of sorts. "Did you know it was me all along?"

"No," he said, without hesitation. "Definitely not at first. I knew when I touched your energy that you were unlike other witches, but I assumed it was because of me."

"Because of you . . . ?"

His laughter was low as he took in my incredulous expression. "Because we're bonded, Precious. And have been since we were very young. It made me a stronger spellcaster, and I figured it had a similar effect on you, only you didn't have my father to train you up in our magic."

"How are we bonded?" I asked, tension pounding in my temples. This was the answer I'd needed all along—what happened in our past to connect us in the present? The reason he'd called me mate.

Logan somehow noticed the ache in my head, and when he brushed his hand across my face, his soothing magic took away the pain. "You're tired," he murmured. "We can talk in the morning after you sleep."

I wanted to protest. I'd followed him here for answers, and we were right on the cusp of real information sharing. But he wasn't wrong about my exhaustion. I'd slept badly for weeks now, and with my belly full of delicious food, I was two seconds from a sleep coma.

Logan had managed to get me to eat my first full meal in weeks; maybe he'd pull off the miracle of getting me to sleep as well. When we stood, I stumbled until I found my footing.

"I've got you," Logan murmured, sliding one hand across my back and the other under my thighs, lifting me into his chest. "We'll talk in the morning. I promise."

I tried to protest, but Logan smelled good, and my feet hurt, and I decided to fight this battle when I wasn't so wrecked. He carried me up the stairs without any use of magic to aid him. He was stupidly strong. All those days of bench-pressing small cars in the gym had paid off.

When we reached the second landing, he strolled down a long hall, stopping only when he reached a set of double doors. They opened for him, and the room was dark enough that I could only just make out the huge bed in the center. There were floor-to-ceiling windows letting in the moonlight, but it wasn't a bright night.

"Shower first?" he asked, lowering his face and breathing me in.

I nodded, struggling for words in the intimate setting of his dark room.

When we entered the bathroom, it was lit only by two low sconces on either side of the mirror. Enough illumination to see the shower and freestanding bathtub, but not so much that it hurt my head.

"Will you be okay on your own?"

My heart flipped at this caring side of Logan; he was completely tearing me apart, the seams of my existence dissolving, until I was nothing more than a mess of emotion.

"Yes," I whispered, swallowing against the tightness in my throat.

He set me on my feet, holding on until I was steady. "Towels and toiletries are there," he said, pointing to a cabinet beside the double sinks. "I'll bring you a shirt to sleep in."

"Always trying to get your clothes on me," I teased, even though I secretly loved it.

"Well, I prefer you naked, if I'm being honest. But second to that is you in my hoodies. Still sleeping in them, Precious?"

Did this asshole have cameras in my bedroom?

I shook my head and lifted my chin. "Nope. No idea where they even went."

His smirk grew. "Don't worry, I've got plenty more for you to borrow and *lose*."

Then he was gone, and on weakened knees I stumbled over to the shower. There were four levers, and with no idea what I was supposed to turn on, I lifted them all to find multiple showerheads shooting water around the large stall. *Okay.* Rich people had better showers too.

Stripping off my clothes, I stepped under the warm streams, groaning at how good the hot water felt. Steam surrounded me as well, and I wondered which one of the levers controlled that. There was a hint of mint and lavender in the spray, and I could die a happy witch in Logan's shower.

A tiled bench ran the full length of the far wall, and I lay across it, letting the water beat over me. Being naked and vulnerable in the house of a Kingston shouldn't be congruent with relaxing, but I found my eyes drifting closed as I enjoyed the sensation of water beating across my skin.

I started at a knock on the bathroom door. "Clothes are just outside," Logan called, and I pulled myself up to sit, knowing I'd fall asleep otherwise. Finishing my shower by using his amazing bodywash, I turned the water and steam off and stepped out. After drying myself with one of Logan's cloud-soft towels, I cracked open the door to grab the shirt.

It was plain black and large enough to fall to mid-thigh. It smelled faintly like Logan, and I was soothed by the now familiar minty evergreen. His hoodies I slept in no longer held that scent, and I'd been secretly mourning the loss.

Before leaving the bathroom, I brushed my teeth with the spare toothbrush he'd left on the shelf. I also found a brush to run through my long hair—if I went to bed with it wet and tangled, it'd be a bitch to tame tomorrow.

When I'd delayed as long as I could, I exited the bathroom to find Logan sprawled on his bed. There were still no lights on, but the moon had moved out from behind a cloud, and its beams filtered through those amazing windows.

When I crossed to his bed, I noticed his hair was damp and he wore a pair of soft shorts, leaving the full expanse of his muscled chest on display. I'd been desperate to examine his tattoos for almost a year now, and in the low light, I noted a large white tiger, and what looked like a dragon wrapping around his shoulder and down his biceps.

He sat up, and I tried very hard to ignore all those flexing muscles. "You okay, sweetheart?"

Fucker.

"Stop it," I said, unable to help my splutter of laughter. "He's a friend."

Logan's expression grew darker. "On your side maybe."

James had been my friend and boss for a long time, and I'd never seen any real indication that he wanted to be more, so I ignored that statement.

"Where am I sleeping?"

Logan patted the bed. "You're with me, Precious. Where I can keep an eye on you."

I blanched, even if almost every part of me wanted to dive into this sexy-as-fuck warlock. But I didn't need him to have a front-row seat to my nightmares. Without my potion and pills, I was going to wake up screaming.

"Maybe it'll be better if I sleep alone. I have no intention of fucking you tonight." My tone was bitchier than needed when he'd been nothing short of amazing, but I was half-panicked at being this vulnerable with him. It was too much, and at the same time, not remotely enough.

Logan stood, his energy sweeping out to surround me. "You're exhausted," he repeated, and I expected a bite in his tone after my comment, but there was none. "This is not about *fucking*, Paisley. This is about you sleeping where the monsters can't reach you. Let me do this for you tonight."

My eyes burned. My *soul* fucking burned.

Trying not to let my tears spill, I decided I was too tired to fight him and stumbled forward to crawl onto the huge bed. Logan waited for me to slide under the thick comforter before he got in after me, on the side closest to the door, nudging me over.

"I sleep between you and danger," he said as he settled under the covers.

There was a moment of tension where I wondered if I'd ever fall asleep with him beside me like this, but then he wrapped his arms around me and pulled me against his hard frame.

"Relax, Precious," he breathed, pressing a kiss to my temple. "I've got you. I promise that I won't let the monsters near you."

The tears I'd been holding back surged again, but only one slipped free. I felt the brush of his fingertip against the moisture, the heat of his power wrapping around me. True to his word, I felt a sense of safety for the first time in weeks.

Seconds later, sleep dragged me under as if it had been waiting for me all along.

CHAPTER 6

Since the bloom of my power last year, I'd been plagued by dreams. Most of them were sexy. Some were downright terrifying. A lot were both.

The two sides of my world collided in ways that drew screams from my lungs even in the middle of sleep. This night with Logan, though, not a single dream marred my slumber.

I had no idea how long I even slept. I only roused when a phone buzzed on the side table.

Snuggling deeper into the delicious heat surrounding me, I realized I was wrapped around the spellcaster. My head rested against his chest, the low thud of his heartbeat soothing under my ear. His hard thigh was pressed between my legs, and I barely managed not to moan as his muscles nudged against my sensitive core.

My lack of underwear beneath his shirt was never more obvious than when I felt my slick heat soaking his thigh.

Not ready for reality to intrude, I kept my eyes closed, hoping for a few more seconds of peace—a few seconds before Logan returned to being the son of my family's enemy and I became a witch with an affinity that would get me killed if anyone found out.

The bright light of day would destroy this perfect, peaceful bubble.

I wasn't ready for that.

Last night, Logan had been open and caring toward me. It had cracked through my walls, and if we went back to hating each other today, it would destroy me.

He'd called me *mate*.

And told me that this was *my* house.

"Stop thinking so hard, Precious," he murmured.

I opened my eyes, needing to see his expression, only for another sight to completely steal my attention. "What in the world?"

My heart slammed hard as I jerked into a sitting position and looked around the semidark room. Blinds covered the windows, but I could still see the mountain lion–sized cat sprawled across the end of his bed.

"Logan . . . is that a cougar?"

He pulled himself up to sit behind me, dragging me back against his body. "Misti likes you," he said, in his husky, sleepy voice.

A shiver traced down my spine, and I glanced over my shoulder. "Misti . . . ?" She had a name like a pet . . . only there was nothing domesticated about this creature. I could see the wild energy in her gaze as she watched us.

She got to her feet and stretched languidly, and I found myself breathlessly waiting for her next move. Turned out, it was morning scratches behind the ears. She prowled forward, headbutting my hand. "Hello, pretty girl," I crooned, my fear fading as she purred. "You're just perfect, aren't you. A pretty baby girl."

Logan chuckled from behind me. "Never thought I'd be jealous of a cougar, but here we are."

I shot a knowing look. "You want to be a good boy, Logan Kingston? You need some praise in your life?"

His eyes darkened as his chest rumbled. "You're playing with fire, baby. But I can definitely be a very good boy for you."

Fuuuck. Well . . . that backfired.

Returning my attention to Misti, I scratched her until she was on her back, purring and pawing gently at me. "Trust you to tame the wild beast," Logan said, watching us both. "Misti is not bonded to me, but she comes around every now and then. I have no idea where she goes when she's not here though."

He was wearing an adorable lopsided smile that only added to his sexiness. I'd never seen him rumpled and half asleep, and his full lips were so close that I only had to lift my head an inch to touch them.

Drawn to his power, I almost kissed him, before he brushed his hand along my cheek. "That was your phone ringing before," he told me, and I jolted at his words. "I brought it up last night. You should check your messages."

Oh shit.

Mom would be wondering where I was, since I hadn't come home last night or called in this morning. I also needed to make sure Sara was okay.

Logan clouded my mind until I forgot anyone else in the world existed. Which was dangerous for more than just me.

Grabbing my phone, I swiped a finger to unlock it and groaned at the multiple messages and missed calls. My ass was in big trouble.

Logan pulled himself out of the bed and opened the blinds with the press of a button. As the morning sun filtered in, I sensed he was done being my sweet spellcaster. His expression remained carefully blank as he rubbed his hand across

Misti, before opening the door so she could head out of the room.

When he entered the bathroom, I let out a sad huff and called my mom. It rang twice before she growled down the line. "Paisley Hallistar, you better be in the hospital."

I managed to swallow my laughter, lest I fanned her current anger into a volcano of rage. "Mom, shit, I'm so, so sorry. Sara and I got a little hammered last night and ended up at a hotel. We didn't want to navigate across town so drunk."

It was a reasonably safe lie, because as I'd dialed Mom, I'd noticed a text from Sara saying she was at a hotel and safe in all ways except for her vagina. *Which was about to be demolished.* Her words, not mine.

"Honey, you know we have one rule about nights out. You have to let us know if you're not coming home, so we don't freak out and think you've been murdered."

"I know, and it won't happen again. I'm sorry I stressed you out with everything else that's going on."

She paused, breathing deeply. "It's okay. I understand your need to escape for a few hours. As long as you're safe, then we're all good. Will you be coming home soon?"

"Yep," I said, resigned to the fact that my time with Logan was coming to an end.

"Okay, good." I could hear her relief. "We need to pack for a few nights in the city for Dad's trial. It starts tomorrow, but they're expecting it to run for at least three days."

Three fucking days for a simple expulsion from Weatherstone. This entire charade was outrageous.

I kept my thoughts to myself because she was already worried enough. "Okay, Mom. I'll see you soon. Love you."

"I love you too, Paisley."

The line went dead, and I let out a low breath of frustration. For one brief night, consumed by Logan Kingston, I'd forgotten that my family's entire future rested on this trial—which probably wouldn't go well because Dad *was* guilty of what they accused him of.

I couldn't understand why anyone cared though.

The bathroom door opened and broke me from my darker thoughts. I lifted my head to find Logan in a white towel, which contrasted against his gorgeous jewel-toned tattoos.

"Everything okay?" he asked, and I was happy to see that he wasn't completely icing me out.

"Just Dad's trial tomorrow," I said shortly, pulling myself out of bed. Logan's shirt brushed my bare legs and I tried not to remember the way his hard thigh had pressed against my center. "I need to get home."

He nodded. "I'll take you."

When I entered the bathroom, I closed the door so I could pee and brush my teeth. Retrieving my dress from last night, I slipped it on but left my panties in Logan's wash basket.

No way was I putting on dirty underwear, not even at the risk of flashing the world my goods.

When I stepped out, I had the shirt in my hands. "Here's your shirt. Don't say I never return your clo . . ." I trailed off as I noticed the view outside the windows.

What I hadn't been able to see last night in the dark was that beyond Logan's gorgeous farmhouse mansion was a field of lavender in bloom. I crossed the soft carpet to press my hands against the glass, staring across the purple expanse.

Logan stood at my side, and while he didn't touch me, it also didn't feel awkward. We might not still be in the bubble, but we also hadn't returned to what we were before.

There was progress, and that was enough for now.

He let me look for many long minutes before he said, "Let's get you home, Precious." Closing my eyes, I fought for composure, and by the time I turned toward him, I'd gotten myself under control.

"Thanks. Mom was about to send out a council search party to find me. She probably would have if she didn't think I'd lose my head at the same time."

Logan's expression darkened. "Don't even joke about that, Paisley. I'll never let them touch you."

He wasn't touching me either, keeping his distance as we left the room and headed downstairs. I had my bag in one hand and my shoes in the other as I followed him out the front door.

As we were leaving, I tried not to drool over his property, with its lavender fields stretching on all sides and a creek meandering behind the house. It was easy to see why Logan's mom had loved this place, and why she'd left it to Logan.

"She left you with her heart." The words slipped out before I'd realized, and as Logan ground to a halt, I wondered if I'd just majorly fucked up.

He spent endless seconds studying me, and I was about to apologize when his expression cleared and he was moving again. "Come on," he said, striding toward the gate. "Let's not worry your family any longer."

I followed quietly, knowing that despite his promise of answers, all I had were more questions. *Typical.* At least I'd gotten a night of amazing food and sleep.

With the unpredictable spellcaster, that wasn't a half-bad deal.

CHAPTER 7

Our hotel in New York wasn't fancy. "Sorry, girls, this is the best we could get," Mom said, handing us a key card each. She'd booked two separate rooms to give Sara and me privacy—my siblings couldn't get away for the three days to be here, but they were prepared to transport across if the trial went badly. "It's safe enough, at least. Not that a regular human could ever get the drop on us."

"Totally fine, Mrs. Hallistar," Sara said with a smile. "I've never been to the city, and I can't wait to explore."

"We can go out now, right, Mom?"

She nodded. "Just keep your phones on you so we can coordinate for dinner. We should get to bed early. Tomorrow will be a long day."

The preliminary hearing started today, but it was closed to everyone except Dad and his coven-appointed lawyer. Tomorrow, though, we would all be there for the main trial. The verdict would be delivered on the third day.

Mom left to unpack in her room. We grabbed our phones and bags, and headed to the street to catch a cab. I'd just waved one down when my phone buzzed, and I hated the way my stomach tightened in anticipation.

Logan had returned me safely home yesterday, as promised,

via another *illegal* transport portal, and I hadn't heard from him since. I swiped to find the message wasn't from him.

Haley: I'm reading a shifter book, and he is scenting her to see if she's clean. He can smell her periods. I mean . . . What the fuck am I even reading? Shifters . . . I tell ya. They have issues.

A snort of laughter escaped me as I slid into the back seat of the yellow cab. After Sara directed the driver to Central Park, I handed her the phone and she lost her shit reading Haley's message.

She replied before I could stop her.

Paisley: I'm going to need the title. For research purposes.

There was a minute before she responded.

Haley: Hey, Sara. I'd know your dirty mind anywhere.

I snatched my phone as Sara shrugged. "Ask her if she's going to make it tonight?"

After shooting off another quick text, I threw my phone into my bag and stared out the window, taking in the sights. When we reached the drop-off near the park, my phone buzzed, and I checked her reply.

Haley: Not tonight. But 100% on for tomorrow.

Sara read over my arm. "I've missed her so much. It'll be great when we're all back together again." She paused, and I knew what she was going to say. "Did Belle reply to your message?"

I'd messaged this morning to see if she'd be at the trial. Her ass of a father was part of the proceedings, which meant there was a chance.

"Nope," I said, feeling grim about it. "She hasn't even read it, and in all honesty, I don't trust her father doesn't have her chained up in the basement."

"I want to laugh," Sara deadpanned, "but since there's a chance it's true, I'm mostly panicking."

"Maybe she's with her mom . . ." I suggested to calm my own panic. "She said they don't get the best phone service near her mom's village."

"We should ask Elder Monroe tomorrow," Sara said, stepping aside as a large group of kids in matching shirts pushed into the park, heading in the direction of the zoo.

Like he'd tell us anything.

Keeping Belle away from her friends and support system was at the top of his to-do list. The moment the school year finished, she'd ghosted us hard.

"No doubt he'll be more concerned about slapping my dad with the maximum penalty he can get," I grumbled. "I'm really not looking forward to tomorrow."

Sara wrapped her arm around my shoulders and gently squeezed. "I know, hon, but let's not let it ruin today. I mean, how often are we in the city like this? Let's experience playing tourist."

As she dragged me along the path, I attempted to push my stress and worries aside. The trial was going to happen whether I worried today or not, so for now I'd enjoy this moment with my bestie.

The day passed in a pleasant haze.

We didn't talk about Dad or the trial again. We ate hot

dogs from food carts, visited the zoo, and, despite the icy weather, explored the park until the sun started to set.

The cab was toasty warm on the way home, and I sank into a relieved heap to thaw out. Sara, doing the same beside me, smiled broadly. "I've been waiting for you to bring it up, but are you ever going to tell me what happened the other night with Logan? He called you mate. Like, *mate*?"

Now it was too hot in here, and I unwound my scarf to free up my neck. "You haven't mentioned what happened with you and Alaric either."

It wasn't that I didn't want to tell her about Logan, it was just hard to describe the night. He'd taken me to his secret house, made the best pasta I'd ever eaten, and then cuddled me to keep the monsters away. There'd been no sex, or anything remotely sexual, and yet the night had felt intimate in a way that went way beyond casual fuck buddies.

Oh, and he'd also told me we were bonded and called me his mate.

Right before he took me home and proceeded to ignore the two messages I'd sent checking in on him. Which were the last messages I would be sending.

Logan Kingston was complicated and frustrating, and I had no idea what was happening.

At the mention of Alaric, Sara's face lit up. "Oh, Pais! Oh my fucking goddess. He absolutely destroyed me. I've never had sex like that. Never. I couldn't remember my own name, even as I screamed his for half the night."

I laughed so hard my stomach hurt. "Never a dull moment with you. Are you going to see him again?"

Her eyes were wide and shiny as she shrugged. "Honestly, I have no idea, but I hope so. He's already messaged today to check in and see if I was still in Spokane. It hurt to tell him that I was away and wouldn't be back for a few days."

"If he's interested, a few days' wait won't deter him."

"I know," she said softly. "And while I'm not sure I'm ready for more than great sex, it's nice to feel wanted at least."

It was nice, even if it was also confusing and terrifying.

When we reached the hotel, Sara and I rushed to shower and change for dinner. We were going to check out a small Chinese restaurant around the corner. Mom and Dad knocked on the door when it was time to go, and the four of us walked the two blocks to the restaurant. "How did today go, Dad?" I asked him.

For most of my life Tom Hallistar had been a larger-than-life warlock, filled with power and the literal fire of his element. But tonight he looked tired. "As well as could be expected," he said, tucking Mom into his side. "They basically went over the schedule for tomorrow, and the order of evidence and witnesses. The trial will be a long day."

"What's the worst punishment that we're looking at? Is it beyond you just losing your job now?"

He exchanged a glance with Mom before he answered; they tended to try to hide the darker aspects of life from their kids. "I think the worst will be losing my job, but there's a chance they could push for more. Students were injured, though thankfully none of them died."

"Shouldn't you already know the charges?" Sara asked, expression serious as she dodged a nasty-looking puddle of melting ice. "They can't just drop new shit on you during the trial, right?"

"They can," Mom said, and I hated how concerned she looked. "If the elders decide there's enough evidence to support further charges, they'll just bring them up. That's why

I said to pack for a week. In case we're here longer than the original estimate."

We'd reached the restaurant now, red neon lights flashing its name, but my stomach was churning so hard I doubted I'd be able to eat anything. This was all so unfair, and I had no idea why Elder Monroe would want to punish Dad. Even if he thought I was a demon-witch, and I could only assume he did based on previous comments, my affinity had nothing to do with my parents. Or was his aim to remove my support system from Weatherstone?

When I returned for my sophomore year, Alice and Jenna would be gone.

If Dad was as well . . .

I'd be more vulnerable than ever.

Later that night, I lay in bed staring at the popcorn ceiling. I sent out a prayer to Selene that tomorrow wouldn't end up a complete knife through the chest for my family.

Sara had fallen asleep half an hour ago, but I couldn't get my mind to settle. Restless energy and anxiety tore me to pieces, and I wished for a brief second that I was with Logan in his gorgeous home. Grabbing my phone, I checked my messages, startled to find there was one unread.

Stalkcaster: Sorry for the late reply, I was tied up on some business. Did you make it to the city okay?

Fire washed through me as my magic surged against the suppression potion, and I forced myself not to shoot back an immediate reply.

I even debated ignoring him, which lasted all of ten seconds.

Paisley: Yep, made it safe and sound. Dad's main trial day is tomorrow. I'll be at the council chambers.

He replied almost instantly:

Stalkcaster: It's going to be ok. I will make sure your dad is safe, so don't stress. I can feel you freaking out from here.

Ignoring his statement about making it okay, because there was no possible way he could help, I replied just as quickly.

Paisley: I bet you can, Stalker. Where is "here" anyway?

Another quick reply.

Stalkcaster: Our bed.

My heart stuttered in a weird arrhythmia.

Paisley: You have got to stop saying things like that. You're confusing me. Speaking of, you didn't answer my questions the other night, and you promised you would.

Stalkcaster: You needed a break. You needed a night to not deal with the stress of life. The questions and answers aren't going anywhere. Now go to sleep.

I clutched the phone tighter and let a moment of vulnerability seep out.

Paisley: I find it hard to sleep these days.

He read the message, and for the first time there wasn't an instant reply. Figuring he was done with the chat, I was about to drop my phone on the green laminate side table, when it buzzed once and then again.

He was calling.

Reflexively, I slid my finger across to answer and whispered, "Hello."

"I'll stay with you until you fall asleep," he said, the rumble of his voice deeper than usual. "Or I can get you and bring you back here."

Oh Hel.

"I'm with Sara," I whispered in reply. "I can't leave."

I wanted to, though. It was scary how much I wanted to.

Even though Logan's actions gave me whiplash, this caring side he revealed was impossible to resist.

"Close your eyes, Precious."

My eyes were closed before I could consider how quickly I obeyed his command.

"Good girl," he murmured, as if he could fucking see me.

Could he see me? Wouldn't put it past him.

"Let me tell you about our last day together," he continued, and despite my sleepiness, I perked up, wanting to hear this story. "We went to the park twice a week. Our moms would take us to hang out so they could gossip. The twins ran off to play together, as they always did. Those two never needed anyone. And Jensen and Trevor were content to wrestle in the mud or throw punches at all the assholes in the park. Which left you and me. You followed me everywhere, and I pretended I hated it, but deep down . . . I thought you were adorable."

At some point, my breathing grew so shallow I felt light-headed.

Was I finally going to find out what happened that day in my memories?

"You ran away from me," I whispered.

Logan's chuckle vibrated through the phone and deep into my body. "I always did, and you always caught me. Or . . . I let you catch me. But that day, you tripped and fell. You hurt yourself. There were shallow cuts on your hands, and I remember being so angry with myself. I scooped you up in my arms, trying not to freak at your tiny tear-streaked face. Our moms didn't see us, too caught up in *Witch Weekly* or whatever they were chatting about, so I took you over to a set of chairs near the back of the park."

I strained my brain, but all I had was that one memory: the falling.

"I cleaned your hands with water from the tap and my shirt. And you looked up at me with the bluest fucking eyes I'd ever seen, and said, 'I'm going to marry you one day, Logie.'"

He paused and didn't speak for so long I thought he'd already gone.

"What happened then?" I pushed gently.

"You pulled a spell from your pocket." He sounded less intense and more amused now. "You'd stolen it from an old book of your gran's. That's why you'd been chasing me—to give me a gift."

A book of Gran's . . . ? *Which gran?*

"We read that spell together, and then I cut my palm to press against the blood already on yours. We were just stupid kids messing around, but fuck . . . it worked, Paisley. Magic bound us, and I felt the bond to you. It was subtle until we bloomed, but there was no denying that day was when you became more than my best friend."

My head spun, and I lifted my hand as if I could see the blood that had bound us.

"*More* than best friends, as in . . ."

"Mate," Logan finished for me. "Mate-to-be anyway. Didn't you think it was weird that when you bloomed, you started dreaming about me? The moment your power emerged, our bond was triggered. The dreams pushed us together until the first time we had sex, needing to seal the spell we set in motion almost twenty years ago."

"But . . . I mean . . . you can't do magic at four and six." It was impossible, even as I felt the connection simmering between us. It'd been there from the first moment I saw him at Weatherstone, even as we fought against it.

His pause was brief. "We did though. We did, Paisley."

My chest grew tighter, the pain sharp and direct. "How could you know this about us and then reject the bond so many times at school?" My voice rose until I was in danger of waking Sara.

He breathed deeply, and that low sound weirdly settled into my energy. "I had to keep you safe, Precious. I've been trying to keep you safe for years, which meant staying away until I was strong enough to protect you."

"Are you strong enough now?" I whispered, broken but not ready to give up yet. "I don't think I can do this hot and cold any longer, Logan."

His reply was soothing. "I know, Precious. We won't have to hide much longer. I promise. Now get some sleep so you're not tired tomorrow for the trial."

I closed my eyes once more, and with Logan whispering soothing words, I found myself drifting off, phone still clutched in my hand.

CHAPTER 8

"It's starting," Sara murmured, holding my hand tighter. "I'm so fucking nervous."

I was beyond nervous, but thanks to Logan I'd had enough sleep to keep exhaustion at bay.

We were seated across a row in the small chambers, waiting for the proceedings to get underway.

A warlock with thinning gray hair and a hard face walked to the front of the stand. "There's been a change in the elder schedule," he said to Dad and his lawyer, who were in the front row. "Elder Monroe will not be able to make it. In his place, we've brought in Elder Catherine."

With those words, six elders entered the room and climbed the steps to take their seats on the raised platform.

Sara and I exchanged a long, worried stare. *What the fuck is happening?* I silently asked her.

She shrugged and mouthed, *Do you think Belle is okay?*

I shook my head, having no idea, but not feeling great about it.

The trial got started quickly. The same warlock laid out the charges, giving facts about the night in question. The night when witch wine had Weatherstone students acting like idiots, resulting in a building being burned down. There were photos of the fire and witness accounts of Dad knowing about the wine and ignoring it.

"Can we call these witnesses?" a female elder on the end asked. She looked to be in her sixties with a stern face and steel-gray hair. All the elders were dressed in dark robes, and none of them looked particularly happy to be here. "We need to question them directly."

The warlock reading the information checked his notes again. "They were supposed to arrive this morning but have now declined to attend."

The elders stared as if he'd slipped into speaking a dialect they weren't familiar with. "Okay, so you have no actual evidence to show us, and no witnesses?" a Black man near the middle said. "Why are we even being called for such a minor triviality? We're busy. This is a Weatherstone issue to deal with."

I was glad I wasn't the only one who thought so.

"Elder Monroe believed it was prudent," the gray-haired warlock said with a shrug.

"So prudent he didn't even show up," the first witch stated, annoyance tingeing her tone. "This case is dismissed. Professor Hallistar, you're free to go. And while we'd normally leave this up to Headmaster Gregor to decide your fate at Weatherstone, he's already informed us that in the event of a not-guilty verdict, your job is to be reinstated. Thank you."

Noise erupted in the room, and I jumped to my feet with Mom and Sara, the three of us hugging. "Holy goddess," I burst out, tears spilling down my cheeks. "Did that just happen?"

Mom's eyes were glassy as she sniffled. "I can't believe it. After all the stress and drama, Tom won't lose his job."

She released me to head for Dad, who was already moving our way. He lifted her smaller frame off the ground, whispering into her ear. "Your parents are freaking adorable," Sara said, sounding sniffly herself. "It's about time we had some luck."

It felt like more than just luck. Of all the scenarios I imagined today, a complete dismissal wasn't even on the list. Yesterday, Dad said it was all going ahead, but everything had changed with the absence of Elder Monroe and their two witnesses. What were the odds that none of them would show up today . . . ?

I would bet my measly bank account that Logan fucking Kingston had something to do with this. He'd told me last night he'd make sure it was fine, but how in the Hel had he pulled it off?

Sara walked over to my parents, giving Dad a hug too, and I took a second to pull out my phone and check for a message.

Stalkcaster: I've got your back.

My tears flowed with abandon, and I shot back a quick reply thanking him before I stumbled toward Dad. I found myself wrapped in his strong arms. "Little Gem," he crowed, "we need to go out and celebrate."

"I'm so freaking happy, Dad," I said, staring up at him. "Best news ever."

Mom, who was snuggled into his side, said, "The girls might want a night out without us oldies before we leave. We'll head home tomorrow now."

Dad's eyes softened as he stared down at her. "The elders offered me theater tickets if you want to see a show, my love."

We were forgotten as they fell into their bubble of love.

If anyone had given me an unrealistic expectation of marriage, it was my parents.

"We definitely need to go out," Sara said as she linked her arm through mine. "Hales will be here in a couple of hours, and this city is our fucking oyster. Or whatever that stupid saying is. Oysters are disgusting, so that's in no way appealing."

"They're snot with shells," I confirmed.

"Grainy snot with shells," Sara corrected, and I laughed. "Come on, let's head back to the hotel and leave your adorable parents to make every other marriage look subpar."

My eye roll told her everything, even though I also thought they were adorable.

Adorable and nauseating.

Outside the council chambers, we flagged down a cab, and as I slid into the seat and Sara gave the driver our address, my phone buzzed.

Stalkcaster: Howling Moon Club. Tonight. 10pm. Mention me at the door. You can bring Sara and Haley.

Somehow, he knew that Haley was joining us tonight. The urge to check for a hidden camera was strong, but when one was a spellcaster, there was no need for cameras.

"Logan invited us to a club tonight," I told Sara. "Up for it?"

Her eyes bugged. "He's here? What the Hel? Why didn't you tell me?"

"I didn't know until right this second."

Sara examined me, eyes narrowed as if ready to catch me in a lie, before she relaxed. "You know I'm in."

"I don't understand what's happening," I admitted as the

cab honked and came to a dead stop in traffic. "Logan barely spoke to me last year, and when he did, he was an asshole."

Mostly. Last night he'd told me it was about protecting me, but I was scared to let myself believe that. To let myself fall into this feeling between us.

Sara, of course, called me straight out on it. "Babe, he saved your life multiple times. Whenever you needed him, Logan was there. The rest, in my expert opinion, was all smoke and mirrors to hide the fact that he claimed your ass." She side-eyed me. "Your lucky freaking ass."

"He said we're bonded," I whispered, clearing my throat as emotion got the better of me. "That's why he called me mate; we have a proper magical bond. He said pushing me away was about protecting me until he was strong enough to keep me safe."

Sara nodded as if she'd expected that all along. "It makes sense, you know. All of us could practically *feel* the energy connecting you two. The air crackled with it whenever you were close. If you want my opinion—" I knew she'd be giving it to me whether I wanted it or not "—stop trying to figure it all out. Allow yourself to care about Logan and accept this bond, and trust that he's got your back. He's never shown you that he doesn't. Not where it really counts."

There was an undeniable truth in what she said. "What about his father?" I pressed. "The feud with my family still exists."

She shot me a droll stare. "Which is no doubt what Logan's protecting you from. Your dads' feud is not yours and Logan's. Don't take it on."

Again, she was right, and I wished it was as easy as simply ignoring the feud started between our parents when we were children. But if Logan had been trying to protect me from it all along, that meant it was an issue we still had to overcome.

By the time we arrived at the hotel, I was a confused, messy lump. As we exited the cab, a tall, slim witch stepped away from the side of the hotel and jumped up and down waving at us.

"Witches!" Haley shouted as we rushed over to her. "I've missed you so much." She wrapped us in her arms, the three of us hugging for what felt like an hour.

When we finally broke apart, Haley turned her sweet smile my way. "Sara told me about your dad's trial. I'm so happy that it's been dismissed. Not gonna lie, I was secretly freaking out."

"Me fucking too," Sara added dramatically.

Having friends who cared about your issues as much as you did was a gift I'd never expected from Weatherstone. "Selene was watching over us for sure," I told them, shaking my head at how the trial had imploded. "And we're all heading out tonight to celebrate."

For once, Haley didn't react like I was about to perform open-heart surgery on her without healers. "I figured. I even left my book at home and packed a dress for the occasion."

"That's my little book-witch," Sara said, wrapping an arm around her and dragging her into the hotel lobby. "I'm going to glam the shit out of you tonight. We're getting you laid."

On our way to the room, Sara launched into a detailed description of her sexcapades from the other night, and the absolute *destruction of her vagina*, leaving Haley and me snorting in laughter.

Tonight was going to be fun.

By 9:30 p.m. we were dressed to impress, our hair straight and sleek, eyes done in smoky tones, and outfitted in the skimpiest dresses Sara could find.

My dress was a deep, shimmery navy that brought out the

blue of my eyes. It was corseted with a flared skirt, and for once, I was out of my boots and in shiny black Louboutin knockoffs.

Sara had on a gold bandage dress that hugged every inch of her curvy figure. Haley was the most conservative in a loose green sheath falling to mid-thigh. She wore heels too, which meant both of us were at real risk of breaking our inexperienced necks tonight.

Sara, on the other hand, could have run a marathon in her five-inch stilettos.

"Night out in New York City," she cried, pushing her coat open to show off her dress underneath. It was freezing, but there was thankfully no sign of snow.

The club Logan had directed us to was in an industrial area, and our cab couldn't get closer than two blocks from the venue. "There must be an event here tonight," I said as we exited to join the streams of people moving along the sidewalk. "Do you think we're in the right place?"

The girls didn't answer as we were swept up in the crowd, leading us right to the warehouse venue. The building was massive, its black walls blending into the darkness beyond. Huge red doors stood out like beacons, open and beckoning everyone forward.

Four security guards were checking tickets, and I looked around wondering what to do.

"This is a ticketed event," Haley whispered as we got closer to the red doors. "Which I doubt we can afford."

"Logan said to mention his name at the venue," I said, stumbling as a drunk chick crashed into me, cackling her head off. Just then a guard shouted, "The line for will call is over there."

We pushed through the crowd, moving away from the doors to join the long line. It moved quickly enough, though, and soon we were at the front. A young chick with platinum-blond hair and heavy makeup looked up as we stepped in front of the window. "Show is sold out, so unless you're picking up tickets on hold, you're shit out of luck."

Right. Okay. Well, that explained why the line had moved so quickly.

"We're supposed to be guests of Logan Kingston tonight?" I tried not to make it sound like a question. *Tried and failed.*

Her gaze grew less flippant as she squinted at me. "Name."

"Paisley Hallistar."

Her demeanor changed dramatically as she reached for an envelope. We even got a smile as she said, "You're our mystery VIPs." She slid the envelope under the glass toward me. "And you use this entrance here. Make sure to put your lanyards on before you go in."

I exchanged glances with Sara and Haley, and they shrugged their confusion. None of us had a clue what was happening. The chick left the glass enclosure to show us to a door hidden just behind her booth. There were two security guards on it as well. "Lanyards," she hissed, and I fumbled to pull out the three black plastic cards with our names already printed on them.

"These are the mystery VIP guests," she said to the first burly dude. He was one of the biggest humans I'd ever seen, with a patch of bright red curls that didn't quite match his roid muscles.

He ran his gaze over us briefly, before he checked our passes and opened the door to let us through. "This is the weirdest club I've ever been to," Sara said, peering down the hall as we stepped through. "I wonder what show she was talking about . . . Maybe it's one of those sexy male dance groups. Or it's a sex dungeon slash swingers club." Her voice grew breathless. "I've heard they have a lot of them here."

Haley squeaked. "I'm not ready for a sex dungeon. I couldn't even get through the shifter sniffing scene."

That cracked us up as we hurried along a dimly lit hallway painted as dark as the outside. When we reached the end, more security guarded a door, and after checking our lanyards, they escorted us into the main venue.

"Holy . . . shit."

It was dark inside, strobe lights showcasing the massive space. Heavy music thrummed through my body and ignited my suppressed magic. The crowds were jumping and screaming already—there had to be upward of two thousand people packing the massive space.

As we rounded the corner into the central part of the venue, I noticed the stage and realized the music was live. The five members of the band were headbanging in time to their music.

The lead singer had hair to his shoulders, his dark eyes made even darker by the makeup lining them. He stared out over the crowd and rasped the words to his song.

"It's a music venue," Haley cried, relaxing. "Thank the goddess my virtue is safe."

Sara threw her head back and laughed at our bestie, before she shrugged out of her jacket. "We need to ditch our coats."

The coat check was near the red-doored entrance, and once we had our passes stashed in our clutches, we made our way toward the bar.

"Are you going to message Logan?" Sara asked as we ordered some drinks. "You're never going to find him in this venue."

Pulling my phone out, I was about to send him a message, when the final beat of the rock song faded away. There was a brief pause, and then the crowd lost their fucking shit.

I turned to find the band leaving as red and purple lights circled the empty stage.

A loud voice blasted through the venue. "That was Burning Chains." Applause filled the venue along with screams and cries. "And now the moment you assholes have been waiting for. You followed them around Europe, stalked their fucking asses across the States, and now . . . the fact that they've agreed to play here tonight means we're the luckiest bastards in the world. Make some motherfucking noise for Casters."

"Did he say Casters?" Haley breathed.

I squinted at her. "He did. And I'm guessing they're part of our world with that name."

She shook her head. "Babe, they're one of the biggest underground rock bands of the last few years. I don't follow them or anything, but if you're into any part of the music scene that's not mainstream, they're a big deal."

That explained the chaos outside.

Wait . . . "Logan said he was in a band," I murmured.

The girls replied, but I couldn't hear a word because the crowd was screaming so loudly.

Three huge men took to the stage, dressed rather casually in black jeans and torn shirts, displaying a lot of their muscled chests and tattoos.

"The masks," Sara choked out, right beside my ear. "Holy fuck me, they're smoking hot. Am I on fire? I feel like I'm on fire."

They didn't actually wear masks, but their faces were painted in red and white, giving them a ghostly serial-killer vibe.

"They're warlocks," Haley gasped, nodding as if she'd suspected that all along. "Can you feel the magic?" Their face paint shimmered under the stage lights, and I recognized the signs of a spell designed to conceal their identities.

But I knew exactly who stood on that stage.

Logan was in the center, one of the guitars I'd seen in his room at Weatherstone strapped over his shoulder, with the slightest of smirks playing around the corners of his lips.

Well, this night just got very interesting.

CHAPTER 9

My drink was all but forgotten as I moved closer to the stage, taking in the sheer size of the drummer as he settled behind his kit. That was Noah, for absolute sure. The bassist I didn't know, but I would bet good money on it being Tobias. I couldn't tell much about his facial features with the magic paint, but while he wasn't quite as tall as Logan or Noah, he was equally ripped and tattooed.

It was no surprise, after seeing them up there, that they were popular.

All three oozed power and sex appeal.

"Good evening, New York City," Logan growled into the mic, and the crowd lost their shit, screaming and jumping, strobe lights flashing around the space, lighting us all in blues and purples. "This is a last-minute gig for us," he continued, locking the crowd into his green-eyed gaze. That part of him wasn't concealed, and as he turned our way, Sara and Haley started to scream.

"Babe! It's fucking Logan!" Sara clutched my arm.

My laughter was lost as the crowd joined her in screaming. The band started to play, the beat heavy as it filled the venue. Haley moved to shout near my ear. "Did you know?"

I shook my head, eyes still locked on Logan as he began to sing.

Fuck. My knees weakened at his low, perfect rasp, lyrics wrapping around me as he sang about broken hearts and unrequited love. The song wasn't familiar, but it felt as if it should be—I had no idea how I'd never heard of this band before.

After staring totally entranced for a few songs, my need for answers drew me to do a quick Google search, which brought up a ton of articles. Casters started in the European scene a couple of years ago, stirring up a ton of interest over the mystery of their concealed identities—along with the fact that their appearances were random, and they gave no more than forty-eight hours' notice of a concert, leaving the music scene in an absolute fucking tizzy over them.

They'd started with American appearances about ten months ago.

No need to guess the whys of that timing.

No doubt a few of those occasions Logan disappeared from the school—especially when Noah was gone as well—were due to them having a gig.

It didn't surprise me that Logan chose to conceal his identity. His dad had grand plans for him to take over the family business, and would no doubt lose his shit if he knew his son was a famous rock star. Not that Logan needed fame or money, but from what he'd told me, this was his outlet in a world filled with responsibilities and darkness.

"I'll be thinking about his voice and how he strokes that guitar when I use my vibrator tonight," Sara shouted near my face, and I wrinkled my nose at her.

"We're sleeping in the same room, you weirdo," I shouted back and tried not to consider hexing my bestie because she was fantasizing about Logan. Between that and fighting the urge to climb the stage and stake my claim on the spellcaster, I was in real trouble.

Haley pushed us forward in the crowd, until we were close to the row of security around the stage. *Protecting the band.* I almost cackled like a cartoon witch at the thought of Logan needing anyone to protect him from humans.

He could level this fucking building without moving from where he stood.

Sara and Haley danced as the song switched to a faster-paced one, but I couldn't move. I was once more just staring up in awe, wondering if it was time to change *my* phone contact to stalker too.

As if he could feel my stare, Logan's gaze snapped down to me, our magic dancing between us. His lips quirked, but he never missed a beat. When the faster song came to an end, Logan's fingers slowed on the guitar, a softer melody emerging.

The crowd went wild, setting off a low pulse thrumming in my center. Logan was already edging me with his guitar skills and orgasmic voice; add in that intense stare resting on my face, and I was a puddle. He released me with the next number, his gaze returning to the crowd, and I was able to breathe a touch easier. Casters moved from heavy beats to slower and intense rock ballads without a pause between songs. The crowd's response told me which were their biggest hits, though at times it was hard to tell because they were all adored.

Finally, after about an hour, Logan stopped singing and addressed the crowd. He didn't halt strumming his guitar, though, long fingers moving deftly across the strings. "You all know that we occasionally bring one lucky audience member up onto the stage for a personal song." The rasp in his tone was more pronounced after an hour of singing, which momentarily distracted me from what he'd just said.

Wait. *Bring someone up onstage?*

He'd better fucking not be talking about me or he'd find that gorgeous black guitar of his smashed over his head.

"Tonight, we're bringing up three."

Haley and Sara gripped my hands, and I was trying to back away, but they wouldn't let me move. Traitors. All of them were traitors.

Logan nodded toward someone offstage who we couldn't see, and two roadies hurried out onstage holding three low stools between them. They deposited the chairs in the center of the band. A second later, the crowd parted, and two burly security guards stopped before us. "Casters want you ladies up there with them," the first one said, his eyes flat as annoyance seeped out of him. "Please don't touch the band. They're not animals for you to pet, no matter how much you want to."

Haley snorted so loudly that she had to cough and cover the sound with her hands.

"I think we'll manage," I shot back dryly. "But what if we don't want to go up?"

Logan, who stood near the middle of the stage, couldn't have possibly heard me over the crowd, but he wore an amused expression as I continued to display my reluctance. My protest died off at how incredibly delicious he looked, sweat dripping across the bare skin of his chest revealed by the torn-up shirt.

"Come on, Precious. Live a little."

The crowd lost their fucking brains, chanting "Precious" in time to his guitar riff, and I knew that refusing was only going to make this worse. Sara tightened her hold on me and Haley, and all but dragged us after the security, who directed us toward a set of side stairs.

"Fuck," Sara whispered, when we reached the stage, staring out into the thousands of faces packing the warehouse venue. "I think I'm going to puke."

Haley was the one now to drag us along and deposit us on the stools.

"Ladies," Logan said, towering over us as he moved closer. "Welcome to the stage."

I nailed him with a glare, anger soothing my nerves. He just chuckled, completely unintimidated by me, even though he should be at least a little worried. I could get very creative in my revenge plans.

"We always serenade with one song during a show," he explained, before he looked over his shoulder and winked at the crowd. Yeah, they lost their minds again—at this rate, no one in the audience would have voices by tomorrow. "We usually sing 'Heart Chords,' but tonight . . . tonight it's going to be 'Pact.'"

That song clearly meant something to the fans, but the title alone sent shivers through my gut. I squirmed on my stool as Tobias moved toward his microphone. "I know this is a fan favorite, the *unicorn song* we only perform once a year, so hold on to your fucking knickers, ladies. Dudes, you too, if you're wearing any. Because we're about to rock them the fuck off."

Tobias had a British accent, smooth and deep without Logan's rasp. He stood right before me, and this close I could see the slight glow of the magic around their painted faces.

Logan got very close, leaning down to stroke a single finger across my cheek. "This one's for you, Precious," he murmured, his mic broadcasting those words to the crowd.

His speed picked up on his guitar, the black pick in his fingers gliding across the strings. It was an intricate melody he wove in what was clearly a rock ballad.

Noah's drums started a beat later, and the layers added

by Tobias's bass had tingles tracing down my spine to leave goose bumps across my skin. The feeling swooped through my gut and settled low in my body, until I swore my clit throbbed at the sensation.

Logan wasn't touching me, but with each chord, it felt as if he did.

Especially when he started to sing.

The three of us were captured in the essence of their magical music, mesmerized as Logan wove a tale of a pact between soulmates. They died together in the end, wrapped in each other's arms, only to be reborn to love again.

It was just a song. But it destroyed me.

Logan's eyes were on me the entire time, and as hard as I fought the tears, there was no holding them back. The stage lights blinded me from being able to really see if the rest of the crowd were bawling too, but the choked silence after the final chord told me there were more than a few tears.

Noise exploded around us as the bubble burst, and I turned to find Sara's and Haley's tear-streaked faces staring at me. "I'm dead," Sara sniffled. "That bastard."

Logan brushed away one of my tears, giving me another second of his full attention before he returned it to his audience. "I know, I know. It's our emotional ballad, and that's why we rarely play it. But with such beautiful ladies, we couldn't resist."

He strummed his guitar again, moving on to a faster beat. He didn't look our way as the security guards returned to escort us off. When we reached the side of the stage, we were told to wait. "The boys will greet you after the show."

Sara and Haley pushed in on me as soon as the guards were gone. "What. The. Fuck. Paisley Hallistar?" Sara's grip was just short of painful. "What's going on with you and Logan? That song was for a motherfucking soulmate. A soulmate. He was dead serious when he called you mate the other night? Like . . . no sarcasm?"

"He sang to all three of us," I shot back weakly.

My *ex*-besties blinked at me before they laughed their asses off, and I narrowed my eyes in an attempt to murder them with my gaze. "Whatever you want to tell yourself," Sara shouted when she caught her breath. "But I think it's better if you're honest about it."

"I really fucking don't know." I had to scream over the music. "I want to trust in this. I want to fall into Logan, I really do, but there's still a lot I don't understand." I thought about the story he'd told me last night—our last day in the park and that magical pact that bound us together. Part of me was relieved to have the information, while another wondered if Logan only wanted me because of the magic binding us from when we were kids.

My pain and doubt were clearly broadcasting across my face, which had Haley and Sara backing off, sympathy in their gazes. "Just stay safe," Haley said near my ear. "Enjoy the journey. Logan is smoking hot and could star as a book boyfriend in any of the books we read. I know we've thought him evil in the past, but he proved us wrong again and again. We owe him for your life, and he has my vote."

It was the truth. Absolute, undeniable truth.

We were distracted by the stage crew bringing us refreshments, and while it was only regular alcohol, I downed two in seconds. They kept them coming thankfully, so by the time their set was done, I almost had a buzz.

"They're incredible," Haley gushed as the guys wrapped up the night and left the stage. "Does anyone know if Noah's single?"

My laughter was cut off as Logan reached my side, his guitar still around his sweaty neck. I'd seen him sweat before—this warlock had a weird penchant for lifting heavy things and then jogging for seventy-two hours after. But tonight, with the mask and the rock star clothes, and the easing of his intense energy—as if his demons were temporarily quiet—it was like seeing him for the first time.

"I am single," Noah said, appearing over Logan's shoulder.

"Me too, you right bastards," the third to their trio chimed in. He flashed a smile my way and held out his hand. "Hello, love. Tobias Brietlin the Third, at your fucking service."

He cursed like a rock star, but his accent was posh and refined. This warlock grew up rich as well. All three of these warlocks were rich, and I'd put good money on them having met at a fancy-ass academy in Europe.

When I reached out to grasp his hand, he gripped my palm tightly before dragging me closer. "Let me get a bloody look at the witch who has Logan's knickers in a twist."

Logan's power surged and Tobias's hand loosened and dropped away.

"No touchy," Noah growled over Logan's shoulder. "You don't want to piss off the spellcaster."

Tobias shrugged, like he wasn't quite sure that was true. "Come on, Loges. You know I would never. But curiosity and all that."

With a burst of magic, Tobias was shifted away from me with such force that the guitar strapped over his chest swung around and almost clipped the roadies working the stage. "Fuck, okay," he said with a laugh, rubbing his chest. "You've got it, mate. I won't touch your witch."

Returning my gaze to Logan, I tilted my head and he shrugged. "As Noah said—" his voice was deeper after the hours of singing "—don't touch what's mine."

I patted his sweaty chest, and it wasn't even gross. Old sweat might smell bad, but Logan smelled delicious.

"No need to piss on me, bestie. I'm not interested in your friends." I lifted my gaze to smile at Noah. "Hey, big guy. Nice job on the drums out there."

His return smile was warm. "Good to see you, pretty girl. Even nicer that you brought pretty friends with you."

He looked at Haley as he said that, and the pink in her cheeks deepened. Tobias glanced toward Sara as well, but didn't show much interest. An energy she returned tenfold.

She wasn't a fan of the snooty Brit, clearly.

Meanwhile, I was locked in an icy green gaze. "You have some explaining to do," I murmured to him, and he just smiled.

"Give us fifteen to get out of costume, and we'll meet you right back here." When I nodded, he leaned forward and tucked a strand of hair behind my ear. "Don't move from this spot, Precious."

It grew increasingly difficult to swallow, but I managed another nod, and that appeared to satisfy him enough to leave, Noah and Tobias trailing after him.

"I think I just came in my panties."

I swung around to Haley and gasped, before reaching out to press a hand against her forehead like she was unwell. "Who are you and what did you do with my bookish bestie?" I demanded.

She sucked in a deep breath, and then another. "Noah actually looked at me," she choked out. "I've been chasing that fucker with my eyes all year, and he finally saw me tonight. What is happening?"

"All year?" I said with a jolt. "I had no idea you were interested in him."

Haley flushed harder. "Fantasy only, Pais. I'm not the sort of witch Noah would go for. He's a bad boy and I'm the epitome of good girl."

"Sounds exactly like a romance novel," I said with a smile. "Don't sell yourself short. You're gorgeous, intelligent, and a badass witch. Noah would be freaking lucky to have you."

Haley dropped her face to hide her expression, but she didn't argue again.

Well, tonight just got a tad more interesting.

CHAPTER 10

The guys were back in fifteen minutes, sweat and masks gone. They were dressed in jeans, boots, and hoodies, and Logan held our coats over his arm, having known to retrieve them from the coat check. He was the most observant warlock I'd ever met; there was a reason I called him Stalkcaster.

He handed Sara and Haley theirs, before holding mine out and helping me into it. "I should murder you," I said as I slipped my arms into the sleeves. "What the Hel were you thinking pulling us onstage? Going incognito doesn't work when you choose friends to serenade."

Noah answered with soft laughter. "That was Logan's attempt at flirting. He's just terrible at it."

The scowl Logan shot his way would have scared a lesser warlock. "I'm terrible at nothing, asshole. Precious might be a tough nut to crack, but I'm chipping away."

An undeniable truth. "So, what's the plan now?" I asked, desperate for a subject change before I slipped up and revealed just how close Logan was to *cracking my nut*. Tobias stepped closer, and without his mask of magic, we could see his handsome features. He had messy blond waves, longer on top and short on the sides. His face was clean-cut, with an aristocratic nose and dark brown eyes.

"We're heading to our place in the city," he said with a casual shrug. "You ladies want to join us?"

Haley piped up first. "Hel yes, we'd love to join you. The night is still very young."

"Speak for yourself," Sara huffed. "We should hit some clubs. I need drinks and dancing, in that order."

"Aw, come on, love," Tobias said, stepping closer even though Sara couldn't be giving off stronger *don't touch me* vibes. "Don't be like that. You'll spoil your friend's fun."

I had no idea why she'd instantly disliked him so much, but she was making no attempt to hide her disdain. "I'm not your love, *love*." She mimicked his accent and I tried not to laugh.

Tobias pressed a hand to his chest. "You wound me, Sara. Shot through the heart."

"If only that was the truth," she said with her sweetest smile before swinging around to Haley and me. "If you two want to go back to their creepy, serial-killer pad, I'll tag along to make sure they don't wear you as skin suits. But that's all I'm there for."

Logan's laughter was warm and enticing, and I wanted to press against the heat of his magic.

"I spent all year keeping this one alive," he said, brushing a hand across the bare skin between my neck and coat, "and as pretty as her skin is, I'd rather it stayed perfectly intact on her body."

Noah—clearly riding the same euphoric high from their concert as the other two—wore an actual smile, softening his scary exterior. "Let's get the fuck out of here."

The party in the warehouse was only getting started by the sound of it, but backstage everything was being broken down and stored. Logan led us to a door off to the side, and after making sure no one was in the vicinity, he opened another portal for us to step through.

"Quickest way," he said when I raised an eyebrow at his continued illegal activities. As long as he didn't get caught, I honestly wasn't fazed by his loose interpretation of the law.

We emerged in a marble-lined entrance, outside of a double set of white and gold doors. Behind us was a single elevator, and there were no other rooms on what was clearly the penthouse floor in an expensive apartment building.

"Whoa. One of you is rich," Haley said, wide-eyed.

"I'd hazard a guess all of them are," Sara said with a huff, as if she were mortally offended by their wealth. Outside of Belle, who had a father on the council, the rest of us were solidly lower middle class. There wasn't any extravagance in our lives.

"Remember, what's mine is yours, Precious," Logan murmured, leaving me flustered as he opened the doors—without touching them, of course.

"I'm extremely rich," Tobias drawled. "Like *my family is related to the royal family and we have billions* sort of rich."

Sara shot him the fakest smile I'd ever seen. "The *third* after your name kind of clued us in on the rich and royal." She made a show of sidling past the warlock without touching him. "And the fact that you *used* the *third* after your name clued us in on your douchebaggery. We know all we need to."

The general air of joviality he'd been rocking faded as he watched her enter the apartment. It wasn't darkness in his gaze exactly, but she'd struck a nerve. It wasn't like Sara to be so judgmental, but this warlock rubbed her the wrong way.

"It's all good, moneybags," I said, patting his muscled arm. "We won't judge you for your bank account, if you don't judge us for our lack thereof."

That sliver of darkness faded from his eyes. "No judgment from me. Your little friend isn't wrong about money turning witches and warlocks into *douchebags*. My family is chock-full of sanctimonious bastards, and I've done my best to escape. This band saved my life. I'd take homelessness before I returned to the Brietlin fold. Thank the goddess for a trust fund that's free and clear of the rest."

It was a shame that Sara missed that little speech; it would have gone a long way to softening her ire.

Inside, the apartment was no less extravagant, but it was warmer. White-and-gold marble floors were covered by thick plush rugs, mostly in shades of black and white. We took our shoes off at the entrance, and I was relieved to be free of the heels.

Padding along the nicely warmed flooring, we ended up in a huge open-plan living, kitchen, and dining space. It spanned across what felt like the entire level and had floor-to-ceiling windows, similar in style to the ones in Logan's farmhouse.

The spellcaster enjoyed having a view, no matter where he was living.

Drifting over to see what lay below, I was caught in the millions of lights and the beauty of the city at night. "Central Park is down there," Logan said, joining me at the windows.

I didn't jump. I'd felt his energy before he reached me. "How many homes do you own?" I asked, turning to face him.

"We, Precious."

I blinked at him. "What?"

"How many homes do *we* own."

I shook my head. "Logan, come on. I mean, sure, I appreciate your continued implication that I'm your true mate and we have this unbreakable bond. It absolutely makes a witch feel good about herself, but you have to stop. Don't . . ." I ran out of steam, unable to finish. *Don't make me fall in love with you, because I won't survive the end.*

The betrayal that I knew was coming.

No matter the sexual chemistry between us, and the undeniable connection between our magic, nothing had changed with his father or mine, and sooner or later that feud would come to collect.

Logan didn't react as I'd expect. He didn't get angry and snarl back at me. His touch was gentle as he reached out and brushed my hair back. "One day you won't have to question my motivations toward you. I promise it will all make sense soon."

"I've heard that before," I responded dryly.

"Drinks!" Sara shouted, interrupting further conversation. "Thank fuck. I was starting to worry that this was a dry party."

Logan and I turned to find three of our four friends crashed out on the black suede sectional, making themselves comfortable. Tobias was the only one still standing as he mixed drinks behind a bar that ran along one wall.

"I've got witch wine in a variety of brands," he said, gracefully depositing glasses onto a round stone coffee table. "I've also got regular alcohol for those who can't handle the buzz." He shot a quick glance at Sara, and she sat straighter on the couch.

"Ah, fuck," I muttered, and Logan glanced at me. "He's challenged her now."

Sure enough, Sara reached out and snatched up two of the witch wines, downing them almost in one gulp. "I'm the goddess-be-damned life of the party," she drawled, the wine taking effect so fast her eyes were already shiny. "Don't question me, you overgrown pubic hair."

Tobias stared at her. Then stared some more. As if he'd never seen anyone like Sara in his life. "Did she just call me a pubic hair?" he finally asked. He was talking to us, but he was still staring at her.

That set Noah and Haley off, as they fell into each other laughing their asses off. They had been sitting rather close to start with, but now Haley was practically in his lap.

"You're as annoying as one," Sara said. "Hence why I spell my coochie bare. Not. A. Fan. Of pubic hair." Tobias's eyes draped down her body, as if he could prove that statement through X-ray vision. Sara got to her feet and prowled across to him—she was tiny enough that he looked massive next to her. "Not that you'll ever find out, *moneybags*."

She'd adopted my nickname, and I covered my mouth to hide my laughter.

Tobias's eyes flashed. "Babe, I'll have you naked before this night is through and you bloody well know it. This pretend hate is nothing more than intense chemistry."

"Chemistry masquerading as hate," Logan murmured near my ear. "Feels familiar."

With a shake of my head, I headed for the couch, grabbing a witch wine on my way. *Just one tonight.* Then I'd switch to regular alcohol.

"Come on, guys," Haley said, selecting a vodka mix. "It's a party. Let's relax."

For once, she was following her own advice. No book in hand, no constantly checking her watch to escape. She was snuggled into Noah's giant side, looking content as Hel there.

I went to drop into the seat beside Sara, who thankfully also had a vodka in hand after her wines, but a firm grip yanked me back onto Logan's lap.

"What are you doing?" I asked, tensing across his hard thighs.

"Just for tonight, take Haley's advice and relax," he said. "Tomorrow you can go back to questioning my every motive."

"Right," Tobias declared. "Truce all around tonight. Think you can handle that, badass?"

Sara narrowed her eyes on him, but Haley's pleading expression caught her attention. "Fine. Tonight only. We're all friends, and *Tobias Brietlin the Third* isn't an impossible dickhead."

Tobias just laughed. "If you want to see my dick, you only have to ask."

Sara smiled sweetly. "Me and every other girl you randomly meet, I'm sure."

"This truce is off to an excellent start," Haley said with a smirk. "I can't wait to see what the rest of the night holds."

Noah got music playing, and I relaxed against Logan, letting myself just enjoy the feeling of being with him. The guys chatted and laughed about their show, and it was clear they knew each other well. The sort of old friends who'd grown up together and had that comfort and familiarity of a true bond.

When my witch wine was empty, a pleasant warmth infused me, and I was boneless as Logan kept one hand wrapped around my waist, while the other stroked along my thigh. Just tiny teasing touches, and the feel of his hand on my bare skin drove me crazy.

It had been too long since we'd had sex, and I hoped tonight he'd put me out of my misery.

"How did you three meet?" Haley asked, reaching for her third vodka. I'd never even seen her drink a full one before, but she was different tonight. All of us felt different. As if for one night we were part of the book world, living out lead-character stories.

My story was that Logan *was* my true mate. A forever partner who would soothe my soul as I'd seen Dad and Mom do for each other over the years.

For tonight, I let myself drift in that fantasy.

"At the academy," Noah said, lifting his huge arm and draping it across the back of the couch behind Haley, who shivered at the sensation of being surrounded by the massive warlock. *Me too, girl. Me fucking too.*

These guys were potent, and we were unequipped to handle their energy.

"Called it," I said, trying to keep my voice even. "I knew you rich boys would have all attended an academy."

"Westminster Prep," Tobias drawled, his accent deepening. "Creating the warlocks of tomorrow."

Logan shifted under me, his hard length pressing against my ass. "Our fathers weren't really fans of being fathers, and none of us have mothers. They either died or fucked off with the hired help. We bonded over our general lack of quality family."

The mention of his mom dying had me tense once more, but he didn't let me pull away, his hold keeping me firm against him.

Truce.

Tonight we had a truce, and I'd enjoy this while it lasted.

CHAPTER 11

A few hours into our night with the guys, we were way too drunk to get home, so I sent texts to Mom and Dad telling them we were fine and would see them in the morning. Sara and Tobias were dancing now . . . together. No doubt she'd have some regrets in the morning. One of which would definitely be drinking that third glass of witch wine. The third was the killer.

I picked up another vodka; I'd stuck to my guns with only the one wine. "Come on, witches," Sara yelled. "Come and dance with me."

Tobias hauled her closer, his gaze focused on her. "I can handle all three of you witches on the dance floor."

Logan grumbled beneath me but didn't try to murder his friend. He appeared well used to the Brit's antics. "Ready for school next month?" Haley asked Noah. They'd been cuddling and drinking together all night, neither moving an inch.

"Not really," he said. "I'm only there because Logan is."

"And I'll be there this year," Tobias drawled. "Finally got out of the family commitment and accepted my Weatherstone invitation."

Sara sighed as she stopped dancing. "You'll be at Weatherstone?" Her words were just starting to slur.

"All year, badass," he said with a pretty smile. "Wanna extend this truce and be fuck buddies?"

For a beat, it almost looked as if she was considering it, before she batted him away. "Enough with the talking, moneybags. Dance."

He didn't argue, his hands falling to her hips as they moved together.

The stress of the day eventually caught up to me, and my eyes closed as I snuggled into Logan's chest. His hold felt safe, and I let myself relax and enjoy the music and my friends' laughter. If only Belle were here, this would be a perfect night.

I hoped I'd see her at school. What if her father didn't let her return? Speaking of . . .

"Did you keep Elder Monroe and those witnesses away from the trial today?" I murmured to Logan without opening my eyes. I should have asked him that earlier, but the whole *rock star* reveal had been quite the distraction.

Logan shifted me higher, and my eyes opened as he brushed his lips across mine. "Of course. It wasn't hard to create a distraction—Elder Monroe is in a bit of trouble with the council for some of his recent activities. Better he worry about himself than whatever vendetta he has against your family."

"Won't your father be pissed that you're helping mine?" I asked, examining his face.

His green eyes grew icy, reminding me of how he used to look when I first saw him at Weatherstone. "Don't worry about my father. I'll handle Rafael. You just stay as far away from him as you can. If you see him coming, you run the other way. Promise me, Paisley."

I swallowed roughly and nodded. "I promise." The last thing I wanted was to go near Rafael Kingston.

Logan stood abruptly, leaving me a touch breathless as he

adjusted my body until I was secure in his arms. "It's Precious's bedtime," he declared to the room. "We'll see you all in the morning."

"I can walk," I said, slapping his shoulder.

He ignored me completely, like the arrogant asshole he was, and I waved at our friends, who were smiling broadly. I could see by their expressions that Sara and Haley would have *many* questions for me tomorrow.

Logan carried me down a hallway, toward a white door. "This is my room," he said as it opened for him. He stepped onto the plush navy carpet, heading toward a huge bed dressed in a blue duvet and pillows, contrasting nicely to the black iron bed frame. Off to the side I noticed an entire wall of guitars, mounted in staggered displays.

"How many guitars do you own?" I asked, wondering if I'd missed more at the farmhouse.

"A fucking lot," he said with a laugh. "I don't have many obsessions in life. Just you and my music. You both got me through the last twenty years."

My pulse thrummed through me, and I found my fingers sinking deeper into the soft hair at the nape of his neck. He didn't set me down, and in the semidarkness of his room—two bedside lamps the only illumination—there was a cloak of comfort around us. "Do you play any other instruments?"

"Piano, drums, bass, violin, and trombone."

Of course. "I mean, the trombone was a given," I said dryly.

Logan shot me a slow smile as he strolled into his gray marbled bathroom. The first thing I noticed was the black bathtub, large enough to fit six people. "Would you like a shower, Precious? I'd like to take care of you."

The ache in my chest was intense, and I was afraid that it might already be too late for me to protect my heart. "That would be nice." My voice sounded weird. I *felt* weird.

But I needed this too.

The water started from the multiple showerheads as he set me on my feet. He didn't remove his hands from me, though, his palm sliding along my spine to unlace the corset tie of my dress. Fire licked across my skin everywhere he touched, and when the bodice and skirt were loose enough, I stepped free, leaving myself in just a white lace thong.

Logan made a low, desperate sound. "You've been sent here to destroy me, Precious." He stroked a fingertip across my bare shoulders. "I'm one of the strongest warlocks in the world, and you could crumble me with a blink of those blue eyes."

It was a heady feeling, this intensity in my chest as it spilled from me. Pushing up on my toes, I brought my lips closer, and when Logan responded, there was an actual collision of power. I gasped against his soft mouth. Logan took advantage of my parted lips and pushed between them, his tongue stroking mine. I almost came undone with that one taste. Pressing against him, desperate to ease the ache between my legs, I barely resisted the urge to hump his side.

Logan's hands roamed up the front of my thighs and stroked across the material of my thong, pressing against my clit as he caressed the silk. "So wet already, Precious," he murmured, deepening the kiss. His fingers slipped under my panties, sliding through the slickness. I was fucking soaked, and as he slid one finger inside me, he captured my moan in his mouth.

A second finger joined the first, moving slowly at first, before he increased the speed, fucking me harder. His thumb circled my clit, and all the while he never released my mouth from his.

The intense buildup of pleasure almost knocked me to the floor, but Logan's free hand kept me upright. "Fuck," I gasped, wrenching my mouth away to breathe and moan. I tried desperately to keep my voice down, hoping the music was loud enough to hide what was happening in here.

"Fuck, Logan," I cried again, as everything tightened, and the explosion of pleasure sent darkness dancing around the edge of my vision.

His fingers didn't halt their assault, drawing out every second of the orgasm, and by the time he slowly withdrew them, I'd have been sprawled on the floor if it wasn't for his strength holding me up. I gasped when he lifted his fingers to his mouth, lapping up my release. "Goddess be damned, baby," he groaned. "You taste even better than I remember." His voice was a low caress across my sensitive nerves, and I had no words as I watched him. "Now, let's get you cleaned up."

He stripped away his clothes in a heartbeat, and my head spun as he removed my thong and shifted us both under the warm water. Expecting him to grab the bodywash, I was completely unprepared when Logan dropped to his knees, burying his mouth in my pussy, devouring whatever remained of my orgasm.

Getting "cleaned up" had never felt so fucking good.

"You taste like forever, Precious," he groaned, and I slid my hands into his hair as the building pleasure destroyed my ability to talk.

The second orgasm was no less intense than the first, and once again it was only Logan's hands on the back of my thighs that kept me upright. He was destructive, this spell-caster, in every fucking way.

My mind floated in blissed-out ecstasy, and I reached for his hard length, wanting to return the gesture. Logan's dick was as impressive as the last time I saw it, thick and hard, the end red and already seeping pre-cum.

Eating my pussy had turned him on, and I was desperate for a taste of him.

"Not tonight, Precious," he said, capturing my wrist before I could touch him. "Tonight is about you. I want to take care of you."

I had no idea what to say, and by the time I formed a protest, he had the bodywash in his hands and was doing what I'd expected earlier.

Cleaning me up.

With his hands, he gently rubbed soap over every inch of my skin, the minty gel coating me in his scent. Once I was clean and rinsed, he shut off the water and dried me with a fluffy gray towel. Then he nudged me toward a shelf of toiletries.

"Finish getting ready for bed while I tell those assholes to shut the fuck up," he murmured, pressing a kiss to my temple. "You're exhausted."

He was gone before I could comment, and I took a few seconds to sort myself out. My legs were weak, my pulse thrummed, and if my magic weren't suppressed, I'd be calling monsters with the intensity of the swirls of energy in my center.

Logan had me off-kilter, and even as I brushed my teeth and used some moisturizer from the bottle on his shelf, I couldn't calm down. When I exited the bathroom, Logan was there, sliding his hands under my thighs to bring me up against his body once more. He strode to the bed and pulled back the covers before he leaned over to place me in the center.

He followed until we were sprawled together, his arms coming around me to hold me close. "It's time to sleep," he whispered. "I'll keep the monsters away."

The care he was taking with me tonight was my absolute undoing. I didn't know how to handle this side of Logan, and a part of me wondered why he hadn't let me touch him in the shower. Or why we didn't have sex. "Do you not want to have sex with me again?"

It was a ridiculous, needy question that I regretted the second it left my mouth.

Logan stilled, lifting his head higher until I was locked in his gaze. "I have waited a long time for you, Paisley Hallistar. A long fucking time. Nothing went the way I expected when we came together at Weatherstone, what with the dreams, and our bonded magic screwing up our equilibriums, but I'm determined to show you how important you are to me now. You're not just a body to lose myself in, you hear me? You're everything, and we're going to take our time. We might have started with sex, and I fucking promise you we'll end with it as well, but for now . . . just let me show you how important you are to me."

The heat of my tears burned, and no matter how hard I blinked, I couldn't stop them from slipping free. "Don't cry," he whispered, tucking me against his bare chest. "You destroy me when you cry, and I can't even kill anyone for hurting you. Because it was me, and I know I'm a bastard who doesn't deserve you, but I can't let you go. Not before, and certainly not now. I tried, Precious. I tried to let you go, but it's beyond even my power."

His words had me sobbing, and I prayed with everything that this was real. That what we had wasn't some cruel trick, about to be stolen away.

Because I'd worried before about falling in love with Logan and losing myself.

When it was already too late.

CHAPTER 12

Sara gaped at me. "So, nothing happened? Like, no fucking at all?"

We were back in Spokane, the three of us sprawled across my bed, and it was hard to believe that only this morning I'd woken in Logan's arms in his fancy New York penthouse.

He'd kept his promise. There'd been no monsters or bad dreams, and he'd kissed the heck out of me before his driver delivered me and my friends back at our hotel.

Just in time for us to check out and make our way to an *official* transport back home.

"No sex," I confirmed. "Just some amazing orgasms, and then I slept like the freaking dead."

Sara shook her head. "The warlock is into you, Pais. Like, really into. He threatened to destroy us if we disturbed your sleep by being too loud. He knows you're not sleeping very well. It was sweet and—"

"Utterly terrifying," Haley breathed. "Lucky for me, Noah blocked me from most of his wrath."

"Noah, hey?" I said as my smile grew. I was genuinely dying to know what had gone on with those two. "Anything happen with that tank of a warlock? You're not walking funny, so I'm guessing not yet."

Haley blushed, her pretty face pink and flushed. "Nothing happened outside of cuddling and a few intense conversations, but I think I fell in love last night. He's so attentive. He asked me about my books, and fuck me dead, he reads too. Mostly thrillers, but he requested my favorite book titles so he could check them out."

"Get him to read that one with the gargoyle who has two dicks," Sara suggested. "The sex scenes in that were fucking hot, and it's always good to train them up early."

"Great suggestion," I said, backing her choice. "I'm still waiting for the author to expand that world."

"How about you and Tobias?" Haley shifted the focus to Sara.

"Tobias Brietlin the Third, you mean," Sara said with a sarcastic drawl. "Nothing happened. We fought. We danced. We fucked. End of story."

Haley and I stared at her, our mouths agape, and I wondered if I'd misheard. "How is that nothing?" I finally said around a shocked laugh. "Girl. Friend."

Sara shrugged. "Look, I dislike his personality, but the package is very pretty. And huge. A huge package that I seriously enjoyed. He talks a lot of shit, but he fucks like a god. That's the end of it though."

Haley and I exchanged a blank look for about three seconds before we both lost it. I had to press the bridge of my nose in an attempt to stop myself from spluttering as I said, "Sara, please never change." She shrugged like there was no chance of that ever happening.

"What are your plans for the rest of break?" Haley asked. "I've got to get back home to help with Dad, but I can't wait to see you all next month at Weatherstone. Sophomore year."

"No plans for us," I said with a yawn. "Work, keep my magic suppressed—" Haley was aware of what had happened now too, and thankfully didn't think I was an evil demon-witch "—and try to figure out why Belle is MIA."

Haley grew serious, her eyes locked on me. "Do you think it's a good idea to suppress your magic the way you are? What are the long-term effects of it?"

Letting out a breath, I shook my head. "I have no idea. Gran would have known, but we have to trust in her advice. The letters didn't give an end date. They just said that without the suppression, I'd eventually call the monsters in a public location where I couldn't hide them, and the council would destroy me."

I was only safe now because when I'd unintentionally used my affinity, I'd been at Weatherstone behind their warding, which prevented the council from knowing. The few who were aware of my long-forgotten affinity might suspect there was a reaper at Weatherstone, but they never discovered who it was.

Haley pressed on: "What about when you're back at school? They expect a spellcaster."

"I can manage basic magic still—the same as freshman year. I'm just going to have to keep pretending my energy is hard to release."

Haley didn't look convinced, but she didn't argue with me further. "We have your back no matter what." She gave me a hug, holding on for a few seconds longer than normal. "I love you both. Keep in touch."

After Haley left, for the rest of winter break, Sara and I fell into a routine. I went to work and she followed. Even with daily skate lessons, she was woeful, but it was nice having her around.

My parents kept tiptoeing around me, and while my siblings came home for one night to celebrate Dad's trial dismissal, the rest of the time they remained with their coven or at Weatherstone. Both, I was sure, preferrable to dealing with the weird tension in the house.

Logan wasn't around either, with his father dominating his time, but he called me every night, and I wondered how I'd ever sleep again without his deep voice whispering sweet stories into my ear. He'd stuck to his promise of slowly building a bond between us, and I was falling hard and fast.

Though, as nice as a slow build was, if we didn't get to *hard and fast* soon, I might actually combust.

A few days before school was about to start, I found myself alone with Mom in the kitchen. "What really happened that night in the graveyard?" I asked her, unable to keep avoiding all topics related to reapers. "You say you're not like me, so how were you there? How did I call you?"

She sucked in a deep breath, and I thought she was about to leave the room, but as the shock slipped from her features, she settled her breathing. "I wish I knew. I was in the middle of reading Mom's letters when I felt a pull toward you. A tugging in my gut. Moms are connected to their children's magic in ways only another mom would understand. Though I'm sure your gran had a small hand in getting me where I needed to go."

I'd read through Gran's letters too, but there'd been very few revelations outside of her suppression potion. She'd been careful in case they fell into the wrong hands.

They were all gone now, thrown into the fire by Mom as a precaution against my secret ever getting out.

"How could they just wipe a fifth affinity from existence?" I whispered, finding it hard to believe this was my life.

"You're quite possibly the last night witch slash reaper alive," Mom said, just as quietly. "Powerful magic is at play to hunt your kind down. They're afraid of this power, sweetheart. They're afraid of what you are and can do. You can never let anyone know about this. You shouldn't even go back to Weatherstone."

My mind rebelled against the notion. "So, no future for me at all? I just give up now because of some centuries-old prejudice against this affinity?"

Mom swiped hard at her eyes. "No . . . goddess no. I won't allow it. I said you *shouldn't* go back to college. Not that I was going to stop you. But you must be aware of the risks. The suppression potion is so important. You can't ever forget to take it."

"Okay," I agreed hoarsely. "I'll pretend to be a weak spellcaster, the same as last year. I can do it. I can keep this secret."

Providing Belle's father didn't already know and was launching a plan to attack me.

Best I didn't mention that to Mom.

"What killed Logan's mom?" I asked, hoping that her sharing mood would extend a little further. As much as I'd like the past to stay in the past, this unanswered question could be what would tear Logan and me apart.

She hesitated before taking a deep breath. "I have a theory, but I'm not sure I should speak on it. Not while there are feuds and oaths lingering in the magic of our world. I don't want to speak it into existence."

I read between the lines of what she was saying. Rafael was powerful, and we had no idea how well he had us under surveillance. Though, that would mean he was aware of my relationship with his son, unless Logan had his own means of keeping his father's magic away.

"I love you, Mom," I said, thankful that we'd managed to talk like we used to. Even if only for a few minutes. "Thanks for accepting and protecting me."

She reached forward and hugged me hard. "I love you, Paisley. We will make sure you're okay. No matter what else happens."

I nodded, throat too tight to say anything else.

That night when I got into bed and settled under the covers, I sent off a text to Logan, who was no longer Stalkcaster in my phone.

Paisley: Why did you transfer to Weatherstone last year?

Logan: Your power bloomed. I wasn't
leaving you unclaimed.

Whatever magic we'd woven as children was indelibly imprinted on my being.

A permanent mark.

Logan had told me it was the same for him.

Paisley: Is everything okay with your
dad? You're safe, right?

Logan: I'm safe, Precious. And you need to sleep—I
can feel your exhaustion from here. It's not long until
the start of school. I'll be with you very soon. Just have
to make sure everything is dealt with on this side.

I didn't know what he was doing, but I found myself trusting him all the same.

Stupid or not, I was all in with Logan Kingston.

And I couldn't wait for the new year and Weatherstone.

The night before we were set to return to Weatherstone, Sara and I spent a few hours packing our bags.

"So, are you ready for school tomorrow?"

She sprawled back on my bed, cradling her head in her hands as she stared at the ceiling.

"Yeah, I am actually," I replied as I sat on my suitcase to zip it closed. I'd snuck a few crystals in even though I wasn't supposed to spend too much time around them. Mom had locked most of them away, but I'd managed to smuggle out a couple.

Being cut off from them was almost painful, and while I wouldn't take them with me in my pockets or wear them around my neck again, I needed to know they were close.

"I'm ready for some normalcy in my life," I told her, when my bag finally closed.

"And I bet you miss that hunk of a spellcaster . . ." She almost sounded wistful, and I was fairly sure I'd seen a message from Tobias on her phone earlier.

Maybe I wasn't the only one ready to get back to Weatherstone and see a powerful warlock.

When we headed down for dinner, Dad was in a celebratory mood, bouncing around the kitchen. "It'll be great to get back to teaching and guiding my students, Little Gem," he said as he ruffled my hair and pressed a kiss to my forehead. "Your sisters said they'll be back to see you before we leave."

"What about J and Trevor?" I asked.

He shook his head. "They're already at school. They'll see you there."

I shouldn't be disappointed—they'd all been here again

for my birthday and Christmas Day, but this distance between us all grated on me.

No matter what happened over the next year, I was going to work on getting my family and me back to the place where we were so close that they knew what I felt before I did.

I couldn't let this affinity steal that from me.

CHAPTER 13

"We're back, witches," Sara shouted, dancing around the front gate while I hugged Haley. The Weatherstone College gates looked as impressive and imposing as the first time I stood before them, and I couldn't wait to step into the Victorian-Gothic buildings of the prestigious magic college.

"I'll catch you ladies later," Dad said as he gave us all a gentle bop on the head, like we were cute puppies. "Stay out of trouble."

"Always, Professor Hallistar," Sara said, looking far more angelic than she actually was.

Dad just shook his head. After her extended stay over the winter break, he knew she was a brazen ballbuster masquerading as a meek witch. "It's nice to be back," he said, glancing around, his aura infused with a calm that had been missing during his suspension.

It was hard to keep my emotions at bay—I hadn't been sure I'd see Dad walk through these gates again.

"Yep, sis, we'll catch you at dinner tonight," Jensen said, dropping an arm around me for a hug before he took off.

"Later, sis," Trevor called as well.

They'd both been standing at the gates when we arrived, and combined with my sisters' send-off this morning—which included hugs and tears—it settled a part of me that had been in turmoil since last October. "Stay out of trouble," I shouted after them, receiving a wave over their shoulders in response.

Assholes. I loved them, but they were both assholes.

"So, how have the last few days been?" Haley asked as we started up the path, dragging our bags behind us. "We haven't really had a chance to chat since Paisley's birthday."

She'd stopped in for my tiny party to celebrate turning twenty-three, after spending Christmas morning with her family. The night was fun, outside of Logan not making it, but he'd called and sent twenty-three gifts, which had included books, jewelry, crystals, and a small greenhouse with dozens of herbs. Not the same as the warlock himself, but he was showing that this bond between us was real, which helped to push my doubts aside.

"It's been . . . good."

Haley shot me a rueful glance. "Still no face-to-face meeting with a certain spellcaster, I see."

My sigh was extended . . . revealing too much.

"I mean, he gave her a shit ton of presents on her birthday," Sara cut in. "He can't help it if he's in Europe doing dumb shit for his evil daddy."

Rafael was the reason he hadn't come back to see me, and it worried me that Logan was balancing on a precarious tightrope between his father and me. The thought of him so far away *and possibly in danger* had my magic swirling against Gran's spell.

"I spoke with Noah a few times," Haley said, her voice lowering to a dreamy note. "He was with Logan in Italy and Germany, keeping him safe. Or so he said. They appeared to mostly be attending events. Did you know Rafael's company is the largest distributor of integrated circuits? Going hand in hand with their innovative work in robotics."

I knew because I'd googled them and found out they were the go-to for microchips, making them integral to the creation of computers, cars, home appliances, cell phones, and much more.

"All a front for their underhanded and shady practices, right?"

No one made it to billionaire status without some corruption.

"Goes without saying," Haley said, sobering. "I asked Noah if Logan and he were the muscle for Rafael, and he didn't deny it. I really, *really* don't like Rafael."

"Bastard must have loved the day his son's magic bloomed and he was a powerful spellcaster," Sara drawled as we joined the masses entering the school. "Imagine having that extra power at your fingertips to control."

It was hard for me to believe that Rafael had always been an evil megalomaniac—Dad wouldn't have been best friends with someone like that, but there was no denying who he was now.

"Has anyone heard from Belle?" Haley asked when we reached the front steps, pausing behind the dozens of other students already dragging their bags inside. "I've been texting her for days."

"She called me on my birthday." I hefted my bag up the steps to reach the front hall. "She said she'd been in India with her mom for most of the break and then got really sick and couldn't stare at her phone without vomiting. I don't know." I shrugged. "She's been acting weird since the end of freshman year."

"Super weird," Sara said, her tiny nose wrinkling in annoyance. "I don't like it. Especially after the way her father spoke to you. He's been in her ear for months now, and I'm worried about the Belle we'll get back."

"There's no way Belle would turn against Paisley just because her affinity isn't following normal protocols," Haley said, shaking her head as if it was beyond reality. "No way."

Haley's optimism was lovely, but I didn't feel the same way. Just thinking about Belle had an unsettled sadness whirling inside me, so I changed the subject to our classes for this year.

"I think the only class we'll share now is History of Necromancy," Sara said, air swirling around her as she called her element.

"You might share more with me," I said. "I'll be taking a wider range as a 'spellcaster.'"

"Right right," Sara said, bopping her head. "Yep, you'll be in everything except specific necro subjects."

"I'm looking forward to finding a familiar," Haley, our nature sprite, said with a happy sigh. "I've been dreaming about it. Imagining what incredible little soul I'll get to share my life with."

"Still jealous," I grumbled, dragging the wheels of my suitcase toward the next set of steps.

Haley managed to smile even as she struggled to get her bag to the top. "Didn't get your kitty over the break?" she huffed.

Not unless a brief encounter with a mountain lion counted. "Nope. I was too busy having a midlife crisis twenty years before my time."

The girls shot me looks of sympathy. "There's plenty of time for pets," Sara said, patting my shoulder. "We have more important animals to worry about." Somehow, I knew she was referring to the warlock variety.

By the time we made it through the Zoo and to the halls with the dorms, exhaustion pressed down on me. I hadn't been sleeping well again, but this felt deeper than that. My excitement over being here was fading into a weariness that I hoped would vanish with one decent night of sleep.

"I'll see you guys at the welcome ceremony," Haley said when we parted ways. "I need a nap. Dad didn't have a great night last night."

Dropping my bag, I reached out and pulled her into a one-armed hug. "I have some cash saved from my job that I can put toward a healer," I said to her. "Now that Dad's back here again, and the twins are out making their own money for the coven, money isn't that tight at home. I'm happy to share everything I have."

Sara nodded. "I've got a small savings that is all yours, babe."

Haley's eyes filled with tears as she sagged against me. She'd been working to hide her own exhaustion with her dad's accident hurting her family in many ways. He'd been the main breadwinner, and Haley and her mom had to pick up the slack.

"I love you both so much," she sniffled. "I can't tell you how much I appreciate your offer, but it's okay . . . Dad's mostly on the mend, and Mom just got a raise at her job, so we're doing better. But thank you."

"Let us know anytime." I gave her one final squeeze, and she kissed my cheek and then Sara's before she strolled down the hall to her room. Sara waved as she headed off to her dorm as well.

We were all in Florence Wing, one of the five halls in the pentacle that made up Ancot Residences. Belle was the closest to me—I could see her room from mine—but her door was firmly closed. When I knocked, there was no answer, so I carried on to my room.

I pressed my palm against the reader, and it clicked open. After dragging my heavy bag inside, I left it standing near my desk and crashed onto my neatly made bed.

The scent of lavender filled my senses from the thorough magical cleaning everything would have had just before our arrival. I gave myself ten minutes to exist in the joy of being back here, before getting to work unpacking and organizing for the new school year.

The crystals I smuggled in my bag went on the window-sill first, settling between my potted herbs. I'd cast a self-watering spell over them before I left last year, and I was relieved to see they'd made it through the long winter break. "Hello," I cooed, running my hands over their soft foliage. "I missed you guys."

I wasn't a nature sprite, but all of us with magic in our essence were connected to nature and the energy of the Earth.

When I was done unpacking, I took a long nap. Thankfully, Sara managed to remain awake and got Haley and me up in time for the welcome ceremony.

"I knocked on Belle's door, but there was no answer," she said when we started down the hallway.

My gaze shot along the crowded hall to find Belle's door just as closed as it had been before. *Fuck.* I didn't like this. A tingle traced down my spine, and it wasn't the monster tingle, but . . . it wasn't a good one either.

If Belle didn't show up to classes tomorrow, I'd go to Headmaster Gregor to see if he would tell me anything. Our regular phones didn't work at Weatherstone due to all the magic and wards around the college, but I'd try her from the landline.

One way or another, I was determined to find out what was going on with Belle.

Even if it meant that the truth about how she felt toward me, and my affinity, tore us apart.

If she was safe, I'd accept the rest.

CHAPTER 14

My exhaustion had returned by the time I tumbled into bed that evening, having sat through the welcome ceremony and the family dinner, where Trevor elbowed me out of the way to get to the food first—yeah, I might have teared up at the familiarity of his assholeness.

He was no longer holding my silence over the winter break against me and had decided to just go with the flow and get back to being family.

There'd been no sign of Belle, Logan, or Noah through any of the first evening events, and without my phone to check in, worries mingled with my weariness.

Sliding under the covers, I let my mind wander to dinner. Trevor had acted completely normal with me and Jensen, joking and throwing his fire powers around, but I hadn't missed the way he'd searched the hall, just as I'd been doing.

I'd been hoping for a glimpse of Logan and Belle.

Trevor was only interested in one of those two.

Our missing friend was playing on all of our minds, and I was determined that tomorrow I'd get some answers. Eventually, I fell into a restless sleep, tossing and turning. Darkness crept around the edges of my mind; heavy energy and shadowy magic oozed into my subconscious; the tracing tendrils of monsters scraped across my skin until soft music filtered through the carnage.

Consciousness returned in slow increments, and when I realized I wasn't alone in the room, my eyes shot open, my heart pounding hard. The moon was hidden behind thick, ominous clouds, and I searched my dark room, noticing a large shadow perched in my desk chair.

When my eyes adjusted, I relaxed. The monsters hadn't found me yet . . . It was my very own monster slayer.

Logan was sprawled back, his legs spread out before him while he softly strummed his guitar. I wasn't sure if he knew I was awake as he continued to play his soft, soothing melody.

Magic swirled within me, and I could have cried as it smashed against the suppression potion, unable to reach the warlock. We'd been apart for weeks now, and I was desperate to feel our connection. To feel our bond. A bond that I'd come to accept over our time apart, because nothing else made sense.

"Precious," he rasped—he'd known I was awake all along. "Sleep, baby. I'll keep the monsters away."

Tears spilled down my cheeks, and I wished I wasn't always crying when he came back to me. I'd just missed him so fucking much, and having him here with me again was too much emotion to contain. "Why did you choose music as your escape?" I whispered. He'd spoken about it briefly, but I wanted to know more. To dig deeper than what he showed the world—I wanted the real warlock. His soul-deep essence.

He didn't stop weaving the song around me, but he did shift closer, until my arm that was resting along the side of the bed pressed against his hard thigh. His eyes fluttered as we touched, and I wondered if he'd been as desperate for this reunion as I was.

"It started as a *fuck you* to Dad," he murmured, his stare burning into me. "He thought music was stupid and frivolous, and while he allowed me to take lessons and form a band, it was only so he could use it to force me to do his bidding. If I wanted to hang out with my friends, I had to swim in his evil world first. In truth, music saved me. It was a piece of my magic that he couldn't touch, and it gave me an outlet when I was drowning without you."

The last of my control snapped at those words, and desperate to comfort him, I swung my legs off the bed and stood between his spread thighs. I wanted to be closer, to feel his power and mine connect. It was a need that eclipsed everything else in my existence.

His strumming halted as he stared up at me, and in a move so fast I almost missed it, his guitar was set to the side and his calloused palms wrapped around the back of my bare thighs. He squeezed gently at first, his huge hands spreading warmth across my skin. As his hold turned firmer, my breaths sputtered in and out.

"Rafael believed that he owned my soul," he whispered, and even in the low light, there was no hiding the intensity of his stare as he slowly dragged me closer in slow, teasing increments. "The evil fuck had no idea I'd freely gifted it to you years ago."

My body felt as if it were about to combust as fire raced through my veins, and I was helpless to do anything except hold on and hope I survived.

Logan tightened his hold, and even though he sat while I stood, he lifted me with ease until my legs were settled on either side of him, straddling his body. The chair groaned under us, the giant warlock already overflowing around it, but it didn't collapse.

I rocked my pantie-clad core against his hard length. The black sweats he wore did little to hide his need, and I had no doubt that I was dripping for him.

Our lips met in a searing kiss. He didn't wait for me to open, demanding entrance as he stroked his tongue across mine. He kissed me like a dying man seeking his last breath, and I was swept up until I forgot everything else in existence.

It was just Logan and me.

Surrounded by his scent, his hands slid up and down my back and I rocked against his cock, desperately seeking friction to ease the ache. "I missed you," I groaned, unable to keep my feelings locked down. Even knowing how much power I'd just given to him, I couldn't bring myself to regret it.

A rumble rocked Logan's chest, and his hold grew firmer, the smallest bite against my skin. Marking me as his. "If you knew what I wanted to do with you, Precious," he growled against my neck, breathing me in, the tip of his nose tracing across the bare skin and up to the shell of my ear, "you'd be running from this room."

When my tongue darted out to taste his skin, his spicy energy shattered across my tongue. My teeth pressed against his throat, and I moaned at the hint of his blood. I'd broken the skin, and all I wanted to do was press harder. Taste more. Devour this warlock.

He rumbled again, standing so fast that I would have fallen if his arms weren't banded around me. His lips crashed against mine, flooding my system with his taste once more. The hint of metallic from the blood had me gasping as he kissed me harder.

"Precious," he groaned, his teeth scraping down my throat, adding more marks. "I can't be gentle tonight."

Threading my fingers into his hair, I yanked his head

back. "I don't want gentle. I need you to fuck me, Logan. Please."

His growl was animalistic, and if I hadn't been completely out of my mind with need, I might have worried that I'd pushed him too far. His cleverly cultivated cloak of civility—alliteration be damned—had finally snapped, and I got the true power of this spellcaster.

He threw me onto the bed, and before I bounced once, his fingers were in the sides of my panties, tearing them from my body. My flimsy tank top was gone in my next gasp, and I was breathlessly naked . . . and desperately horny.

Shifting myself up on one arm, I used the other to grab his hoodie, yanking it up so I could touch the hard muscles below. Logan reached over his head and, in that sexy way men loved to get undressed, yanked the offending material off to leave his top half gloriously bare.

His sweats were shucked in a similar manner, and as he stalked me across the bed, I forgot how to breathe. Autonomic nervous system or not, it was failing in its involuntary responses.

I'd seen Logan naked before, but this felt like the first time.

When he crawled on top of me, I ran my hands across his broad chest, which was covered in jewel-toned creatures and black-and-white symbols. I wanted to touch and taste every inch of him. Especially those hard, thick inches hanging between his muscled thighs.

A witch needed to write sonnets about his perfect cock, the swollen head glistening with his arousal.

"If you keep looking at me like that, baby," Logan groaned, "I'm going to embarrass myself."

A brief burst of laughter escaped me at the thought of this powerful, confident warlock losing control. It was hard to believe that I could do that to him, and yet the evidence was clear. An inferno burned in his gaze.

"Paisley," he warned again, and my laughter turned to moans as he pressed down until his huge body covered mine. The feel of his skin against mine, his hard lines crushing my softer frame, was worthy of the second sonnet of the night.

I'd be a fucking poet by the time Logan was done with me.

He kissed me slower this time, drawing my lower lip into his mouth and between his teeth. The slow pace didn't last long as urgency overtook us both. "Hold on, baby," he murmured. "Stay with me."

Digging my nails into his back, I did exactly as I was told and held on to him. Logan thrusted forward, the thick head of his cock sliding through my slick heat. My pussy was so wet that my arousal seeped down my ass and onto the sheets, but there was no readying myself for Logan's size. He thrust again, and the burning stretch was deliciously painful.

"That's my good girl," he crooned, giving me not even a chance to adjust. His gaze devoured me, and I was completely lost. "You take me so well. You were made for me, Paisley. Absolutely perfect."

The praise had my walls clenching around him, and as he started to slam into me, my cries were too loud and I pressed my hand over my mouth. The dorms were not fully soundproofed, and the last thing I wanted was for my screams to bring an audience. Logan's mouth replaced my hand as he kissed and fucked me into the most intense orgasm that stole my air and ability to even scream. I soundlessly cried out, losing all sense of reality.

If I'd had full access to my magic, I'd have released every monster in the planes of existence with my complete loss of control.

"Fuck, baby," Logan whispered huskily against my throat,

his thrusts slowing as he followed me into Orgasm Land. I fucking loved Orgasm Land. I wanted to buy a house there and never leave.

As he lifted his head, the moon decided to make an appearance from behind the wintry clouds, and I could see the shine of his green eyes. "Did I hurt you?" he rasped, examining my face as we both breathed heavily.

Placing my hand against his cheek, he briefly closed his eyes and pressed against my palm. "You destroyed me," I said softly, rubbing my thumb over his skin, "but in the best way I could imagine. As you said, if we're truly bonded, in a goddess-accepted bond, then I'm made for you, Logan Kingston. You can't hurt me."

At least not physically.

His hard length was still buried inside me, and I moaned as he started thrusting in and out, through the mess left after our last orgasms, and I could feel that swirl of pleasure building once more. Slower this time. "This need I have for you," he breathed against my lips. "It's never-ending. It never eases, and holding you all those nights, offering comfort . . . it took every ounce of my control . . ."

I cried out softly as his thrusts picked up. "Please d-don't exercise con-control on my behalf," I huffed out.

Logan chuckled, and I was nearly delirious. "Already giving orders, Precious."

I wanted to reply, but I was too busy detonating around his hard length.

This was what I'd dreamed of after my magic bloomed, and it was better than I could have ever imagined.

CHAPTER 15

The alarm jarred me awake the next morning, and as I opened my eyes and stretched, I found myself sprawled across six and a half feet of warlock. His heat and energy surrounded me completely, and as small pains made themselves known through my body, I recalled how little sleep we'd gotten through the night.

Logan's arms tightened, keeping me flush against his chest. "Let's skip classes today," he murmured against my skin. "I've got more important lessons to teach."

I snorted—in a *very sexy and elegant way.* "You're taking your spellcaster classes a little further than Headmaster Gregor asked of you."

His response was to shift me higher, my legs falling open on either side of his hips. My mind checked out for a second as the head of his cock pressed against my entrance. "I declined to teach any further lessons," he said, and I tried to remember what we'd been talking about. "My priorities have changed, and I don't have time for whatever deals my father struck."

He pressed a kiss to the curve of my shoulder and ran his nose up my cheek as he breathed me in. "Priorities?" I managed to say.

"Yep," he whispered, and I shivered as goose bumps traced across my skin. "As in, I only have one right now."

It grew harder to speak. And breathe.

We did not have time for fun this morning, but I wasn't strong enough to halt the direction this was heading in. "What one?"

His chuckle was dark, and I cried out at the hot pulse of his cock against my core. "You, baby. Just you."

He thrust up, and I gasped, opening my legs wider to slide down his shaft. It took a few seconds for my body to adjust— every part of this warlock was huge.

"We really don't have time for this," I whispered, all the while knowing nothing short of a monster attack was getting me off Logan. Maybe not even that.

With limited time, he took control, capturing my hips in a firm grip as he thrust faster.

He leaned up to taste my mouth. "Come for me," he commanded, and I was screaming into an orgasm before his next powerful thrust. Logan muffled most of my noise as he changed angles, sending me into a second spiral of pleasure.

"Precious," he groaned, and I felt the hot swell of his release.

I collapsed against him, a sigh escaping as he traced his hands up my spine. "You're in my bed from now on," he murmured against my throat. "Let's make a deal. No more sleeping alone. It's been torture staying away over the past few weeks. I never want to wake up without you again."

"I wasn't the one who disappeared to Europe," I whispered, my head spinning. The thought of waking up every morning with Logan was like a thousand Christmas-birthdays coming at once.

"I know, Precious. I'm sorry. There were a few unfortunate loose ends that had to be wrapped up. But I'm back now, and I'm not going anywhere."

I wanted to believe him, but I knew how deep Rafael had his claws in his son, and I worried that this was nothing more than a Weatherstone bubble that could be burst with the slightest of pricks. Not that I'd ever refer to Rafael as only a *slight prick.*

Knowing I had to move now or I'd miss all my morning classes, I reluctantly shifted off Logan, mourning the loss of his hard length inside me. Yep, he was still hard. Turned out my warlock was insatiable, with an almost nonexistent refractory period.

No witch would ever complain about that.

"Goddess, I wish we had private showers," I grumbled as I stumbled around searching for clothes to throw on before making my way to the bathrooms. I didn't want to wash Logan from my body, but with our combined release dripping down my thighs, it seemed prudent to at least attempt a quick rinse.

Logan reached down for his hoodie and I shivered as his arm banded around my center. He gently pulled the material over my head, and I tried not to show him how much it affected me, but we were too close for him to miss my reaction.

"Your pupils dilate when you're turned on and happy," he murmured, and I found myself locked in his icy gaze, the mossy center expanding as he stared at me covered in his hoodie. "You like wearing my clothes, don't you?"

There was no point in lying. He'd caught me too many times in his hoodies to deny the truth. "When they still smell like you," I admitted, with a shrug. The small pieces of myself I kept giving Logan were really adding up, but I was trusting that his feelings and actions were real.

"In that case, whatever I'm wearing is yours," he said, brushing his lips down my throat. "Fuck knows I like seeing you in my clothes. Tells everyone else that you belong to me."

Just take my feminism card, because that line was my undoing. "Always with the smooth words, bestie," I murmured.

Logan saw straight through my bullshit. "Not smooth words. The truth, Paisley." His expression had never been more serious. "I know you need actions to back up my words, and I will prove it to you."

He released me to pull on his sweats, standing there delicious and shirtless. He showed no physical signs that he'd had less than a few hours of broken sleep, and I'd bet good magic I wasn't faring as well. A quick brush over the tangles in my hair told me I was a hot mess and would need every second in the bathroom.

"Will you tell me the truth," I asked as I gathered up my toiletry bag, "about why you came to Weatherstone last year? What your dad has planned for my family? Will you clear up all the unease about our families and lives so we can start with a clean slate?"

He reached out and brushed a finger down my cheek, expression giving nothing away. "I'll tell you as much as I can, but I don't have Rafael's full trust when it comes to you. He was there when we were first separated, and he knows how badly I reacted to your loss. He didn't know about the bond, but he was aware that I might not fall in line. He's keeping a lot from me as well."

That made sense, but I couldn't shake the unease unfurling inside me. "If you knew we were bonded in an old-magic way," I said, "why did you wait so long to find me? Why weren't we together when we were younger? I mean, I get why you couldn't come to me as a child, but you've been a powerful spellcaster for years. Years longer than me . . . So where were you? We should have been each other's firsts in all ways, and yet . . . you let years go by."

My words grew faster and harsher, as if the pain had been simmering until it finally boiled over. If what Logan said was true and we were forever mates, where the Hel had he been for all of these years?

The familiar flash of ice in his eyes bothered me as he moved closer. "I didn't lie, baby. I couldn't come for you until I was strong enough to keep you safe." He leaned in closer, and I somehow knew that what he was about to say next would tear me to pieces. "And while I might not have been your first, I've never touched another witch. You are it for me. Now and always."

With that, he leaned in and pressed his lips to my cheek and strode out the door, leaving me a broken mess about to collapse on the floor.

Had he . . . ? Did he just . . . ?

Logan had been a virgin?

How was it possible? He kissed like an expert and fucked as if he'd spent his formative years in tantric classes. There was no fumbling or unease in the powerful spellcaster.

How was that possible?

I had no idea how long I stood in my room staring into nothing, my mind buzzing. There was no way to define what was happening inside my head, outside of an overwhelming abundance of emotions. Strongest of all was the devastation that I hadn't waited for Logan. There'd only been a couple of warlocks before him, but that was too many.

The knowledge itched under my skin.

"Paisley!" I jumped at the shout through my door. "Witch, are you in there?"

Forcing my shaking limbs to move, I hurried over, dressed just in Logan's hoodie. I had no idea what expression I wore when I wrenched the door open, but Sara and Haley both jumped back a step, concern creasing their faces. I waved them inside, and when they hesitantly shuffled through, I slammed the door and fell against it, my chest heaving.

"Pais," Haley said, reaching out but halting just before she touched my arm. "What's going on? Did something happen? Is your family okay?"

"Talk to us, babe," Sara said, pressing closer on my right side. "You're starting to scare us."

I was starting to scare myself.

"Logan," I whimpered. "He . . . he—"

"What?" Sara growled, her concern morphing into fury. "What the fuck did he do? Do I need to kill myself a spell-caster?"

Tears burst from me, hot and furious, and I had a suspicion that I might be losing my mind. "He waited for me," I sobbed. "He's never been with another witch. He knew we were bonded and he . . . waited."

My friends stilled on either side of me, and I had no doubt they were exchanging glances, but I was too fucked-up to try to interpret their looks. Haley's voice was softer when she finally grasped my hand. "Honey, that's a great thing, right? What's got you so upset?"

"I didn't do the same," I whispered brokenly, staring into space. "I didn't wait."

It must have clicked then what had me flipping out. "Oh, babe! You can't beat yourself up over this," Sara said, showing her softer side. "You didn't know about Logan. You were too young to remember him." Her words made logical sense, but I felt that in my heart I should have known. I should have remembered Logan.

"I never could find anyone to settle with," I rasped around my aching throat. "There were a few warlocks that I slept with, but as soon as any of them attempted to turn it into anything serious, I checked out. I told myself I was waiting for what Mom and Dad had, but all along I was waiting for Logan."

"Which is exactly what your mom and dad have," Sara said fiercely. "You did wait for him, Pais. In all the ways that count. Your heart and soul waited for him."

"Anyone can own your body," Haley said, her voice breaking. "But only one claims the true essence of who you are."

They cried with me now, and there was a very good chance all three of us would be late for class. "I don't know what I did right to get amazing besties like you," I choked out through my sobs, "but I'm grateful all the same."

"We love you," Haley said, hugging me tighter as we sniffled away the rest of our tears.

Sara chuckled as she stepped back, and I jumped when she slapped my bare ass beneath the hoodie. "Love you or not, you smell like sex, babe." She glanced at her watch and shook her head. "And there's no time to shower, so you're just going to have to go out there smelling like your delicious mate."

A snort escaped me, my mood lightening now that I'd moved past my shock. I still had to speak to Logan about what he'd said, but I was determined that this wouldn't derail what we'd been building here. "I'll just quickly pee and brush my teeth," I said, pulling out a pair of sweatpants from my drawer. "You two get to the breakfast cart and grab some food before it's too late."

"Great plan," Haley said, opening my door and ushering me out.

I sprinted down the hall, determined not to be any later than I already was. My legs shook as I brushed my teeth and then peed, cleaning myself the best I could. By the time I was back in my room, pulling on my uniform, less than five minutes had passed.

I grabbed my books and schedule and raced out the door.

Logan had dropped a bomb on me this morning, and it had detonated that final sliver of doubt I'd held that this was still all a huge Rafael scheme.

That sexy spellcaster was my bonded mate, and I was determined to keep him.

CHAPTER 16

It spoke of the recent chaos in my life that I hadn't had a chance to look over my schedule until I was racing for the breakfast cart. I knew this year would bring a mix of magical classes except necromancy, which frustrated me because moving through the planes and touching the essence of the dead were a part of my affinity. But in the vein of remaining anonymous and *alive*, I couldn't request classes that a spellcaster would never need.

My body felt weaker and out of sorts after my emotional morning and limited sleep. My legs were heavy as I dodged students in the busy hallway. When I reached Sara and Haley, they were just finishing up at the cart.

"Here you go," Sara said, shoving a sandwich and perfectly doctored coffee into my hands. The first sip had my eyes rolling in my head. "I've got to get to my specialty air class, but I'll see you witches at lunch."

She took off and Haley shot me a quick smile. "I'm in the forest this morning. See you at lunch, babe."

"Thank you!" I called after them, and as I took a second sip of coffee, I tried not to think about the fact that Belle wasn't here, inhaling food and sipping her tea with us.

When I was done with classes today, I was going to head straight for Headmaster Gregor to pry information from him.

Glancing at my schedule again, I wished I'd known that Water Elemental 102, down by the lake, was my first class. I'd have grabbed my swimsuit before I rushed out the door. Now I needed to return to my dorm first.

As I headed back along the hall, I tucked my sandwich into my bag so I could drink coffee and read over my classes. Because priorities.

Water Elemental 102
Air Elemental 102
Fire Elemental 102
Alchemy 102
Spells for Defense and Attack
Defense and Attack Training
History of Necromancy and Weatherstone

As a spellcaster, I'd have different elemental training next year, and in my fourth year I'd focus on my strongest magical affinities. Doubtful any part of me would show strength, considering everything I was concealing.

By the time I reached the lake, finishing off the last bite of my sandwich, I was ten minutes late. Thankfully, Professor Mordock was still in the process of greeting everyone. He'd been my professor last year—we didn't switch up until junior and senior study—and while he noticed my arrival, he didn't reprimand me for my tardiness.

"You'll be focused on drawing the water around yourselves," he continued, "and using it to move through the lake. We will have speed and agility tests, so you can continue to improve as the year progresses."

He waved the already swimsuit-clad individuals toward

the icy lake and made his way over to me. A few witches and warlocks glanced my way, assessing the possible spellcaster in their midst, but then they focused on their task and I was forgotten.

"Ms. Hallistar," the professor greeted me with a nod. "I'm surprised but delighted to see you in this class. I heard rumors about your *parting of the lake* last year, and I'm intrigued to see what you will achieve with more specialized training."

Forcing a smile, I returned his nod. "My magic is still weirdly locked, unless I get a boost from a powerful source." *Usually in the form of a sexy spellcaster.* "But I'm hoping to keep advancing and finding the key to unlocking my full potential."

He didn't look perturbed, which told me he was fully aware of my *limitations.* "Your dad already gave us all a rundown and expressed that you will not take the usual path of a spellcaster. We've got you, Paisley—we understand that all magic develops in its own way. Don't stress."

As the baby of my family, it didn't surprise me that Dad had already eased my way into classes. My family had my back, even when, at times, I maybe didn't deserve it.

I hadn't been the best daughter or sister lately, but I was determined to make it up to them.

"Thanks, Professor," I said. He left me with a brief nod and returned to teaching the class.

I'd thrown my swimmers on in my dorm, so it was easy enough to strip off my uniform and use the minimal access I had to my energy to warm the air. Small elemental manipulations were easy. It was only when I attempted more that my magic crashed against the effects of the suppression potion.

"Hey." I jerked at that low voice, turning to find the other spellcaster in my year, Marcus Lofting, standing uncomfortably close. "It's good to see you again."

"Hey," I replied, moving a step away. "Sorry, I didn't see you there."

Despite the warmth of magically heated air around us, I found myself shivering and crossing my arms over my chest. His presence used to feel comforting, but he was throwing off weird vibes this morning.

"You never contacted me over the winter break," he said, his expression calm, but his eyes swirled with an emotion I couldn't read.

He'd told me last year that he might be able to help with Dad, which had been right before my life imploded. I honestly hadn't thought about Marcus once over the break. "I know. I'm sorry. There's been a lot of personal stuff going on."

He let the silence extend for a few seconds. "You could have reached out about anything," he said softly. "I thought we were friends."

Slashes of guilt tightened my chest. My relationship with Marcus was complicated. Early last year there'd been a very minor attraction between us, but it had fizzled into nothing. After everything that had happened with Logan, the thought of touching Marcus—or any other warlock again—made me feel physically ill.

"It just didn't feel right reaching out to you. So much happened, and I'm consumed with—"

"Logan."

My brow furrowed at his interruption, and at the fact that he'd known the exact reason I'd been consumed over the winter break.

Marcus's gaze lifted over my head, and I felt the swell of magic as tingles traced down my spine. *The good tingles.*

A featherlight touch traced across my cheek. "Precious," Logan rumbled, clearly ready to publicly stake his claim. "I missed you."

I forgot Marcus existed again as Logan moved us out of hearing distance from the other spellcaster. "What are you doing here?" I rasped, my devastation from his confession this morning coming back full force now that he was in front of me.

"Volunteered to help with a few sophomore classes this year," he said, flashing a perfect, if not a touch predatory, smile.

Clearing my throat, I failed to sound unaffected. "Let me guess, it's a range of sophomore classes suited to a spellcaster?"

Logan's grin widened. "How did you know?" He stepped closer until I was breathing him in, and when he tucked a strand of hair behind my ear, my cool composure faded, and I barely held on to my tears.

I hadn't cried this much in years, but my feelings for Logan were so strong that they spilled over with little to no encouragement. "You didn't know about our bond, Precious," he said, his gaze intense. "As long as you never gave away your heart, the rest isn't important. You were my first, and I will be your last. That's all that matters."

A single tear escaped the rigid hold on my emotions. "You always know the perfect thing to say."

His arms wrapped around my waist so he could pull me in for a real kiss, and I barely registered the gasps behind us—clearly the class was watching the famous spellcaster. "We're a true bonded pair," he murmured against my lips, ignoring everyone else. "I know your mind. I know you."

When Logan pulled away, I braced myself for the curious stares, but he blocked my body with his, turning to address whoever wasn't in the water yet. "Start building your connection to your element," he snapped at them. "Get your asses in the water."

"Ah, yes," Professor Mordock called, sounding farther away. "Logan will be helping you hone your elemental connection today."

Stones scraped as the rest of the class entered the lake, and I was about to do the same, hoping the water would cool me off. Logan's gaze dropped to the hard beads of my nipples, pressed against the school-issued swimsuit, and he groaned. "This is a bad idea. Let's just ditch college. We don't need it. We'll start our own coven."

I shoved him gently, shaking my head. "Come on, big guy, time to teach your mate how to connect to water."

The green of his eyes darkened. "Say it again?"

"Teach me how to connect to the water?" I teased, knowing that wasn't what he wanted.

His chest heaved as he groaned. "Precious . . ."

It was a warning, but with the heaviness of this morning easing, I was in a playful mood. "*Come on, big guy?* You like me calling you *my big guy?*"

Logan's eyes were a mossy pit as he yanked his shirt off, and now I was the one losing all focus as I stared at his delicious muscles and tattoos. "Mate," I choked out, huffing in air like a drowning victim. "You're my mate."

He hauled me up into his arms and raced us into the water. "Mate," he agreed, diving below, the icy water washing over us. It was so cold it stole my breath until his power warmed me a beat later when we resurfaced. "You're my mate, Paisley Hallistar, and I want everyone to know it."

"Aren't you supposed to be teaching all of us, Oh Great Spellcaster?" Marcus shouted from nearby, snapping us out of our love bubble.

Logan, without releasing his hold on me, leveled him with a look that would have had me running, screaming, and hiding. Marcus just flipped him off—arrogance was part of the spellcaster package. "Should just kill that fucking ass-hole," Logan muttered, but he did release me. "You spend some time connecting with the water. I'm going to hurt a few students."

When he left my side, I swam out to the main group with the professor. "Since it's your first day back," he said, sitting a few inches above the water, held up by a small stream, "let's get into the basics before you use the water to move yourself around. Taste the elements in the water. I released a few additions this morning, some natural elements that will dissipate in a few hours. If you connect fully, you'll be able to tell what's new. Start exploring."

To my surprise, with small tendrils of my energy seeping through the suppression, I could break down the particles in the lake water. There was hydrogen and oxygen, bacteria and algae, along with fine traces of nitrogen. The professor had released a combination of lavender and oregano, and I separated them into a sheen of oil across my hands.

Logan and Marcus were the only two in the class to list every element that made up the water, but I was mid-level and quite happy with that effort.

"Your gran's spell is clever," Logan said in a low voice, standing close as we dried and got dressed. "It's not fully suppressing the base magic we all have, just the part specific to your affinity."

"Gran said it was a spell passed down through our family." My reply was barely audible. "I can only assume that's why it works so well on *me*."

"It still doesn't feel like a long-term solution," he added, concern leaking into those words. "We need to learn more about your affinity, and we need to learn how to control it."

His usage of the word *we* settled nicely into the spot reserved just for this bond with Logan. A fundamental, integral part of who I was now. "I've had a lot of sleepless nights think-ing about who I am, and you might be right."

Being a reaper was my identity, and I was desperate to embrace it, but I hadn't forgotten what Gran had told Mom: Whenever one of us tried to express our unique brand of magic, it got us dead.

Dead without a head. Because the council were poets.

So, until we figured out a work-around for that, I had no choice but to keep my power locked down and hide half of who I was.

CHAPTER 17

Logan was in my next class as well, which was Fire Elemental 102. He was busy helping the professor, and on my own I managed to control a small flame—and almost light a candle without any assistance.

Professor Johnstone, a tiny blonde witch I hadn't had a class with before, was aware of my locked-down energy. She mostly left me alone, making no comment on my lackluster power.

I might not be a standout in the class—other students were already growing their flames into an inferno—but I was touching the element. "I heard you managed to extinguish an everlasting flame in the end-of-year test," she said when I was packing up my candle and cleaning ash and debris off the table.

"I did, and I have no idea how I managed that."

Her smile wavered briefly, before it returned. "The only way I know of to extinguish such a flame is to remove not only the oxygen in the air, but all matter completely. You have to create a vacuum, which should be impossible outside of the Purgatory realm. There's no atmosphere there at all."

Purgatory. Forcing out a laugh that was seconds too late, I shook my head. "Maybe it was a faulty flame, because no one can touch that plane of existence. Especially not a low-powered spellcaster."

Her head tilted, as if she were sizing me up. "Right. Of course. That was the consensus from the assessors as well. A faulty candle. At least it got them to check the rest of our stock and ensure we had no other issues."

"That's good." I cleared my throat, hoping I didn't look as freaked-out as I felt. With the suppression potion, staying under the radar should be easy, but I'd already made too many mistakes last year. I couldn't make a single one now. "Thanks for a great first lesson."

The professor nodded and thanked Logan, who was standing nearby, for his help, before she strode off to chat to a few lingering students. "You okay, Precious?" Logan asked as I got to my feet.

There was no way to truthfully answer that in public. "During my assessment last year, my affinity must have broken through the suppression spell to touch the other realms. How else could I have extinguished that candle?"

Logan didn't look as worried as I felt. "Yes, but the spell over the school wasn't as *tailored* to your needs. You don't have to worry about that again."

He said "that again," since we both knew there was plenty of other shit to worry about.

As we headed for the door, Marcus fell into step beside us—as the only other second-year spellcaster, we would be sharing all our classes this year. Which was turning out to be a bit of a problem. His animosity toward Logan grew with every interaction, and two spellcasters sparking off each other would eventually end in an explosion.

"Aren't you a little old to be in every second-year class?" Marcus said as we exited into the hallway. "Paisley doesn't need a fucking bodyguard. Let her breathe, bro."

Logan stilled, turning slowly toward Marcus, his power swelling until the hairs on my arms stood up. "I will say this one time and one time only. Paisley is mine." His voice was devoid of inflection. "Don't ever question my reason for being around her. *You* are the one with no rights here, and if you overstep again, I will kill you."

Marcus, finally showing a modicum of sense, backed away with his hands up. The heat pouring off Logan was enough to scorch, but I pushed closer. "Ignore him," I whispered, wrapping my hand around his. He didn't look away from where Marcus had fled until I tugged gently. "He's not important. And I'm hungry . . . Let's go to lunch."

That wasn't even a lie. Between classes and my overall fatigue, I needed a boost of energy before my next lesson. With a grumble, Logan swept me closer, pulling me against his side until I could feel the fine tremor in his limbs—that promise to kill Marcus had not been an empty threat.

Logan was on the verge of losing control.

"He's not important," I repeated, keeping my voice soothing. "He means nothing to me, and I have no interest or feelings for him."

Logan's exhale released a fraction of his tension. "Fucker knows exactly how to get under my skin."

I'd never seen any other student affect him in such a way, and I wasn't so stupid that I didn't see my part in that. I'd let Marcus get too close, and now he thought he had the right to step in and dictate shit in my life. I needed to talk to him before he got himself killed.

He did not want to go up against Logan, who was immensely powerful due to not only our magical bond, but all the years his crazy-ass father pushed his power.

I might not know every aspect of Logan's life story, but I knew Rafael would have expected nothing less than exceptional from his son.

Logan's energy remained heavy as we headed for the

dining hall, but he did take a second to lift my bag from my shoulder and sling it over his. Even in his anger, he still thought of my comfort, and that was just one of the many ways he proved the truth of our soul-deep connection. Actions spoke louder than statements ever could.

By the time we entered the crowded dining hall, Logan's energy was calmer. I spotted our friends already seated in the middle of the room, surprised to find it felt normal to see Noah and Tobias with Sara and Haley.

Ready to join them, and my stomach already growling, I picked up the pace toward the buffet. Logan's long legs kept up easily, and I groaned as the scent of food hit me. "I'm starving." I bounced impatiently at how slow the students in front of us were being.

The smallest laugh escaped Logan, relieving a fraction of the heavy tension he'd been holding. Heat crept into my cheeks as he watched me with a look that felt . . . intimate. "You're so fucking cute, Precious," he said with an attractive shake of his head. "You were an adorable four-year-old who had me wrapped around her finger, and almost twenty years later, nothing has changed."

My nose wrinkled. "I'm not sure I want you to think of me as cute or adorable. That doesn't sound sexy."

His stare didn't ease. "You're beyond sexy. You already know you drive me out of my mind, but don't underestimate cute. Every part of you turns me on."

Goddess above. "Who are you?" I whispered, trying to wrap my head around this new Logan.

"I'm done fighting who I am," he said, and he sounded happy. "I'm done fighting our destiny, and letting an asshole control my life."

"I'm really looking forward to that," I whispered, wondering if you could die from *feeling so fucking much*. "But for the record, despite me questioning it in the past, I now fully believe in this bond. I can feel it in my magical essence."

Logan pressed a quick kiss to my lips, and as students moved in front of us, I had to debate which need I should feed first. This time he gave an honest-to-goodness laugh. "Come on, Paisley. Let's get you your sushi."

The students had finally moved, and I sucked in deep breaths, returning my focus to food. I filled my plate with sushi, fruit, and yoghurt, along with a bowl of Irish stew. The fried chicken caught my eye at the end, and I examined my plate, hoping to find a spot to fit a piece.

Logan nudged me gently. "I'll get it. Go and sit down. You look exhausted."

"Someone kept me up half the night," I huffed, breathlessly.

He leaned down and skimmed his lips over my neck, in the spot just behind my ear that I was starting to think he'd claimed. "And you'll need that same stamina tonight. Go and eat."

My head spun as I wobbled on weak legs toward our friends, all but collapsing into a chair beside Noah. Sara and Haley regarded me for a beat before they cracked up. "Holy shit, Pais, you look like you've been thoroughly fu—"

"Shut up," I gasped. "Come on. I was just getting food."

Tobias leaned forward. "You clearly *enjoy* that buffet a lot."

I flipped him off while mentally cursing Logan and his stupid ability to weaken my knees.

"I'd change the subject before Logan gets here," Noah said, the only one not openly laughing at me. "He's not above destroying anyone who upsets his girl."

His girl.

Dammit. "She's blushing again," Sara chortled. "Fuck, this is great. Our precious Paisley is *in love.*"

Logan strode over with my bag and two plates. He set one next to me, and the other in front of him. I glanced down to see he'd gotten me not only the chicken, but also mashed potatoes and gravy.

Dammit. Sara was right . . . *I was* in love with this spell-caster.

When I lifted my gaze, the dining hall and our friends faded into background noise as I attempted to convey everything I felt in one charged look. Logan's eyes flashed with surprise and then heat.

Sara's loud groan broke through my haze as she flapped her hands in our direction. "Goddess be damned, get a freaking room. I think I just got pregnant sitting near you two. Stop rubbing your amazing bond in our faces, or we'll be forming a poly relationship to be part of *whatever the fuck you two have going on.*"

Logan, who was thankfully used to her by now, just shook his head as he leaned back and slung his arm behind me. "Sorry, I don't share my mate. Not ever."

Sara grumbled and let out a long sigh. "Typical."

Tobias leaned closer to her, his accent deepening as he said, "If you're looking for a warlock to add to your life, my schedule is suddenly wide-open."

She wrinkled her nose at him. "I said *sexy* warlock. You've got to learn to listen, Toby."

Logan and Noah stilled on either side of me, and when they side-eyed their friend, I got the distinct impression he didn't like to be called Toby. Sara had her little nose in the air, as if daring him to comment back.

Tobias leaned so close his face was only an inch from hers. "You're pushing all my buttons today, badass. Just know . . . you're up to two."

Her bravado wavered minutely. "Two what?"

A feral smile crossed his face. "Punishments, love. Want to go for a third?"

Sara's throat worked and I swore there was more than a hint of desire mixed with her panic. "Maybe I do," she rasped as she shot to her feet. "Getting water," she muttered, running away.

Tobias chose not to follow, relaxing in his chair, even as his gaze settled on her retreating back. Turning to Logan, I raised my eyebrows and silently asked what the heck was going on. He gave the slightest shake of his head and shrugged. He was just as confused.

When I continued to look between Tobias and where Sara disappeared to, Logan nudged my plate closer. "Eat up," he said.

My stomach rumbled in agreement, so I focused on eating everything in front of me.

When I was finally satisfied, I collapsed back into my chair, the warmth of Logan's arm cocooning me as I listened to our friends chat about their classes.

It was pleasant and comforting, and I was hazy minded enough to almost forget my problems.

It was only when Trevor entered the room with a friend that I was reminded of Belle.

I didn't have classes for another hour, which meant now was the perfect time to speak with the headmaster.

CHAPTER 18

"Elder Monroe called in this morning," Headmaster Gregor said, steepling his fingers and peering over the top at me in his signature power move. "Belle will be back tomorrow. She's been in India with her mother and was delayed in returning."

I eyed him, wanting to push harder, but also knowing it wasn't in my best interests to draw any attention to my distrust of Elder Monroe. "I'll wait to see her tomorrow, then," I said, getting to my feet. "If she's not back, I'll check in again."

A not-so-subtle reminder that I wasn't going to let this rest until my friend was here, visibly safe. He didn't show any surprise by my declaration, and I had a sneaking suspicion that he knew a lot about what was happening in the magical community, far beyond his role at Weatherstone.

I'd never been keen on spending prolonged time around necromancers. Their energy had always stirred my own—and now I understood why—but today the headmaster's didn't bother me. If anything, I enjoyed the chill of his power, even if it created a new craving to connect with my own.

After exiting through the concealment spell hiding his office, I paused to see Noah perched against the brick wall.

When our gazes met, he straightened. "Hey, Pais." His voice was soft, expression concerned. "Is everything okay?"

I was late for my next class, so I waved for him to join me as I started to walk. "Totally fine. I just wanted to chat to the headmaster about Belle. He said she's supposed to return tomorrow. I'll push harder if that doesn't happen." Tilting my head back so I could take in his expression, I asked, "Is everything okay with you? Is Logan okay? I mean, it's not that I don't enjoy our brief but scintillating conversations, but I'm guessing there's a reason you tracked me down."

His lips quirked, and I was shocked when he reached out and ruffled my hair. "Just keeping an eye on you when Logan can't be here."

A soft huff escaped me. "He's a bit of a possessive psychopath, isn't he?"

Noah's smile grew as he shrugged. "He's your possessive psychopath at least."

There was that. "So, where is my psychopath? I thought he'd conveniently offered to help out in every class I had in my schedule."

A crowd of warlocks pushed into the hall, loud and large, and I was almost trampled until Noah stepped closer, using his bulk to keep me from being touched. No one would dare trample a warlock of his size and power. "He has a class of his own that he can't miss, so you're mine for this afternoon."

Excellent. "And why do I need a babysitter exactly?"

Noah's face tightened, his easygoing facade vanishing. "Logan's decided that we're done playing Rafael's games—he won't stay away from you any longer. That asshole doesn't take well to being ignored, and we have no idea what he might do in retaliation."

In all the time I'd known Logan, there'd been the sense that he was at war with himself, torn between his feelings for me and what was expected of him. No one had confirmed it so much until right now. Along with the fact that he was taking a massive risk in so openly choosing me.

"Paisley?" Noah's voice broke through my confused panic. "Honey, what's happening?"

"Logan's in danger," I said in a rush, meeting his worried gaze. "You are both in danger. What are we going to do to stop Rafael?"

Noah's expression eased up into relief. "Dammit, Paisley. I was ready to kill someone and I had no idea who to kill. Don't worry about Logan or me. We'll be fine. You're his priority, as it should have always been. His loyalty is yours, his love and magic too. I've known Logan almost my entire life, and I can promise you that he will destroy anyone who tries to take you away from him. You're his."

You're his.

And he was mine.

Whatever this was between Logan and me, it was potent and destructive, and . . . absolutely the best thing to ever happen to me.

"Let's go to class," Noah said, scooting me along again. My last class of the day was spell making, which was a branch of magic where I really shone—mixing and concocting spells and potions, following directions, and then adding my own little touch to bring them to life.

If I had really been a spellcaster, there was no way anyone would expect me to love crafting spells. It was considered the artform of those not quite powerful enough to use their affinities, but the subtle magic of hexes and spells, potions and tinctures, really spoke to me.

By the time class was over and I'd dropped my bags off in my dorm, after assuring Noah I would be at dinner in ten minutes, my ever-present exhaustion had pushed itself to the forefront again. My limbs were heavy as I changed into jeans and a sweater, and pulling on my black, fur-lined boots felt like torture.

With it being only the first day, classes hadn't been particularly difficult, and especially not with all the professors going easy on me.

I really had no idea why I felt so wrecked.

Throwing on Logan's hoodie against the chill of winter, I forced myself to leave my dorm and head for the dining hall.

Food would help with my energy level.

When I reached the entrance of the busy hall, Trevor was waiting, perched in the doorway. He looked like shit, dark rings under his eyes as if he hadn't slept in days. "Hey," I said, when he noticed me. "Is everything okay?"

"Do you know where Belle is?" He watched the witches and warlocks who passed by, as if searching for her face. Fires burned deep in his eyes, and the heat of his energy washed over me until I was almost too hot. "Why isn't she here?"

He'd brought Belle up more than once over the winter break, but I'd been too caught up in my own shit to really think about why. They were friends, I knew that much, but the way he was acting now . . . it was so much more than that.

They were more than that.

Like a slap up the side of the head, I finally understood what the Hel was going on. "You're the one she was seeing last year," I said softly. It wasn't a question. "She told me he was older, but she never mentioned a name." For reasons that now made a lot more sense.

Trevor's big body lurched forward, and by instinct I reached out to steady him. I'd never seen him so out of sorts. "I didn't mean for it to happen, Pais," he whispered miserably. "We just kept running into each other, and the snarky banter morphed from annoyance into . . . more."

For goddess's sake. "I'm not mad at you, moron," I said, pulling him into a hug. "Belle is great, and you are great, and it's nice to see you actually caring about a witch rather than treating them like a revolving product line you need to test out."

He laughed hoarsely and rested his weight on me until I almost collapsed. My brother was heavy, but he'd held me up more than once over the years and I was determined to do the same for him. "She was so reserved over winter break," he murmured in a distant voice. "But I know it's hard for her at home with *him*. I let her have the space and offered my support, but I haven't heard from her for a week. And today . . . she's not here."

I tried to rub my hand up and down his back, but I was barely keeping the both of us upright. Just as my knees buckled, a hard body slipped in behind me, taking mine and Trevor's weight with ease. Mint and evergreen filled my senses, and my exhaustion lessened as I let Logan hold us.

"Headmaster Gregor said she'll return tomorrow," I told my brother, and his head shot up as he scanned my face. "She got delayed in India, but we'll have her back tomorrow. Then we can demand answers for whatever weirdness is going on with her. She's ignored me and the girls for the winter break too, and I'm worried about her."

My brother's sadness turned into a frantic energy. "Whatever it is, we'll deal with it. I won't let her suffer any longer, even if I have to steal her away from her fucking father."

Logan laughed behind me, and I tilted my head back to meet his amused expression. "Of course you'd think his possessive tendencies are funny," I grumbled.

Logan pressed his lips to my cheek. "The fact that he hasn't kidnapped her yet, baby, means he's got a lot to learn."

Trevor finally noticed the third in our little group, and

as his gaze moved between me and Logan, he jerked away and sucked in a lungful of air. "What the fuck, Paisley?" he growled, fists clenched at his sides. "Get away from Logan Kingston."

Oh shit.

So much had happened in the development of my relationship with Logan, but I hadn't exactly been forthcoming with my family. Not even Mom, though she at least knew there was *something* between us, thanks to Logan's statement in the graveyard.

It almost floored me to think that this absolutely life-changing relationship was happening and the people I loved the most in the world didn't know about it.

"Logan is my boyfriend," I said simply. Logan's hands tightened as he pulled me away from my angry brother, angling his body in front as if he were worried Trevor might hurt me.

Which, of course, only made my brother angrier. "You have got to be kidding me, Pais. Boyfriend? What are you fucking thinking?"

"Mate," Logan growled. "Paisley is my bonded mate, and if you value your life, you'll stop shouting at her."

Trevor lurched forward, and I was moved farther back by Logan's magic as the two massive warlocks clashed. "Last warning," Logan said coldly. "You're her brother and she loves you, which is the only reason I'm not kicking your ass. But I only have so much patience with this shit."

Trevor was a hothead who never cared if he was out-muscled or outpowered. So, of course, he advanced again, getting right up in the spellcaster's face.

"Hey," I shouted, trying to get around Logan, even as his magic held me in a protective shield. "Trevor, I'm going to need you to back up. *Please.* Logan is telling the truth."

Trevor's aggression faded as we made eye contact. "I have a lot to tell you," I said, softer. "I'm sorry that I kept this from you, but it's new and complicated."

Logan crossed his arms. "If you want to call almost twenty years new. Sure, baby."

Every time he called me *baby*, my body detonated into a hot, needy mess. Which was not particularly appropriate at this current time. "This dynamic is new," I amended. "But we've been bonded since we were kids." It felt nice to officially claim the bond.

Trevor looked between us, but Logan didn't notice because *he was watching me*. His expression filled with heat and possessiveness. In that look I saw every second of the history that had brought us together.

I saw love.

CHAPTER 19

"Clearly we have a lot to talk about," Trevor said stiffly. "We knew you were hiding shit from us over winter, and I had a feeling it was to do with a warlock, but I didn't imagine it was *this* warlock."

Reaching out, I offered him a hand, and Logan didn't stop us from touching. "Let's have dinner together," I said, desperate to regain my former closeness with my family. "Maybe grab J too, so I can explain what's been going on."

His hand locked around mine, holding on tight. "Okay, sis. But no more secrets, please. We're in this together, whatever *this* is."

"Promise," I murmured.

He held on tighter, as if afraid to let go, but he eventually released me. "I'll grab Jensen and we'll find your table."

When he was gone, Logan tucked me into his side, and I let my head fall to his hard chest. "Do you think I'm putting them in danger by bringing them into my mess?" I asked him quietly. "We know what they did to the family members associated with my affinity in the past."

He steered me toward the buffet before he answered. "It's *our* mess, Paisley, and in my opinion, the danger is the same whether they know or not. It's better that they're informed, especially if we need to protect you."

I'd been trying to protect *them*, but in the process had hurt those I loved the most. Mom was doing what she felt was best in pretending none of this was real or happening, but I couldn't hide myself the same way. Not any longer. "You're smarter than you look," I said with a laugh that could easily turn into a sob if I didn't reel it in.

If I wanted to get through this next conversation, I couldn't start crying yet.

"Fucking Hel, Paisley." Jensen stared, his bite of steak on his fork forgotten as he gaped at me. "How could you not tell us this over winter break?"

We'd secluded ourselves at a table right in the back corner, which was just large enough to fit me, Logan, Jensen, Trevor, Noah, Tobias, Sara, and Haley. For the last twenty minutes, in whispers, I shared everything about my affinity and what I'd been through, including what we'd found out from Gran's letters. I even mentioned Belle and my suspicions that her father was the one who tried to get Dad fired and the rest of us thrown from Weatherstone.

As truth poured from me, I felt lighter.

And terrified.

My powers had caused a death at the school, and I was waiting for the person who would judge me for it—who would believe me to be the monster, rather than the creatures I'd accidentally called here.

"Mom never said a word," Trevor growled. "She's just been making you suppression potions and icing the rest of us out. Why would she keep this from us? We're the only ones to trust with this fucking information. We're your family."

"She's scared," Logan said with a snap. He'd been tense

since I'd started speaking, and I got the feeling he was worried about their reactions and how it would make me feel. "The only real information she has about this affinity is from an ancient book that detailed how every other witch like Paisley was murdered, and panicked letters from her mom listing the ways to keep herself and her daughters safe should one of them have the same affinity. You need to cut her some slack."

"So . . . is Mom a reaper too?" Jensen asked in a tone so low we almost missed his question. His gaze darted to Logan. "Did she call the monster that killed your mom?"

The whole table fell silent, and I couldn't bring myself to look Logan's way. "From what she's told me," I whispered, my chest aching, "she's an elemental. She said she has a theory about what happened that day, but it wasn't the time to go into details while trying to keep me safe."

Logan touched my arm and drew my attention. Bracing myself for whatever expression I'd face, I was relieved to see him looking as he always did. "Breathe, Precious," he murmured, running a soothing fingertip along my neckline. "I don't blame your family for her death. Just like I don't blame you for that student's death. You did nothing wrong."

That was a subjective viewpoint, but it helped ease up the pressure in my chest.

Trevor let out a heated huff of air. "Belle's dad is going to be a problem. We need to deal with him before his next attempt to take down our entire family."

We all fell silent again, and I wondered if the tension and unease I now felt was somewhat directed at me. "I'm sorry to have brought you all in on my mess," I mumbled, feeling the full force of my guilt.

"None of this is your fault," Haley said fiercely, reaching out for my hand. "I've said this before and I'll say it again, this is the fault of the magical community. They chose fear, killing off the witches like you in the past. If you were aware of your affinity, trained like the rest of us, none of this would have happened. You don't deserve this, and the cycle has to end at some point. Maybe it ends with you."

Trevor shoved his empty tray away. "I think you need to learn to control your affinity, Paisley. The secret can't stay that way forever, especially with an elder already suspicious. You have no choice but to embrace your affinity and educate yourself, and we will stand by you. We're all powerful, and we have respect in the community."

"You're not powerful enough to take on the entire magical community," Tobias said stiffly, though he cast me a softer smile. "Not even if the whole school stood with Paisley."

"She won't know until she learns how to control her affinity," Sara said, taking a sip of her soda. "How do we know that her affinity isn't a fundamental part of our magical world? Maybe we've been missing a large piece of the puzzle for decades. The spellcasters are still causing issues in Europe. Paisley might be able to kick a spellcaster's ass, knocking them down from their perceived place at the top of the hierarchy."

Logan, Tobias, and Noah exchanged a loaded stare, and I was struck with another suspicion. "Does Rafael have anything to do with the unrest over there?" I asked the trio, who were far too good at concealing their thoughts.

"Let's just say, it's furthering his interests," Logan said. "That many spellcasters in one place, using their magic to battle . . . The overflow of energy is ripe for the taking."

Magical overflow happened in large bursts of energy. It lingered in the air, tainting the land and world around it. Unless someone gathered it up and used it to funnel into other spells.

Rafael struck me as the type of warlock who'd use whatever power he could for his own end, even if it meant encouraging war. Even if innocent people got hurt.

Maybe especially if they did.

As we'd learned in history class, the grounds of this school were powerfully imbued with hundreds of souls. Death left a particularly strong magical essence.

"Why are they fighting?" Haley asked. "At home we tend to exist in the human world, outside of occasional coven events. I only heard about the unrest this morning in class."

I'd learned about the unrest from Belle last year, when she'd accidentally spilled elder secrets, but the information was widespread now. At least in the magical communities.

"They're trying to abolish and reform the council," Logan said shortly. "Spellcasters don't like answering to anyone, and they've banded together to control the narrative."

"Explains why Daddy Kingston is interested," Sara said as she wrinkled her cute nose. "That bastard screams of *I need to control the world and every witch and warlock in it* energy."

"Daddy Kingston," Tobias said with a hoot, before he waggled his eyebrows at Logan. "And here I thought you'd be the first bastard to rock that name."

Fucking Hel. My face felt hot at the mere thought. Logan leaned closer, his scent and magic adding an extra element of heat to my body. "What are you thinking, dirty girl? You want to call me daddy in the bedroom?"

Any denial on my part would only lead to more ridicule, and I was too frazzled to come up with a better reply than "A title you'd have to earn, spellcaster. I'm not sure you have Big Daddy energy."

I mentally applauded myself for trying to make light of it, especially as everyone else laughed. Logan gripped the sides of my chair and dragged it and me between his legs, his lips so close to mine that I could taste his power. "Challenge accepted, Precious."

"Get out of here," Trevor said, throwing a napkin at us. "You might have claimed her with some freaky magic when she was four, but she's still my sister. And I'll still beat your ass."

"Trevor," I groaned, shaking my head at him. "I'll say this once and once only. I'm twenty-three years old. I don't need your advice or assistance with my love life. Especially considering you've banged half the school."

Trevor opened his mouth and then slammed it closed again. "I'm a one-witch warlock now. Belle has more than enough personalities to keep me interested."

I snorted before coughing to cover it. Haley tapped the table with the nail on her pointer finger. "Do you think her dad stopped her from talking with us? Or she made the choice?"

"I think it's both," Sara said, a neutrality in her tone that I'd never heard from her before. She had big feelings usually, but with Belle, she'd gone cold. "He's been in her ear, influencing her. The few times we chatted on the phone, she was distant in a way I'd never felt from her before. We can't expect the same Belle to return tomorrow."

It hurt to think that we might lose her. Belle had been the first friend I made at Weatherstone, and through everything we'd had each other's backs. I couldn't imagine her not being part of my life, but I also wasn't going to beg for her friendship. If she chose to believe her dad after all we'd been through, there wasn't much I could do.

"We need to talk more about Paisley's affinity," Trevor said, a yawn overtaking his face as he rubbed a hand across his eyes. "But not tonight. I need to get some sleep so I can function with whatever bullshit the world throws at us tomorrow."

He pushed to his feet, before pausing and meeting my gaze. "I'd like to read that reaper book if you still have it."

"Me too," Jensen said, also getting to his feet. "We're here for you, sis. Alice and Jenna will be as well, even if you end up as a lonely old spinster with twenty pet monsters."

I glared at him.

"No chance of that," Logan drawled, and as he stood, he pulled me up beside him. "She's my bonded mate, and we'll have babies and monsters, which means she'll never be alone."

Trevor and Jensen replied with jibes and threats to *kill his arrogant ass*, in the way only brothers can, but I didn't hear a word. Logan had my full attention as he swept me out of the dining hall, and when we reached his dorm, our lips clashed in a desperate kiss.

No level of fatigue would stop what was about to happen next.

A night being loved by Logan was totally worth any exhaustion.

CHAPTER 20

Sara and Haley were waiting for me at the breakfast cart. "Well, hello there," Sara said as I stumbled toward them. "Look at what the cat dragged in."

My head felt heavy, and the mirror hadn't been my friend this morning, but there was no containing the pure contentment radiating from me.

Logan was in the running for Mate of the Century, eclipsing even my favorite book boyfriend.

"You just missed Belle," Haley said, and I jerked my head up, focused on more than my sexy spellcaster. "She took off for class but said she'll catch us at dinner."

"She's really back?" They both nodded. "Did she seem upset with us?"

Sara shook her head, brow furrowed. "No, actually. She was normal Belle and asked about you and everything. It was weird after her icy shoulder over winter break."

Haley handed me my coffee and breakfast bagel. "Don't stress, Pais. We'll figure it all out in time. Today, you have nothing more to worry about than class and your *mate*."

"Speaking of," Sara said around a bite of her sandwich, chewing and swallowing quickly. "We stopped by your dorm this morning, and to our surprise, no sign of Paisley Hallistar. Already shacking up like an old married couple."

Tingles crossed my skin at the memories of last night.

Logan was insatiable, and even in the moments when he loved me to the edge of my sanity, I was desperate for more.

"I'm going to need some of this married life," Sara said with a sigh. "Even your facial expression is giving me feelings I don't know what to do with. Needs and wants I am way too young to consider."

"You're the perfect age, pretty witch." Tobias popped up behind her, and she let out a shriek, almost losing her coffee.

Noah and Logan arrived a few seconds later, interrupting whatever scathing reply Sara was working on. Tobias leaned over, took a bite of her sandwich, and she stared at him like he was an alien lifeform that had just suggested they fuck to save the planet.

Logan nuzzled against my neck. "Hey, Precious," he rumbled, still sounding half asleep. "You weren't in my bed when I woke up."

"I needed to shower before classes today," I said with a laugh, letting myself rest against him. For two reasons, one of which was exhaustion, and the other was the pure need to be close to him. He took my weight as if it were nothing, his hands tracing gently down my sides.

It felt so fucking good that I almost purred at the sensation.

Our friends laughed and joked around us, and I chuckled at Sara holding her sandwich protectively against her chest as she berated Tobias. Not that he appeared to mind, his eyes were locked on her face in a way that said he was deep into his feelings.

I hadn't eaten my sandwich yet, and when I lifted it up to Logan, he made an appreciative sound as he took a bite. He nudged it back toward me then, silently indicating it was my turn. Sharing food with him felt intimate, and I couldn't love these little couple-y moments more.

"I finished your book," Noah said as he sidled up beside Haley.

Which reminded me that she hadn't shared any books with me in ages.

"Excuse me." I straightened and glared at her. "Are you book-cheating on me with Noah?"

Haley's eyes were flat-out laughing, even if she did nothing more than smirk. "Kind of figured you wouldn't have time at night for reading. You're living out your own romantasy anyway. You don't need the made-up ones."

I slammed my palm against my chest and narrowed my eyes on Noah. "Don't get too comfortable, big guy. She loves me more than you."

Haley couldn't hold back her laughter this time. "Absolutely the truth. Witches before . . . uh . . . warlocks. It doesn't rhyme, but you get the point."

Relieved that we'd sorted that out, I relaxed against Logan once more, only to find him watching me with a look that said he was seeing into the softest, more sacred parts of my soul . . . and he liked what he saw.

The air crackled between us as he lifted the hand holding my sandwich. "Eat, Precious."

I took a bite, and even cold it was still delicious. Before my next bite, Logan reached out and wrapped his hand around mine, and the sandwich was once again hot and steaming.

"You're so much more than I expected," I whispered, staring at his perfect side profile. I wasn't sure Dad was even this attentive to Mom, and he was the warlock I'd measured all others against.

Logan's touch heated my skin too as he wrapped his fingers gently across my throat. Possessively. "I'll always be more," he said. "And you need to eat. You don't take care of yourself, which is okay, because you have me now."

He refused to take another bite and didn't let me leave until I'd finished everything.

"I've got alchemy and Attack and Defense this morning," I said when we eventually headed for class.

His smirk told me everything. "Same."

The rest of the day was a repeat of yesterday, with Logan shadowing me through the classes, all of which were easily within the scope of my limited abilities.

"Wanna hang in the gym for another couple of hours?" Logan asked after our fight class. I'd just emerged from the locker room, showered and in my uniform. "I'm going to get a quick session in."

"Sure," I said, not wanting to be away from him. "I can get started on some assignments while I wait for you."

Okay, I was mostly going to ogle him for the full workout because he'd have his perfect body on display. But he didn't have to know that.

We entered the weights room together, and by the time I sat against the wall with my alchemy text and a notepad, Noah and Tobias had joined Logan. All of them wore fitted shorts and tanks, and I tried not to groan at the sheer level of ripped, gorgeous warlock assaulting me.

Tattoos. Muscles. I wasn't witch enough to look away.

Neither was Sara: "Fuck me dead."

Everyone in the gym spun at her loud exclamation.

She stood in the doorway, her bag spilled at her feet as if she'd just dropped it. Her eyes were wide and she was staring at Tobias, who was in the middle of taking off his sweat-soaked tank top.

"Sorry, she's having a seizure," Haley called as she leaned down and gathered up the fallen bag.

Sara shook her head, cheeks fire-engine red, as she pulled herself together and strolled past the hot warlocks, heading straight for me. Tobias's eyes were dark and predatory as he tracked her, and I wondered when their banter was going to turn from annoying snark to sexy fucking. *Again.* Without the help of witch wine this time.

Sara sat at my side, back to the wall, unnaturally silent. "You okay?" I said with a laugh. I turned to Haley. "Did she really have a seizure?"

Haley rolled her eyes as she settled in the empty spot on my other side. "It's quite possible her vagina did."

That snapped Sara out of her daze. "How could you hold out on us, Paisley?" she whispered. *"How. Could. You?"*

I laughed so hard that I drew Logan's gaze. "The guys surprised me with this random gym session. But . . . it wasn't like I could turn it down."

Sara slumped against the wall. "Toby rocks around in ten-thousand-dollar suits, but he should just be naked . . . all the time?" Logan and Noah chose that moment to ditch their shirts as well and she choked. "What is actually happening here?"

"They're weirdos who love to lift the equivalent weight of cars for fun," I said with a shrug. "It's no surprise they're all ripped."

"They are," Haley whispered, her gaze locked on Noah as he bicep-curled a minivan's worth of weight. "Very, very ripped."

"You've got a little drool right there," Sara said, casually flicking under Haley's lips.

Haley narrowed her eyes. "Like you can talk."

"They swim after this," I added, pouring some extra fuel on the horny fire.

"Well, it's settled," Sara said, throwing her hands in the air. "We're going to be late for dinner because I'm not leaving until I see everything. Paisley, you are an absolute witch. You're on my shit list for not sharing this."

"Fair enough," I said, forcing my expression to fall into remorseful lines. "I acknowledge this is too much warlock for me to keep to myself. It'll never happen again."

Sara stared me down for a beat before nodding. "Okay, I'll have a contract over to you tomorrow. I'll need you to sign and add your magical seal."

She was insane, but I loved her.

Haley held a book in her hands, but she hadn't cracked it open as she watched the workout happening before us. Or more specifically, one giant warlock who'd moved on to bench-pressing a small country. "I have feelings for him," she whispered, sounding shocked. "Holy shit. I have feelings for him. Actual real ones. I've never had feelings before." Her voice got higher and faster. She swung toward me, panic on her face. "What do I do?"

"Annnnd we're two seconds from a breakdown," Sara said. "Witch, you don't do anything. You just keep flirting with that hunk of warlock and see where the moon goddess takes you. I mean, he read one of your smutty books. Bro is into you as well. You're golden."

Haley didn't look convinced, and it wasn't that she was a virgin, but I knew her experience was limited. She'd spent most of her life living in fantasy books, and through them she knew what she wanted. An alpha asshole who was obsessed with her.

She'd told us before that it was almost impossible for a

warlock to live up to her expectations, but then Noah had come along and blown her mind, and now she had no idea what to do with him.

A sentiment I was all too familiar with.

Grasping her hand, I squeezed it tightly. "Life is all about risk," I murmured, my gaze on my mate. "But without it, there'd be no reward. Don't be scared to take a chance. Noah might just be worth it."

The tension took a few seconds to ease from her slender frame. "He is. He's worth it."

Her words resonated within me.

Whatever happened with Logan, this time with him was worth it.

Every single second.

CHAPTER 21

By the time we made it to dinner, my magic was slamming against its cage. I didn't need two guesses or a spell to tell me why that was: the gym, the swimming after, and a shirtless Logan hauling me to his room so he could get changed. My energy wanted its mate, and the bond was done waiting.

I'd attempted to delay dinner by crawling into his lap, but he'd just dropped a kiss on my nose, pulled one of his hoodies over my head—*a very nice distraction*—and told me I needed to eat because he could feel my exhaustion.

Exhaustion was fast becoming our word of the day as we discussed the ways I needed to sort my energy out. "I can multitask," I complained as we entered the dining hall. "What if I ate my food off you?" I tilted my head back to see his reaction, and he both laughed and groaned, lifting his gaze to the ceiling as if praying to our goddess.

The moon couldn't help him here.

"Soon," he grumbled, sounding pained as he flashed his beautiful eyes my way again. "Now behave."

"Ugh," I grumbled. "Fine. Food me, and then fuc—"

"Paisley!" Haley's shout drew my attention to their table. As I waved back, I noticed a familiar redheaded former best friend. Belle's eyes met mine briefly, and my desperate need for Logan eased enough that I could focus on getting food and getting to our table.

I raced around the buffet, and on my way to the table with a full plate balanced in one hand, I almost got bowled over by a group of warlocks. A pissed-off sound escaped Logan as he caught my arm with his free hand, and by the blessing of Selene, all of our food remained on our plates.

"Logan, shit. Sorry, man," a tall guy with dirty-blond hair and freckles said.

"It's okay," I burst out before Logan could let loose his annoyance. "I should have been watching where I was going."

None of them got another word in as Logan waved his hand, his magic physically moving them to the side. I shot them an apologetic stare as he guided me through the crowd. "You don't have to go all alpha on me, mate. It was an accident, and I wasn't hurt."

He was the one to grind to a halt now, and I looked about for the new disaster. "Say it again."

My gaze shot to him. "Wh-what?" I murmured.

"Say it again, baby," he whispered, his face filled with a deep, devouring emotion.

Racking my brain for what I'd said, it took me a few long seconds to figure it out. "Mate," I breathed. "I've called you mate before."

His eyes closed briefly, and if he was praying this time, it was with thanks. "You've never said it like that," he said, capturing me in his piercing gaze as soon as he opened his eyes. "Like we are forever. You're mine and I'm yours."

"This possessive side feels weird," I admitted, my heartbeat slamming against my chest. *And fucking amazing.* "After last year."

His expression darkened. "I've had to suppress that side of

myself for too long, but it's flowing freely now. You better get used to an obsessive and possessive mate."

Oh. Oh. I was a big fan of that declaration.

Logan's eyes turned mossy green as he leaned closer. "You like that, don't you, baby?"

With that, he guided me through to the table where all of our friends were already, and I was highly distracted by finally having Belle in front of me.

"You're back!" I said, unsure if I should go in for a hug or not.

She stood and stiffly wrapped her arms around me, almost as if she'd rehearsed how to make this gesture but still didn't quite have it right. The cool wash of her water magic was familiar, and I mourned what had once been. "Missed you, girl," she said.

When we parted, I examined her closer, but she looked just the same as always. Tiny, pretty, with vibrant red hair and perfect skin. Belle told me on the first night we met that she never slept much, with all the travel between America and India, but it never reflected on her face.

"How was your break?" I asked, sliding into the chair across from her, between Logan's and Noah's hulking forms.

Belle's smile didn't quite reach her eyes. "I stayed with Dad for the first half. We traveled around checking out complaints from covens. Then I was with Mom for the last weeks."

Sara piped up, "She went to Europe to look into the spell-caster rebellion."

Logan stiffened. Not that anyone else could have known it from looking at him, but I felt it in the energy caressing my side. "Were you near the rebellions too?" I asked him, taking a bite of pasta. "When you worked for your father?"

"Rafael had us all over Europe," he said, his tone indicating he wouldn't be answering further questions about his time away, at least not in front of others.

"I hear you three are rock stars." Belle changed the subject, looking between the huge warlocks. "Sad that I missed the show."

"We've got another one soon," Tobias said as he finished his cheeseburger. "We lose our bloody minds when we go too long without rocking out." He sat across from Sara tonight, and she blanched when he locked his gaze on her. "You need to be there again. That was a fun night."

Sara swallowed roughly, her cheeks slightly pinker as she no doubt recalled the night she'd gotten wasted on witch wine and had sex with Tobias. He'd been playing a game of seduction ever since, but she'd managed to hold out. "Yeah, I mean . . . if it's a weekend, we can probably make it."

"Dad has me locked down at Weatherstone," Belle said, ripping up the bread on her plate. It looked like she was moving food around rather than eating it. "I can't get weekend passes away this year."

"What about your mom?" I asked, moving on to my sushi pile. I'd saved the best for last. "Surely your dad doesn't get the only say."

She stared at me for a beat longer than normal. "He's taking point on safety issues," she said with an undercurrent that I didn't need an interpreter to understand. "All the unrest has him worried about his little girl, and I trust his judgment. He's my dad after all."

Sara met my gaze, her eyebrows briefly lifting before she went back to her food. We all knew why Belle had been distant over the winter break. Or at least we'd had a very good idea, and she'd just confirmed it.

Belle was firmly on Team Elder Monroe, who, by all indications, thought I was a demon-witch who needed to be put down.

The only part I couldn't figure out was why he hadn't tried to take me out yet. Was he waiting for evidence? Was the suppression potion screwing with his plans to catch me in the act and justify his murder to the council?

Whatever the reason, I couldn't let my guard down around Belle. No matter how much I wanted to confess everything to her, she was her father's little spy—this time with full knowledge of what she was doing.

The rest of dinner was quiet and awkward, and with my stomach in knots, I found it difficult to eat my sushi. It was only Logan nudging my plate and keeping his flinty gaze on me that had me choking down the remains.

Every time I took a bite, his hand slid up my bare thigh, tracing the sensitive skin. Rewarding me. "I know what you're doing," I muttered, glaring at him. All the while my magic writhed inside, happy and buoyant. My energy liked it when our mate touched us.

"Good girls get rewards." A finger traced over the wet lace of my panties, and my breath hitched.

"Belle!"

Trevor's shout had me jumping in my chair, and Logan withdrew his hand, looking far too pleased with himself. When my brother raced to our table, Belle's face crumpled, filled with sadness and need. Her first real display of emotion. She tried to school her features back into neutral lines, but she couldn't quite manage it. Her eyes were screaming for him, and even as she iced me out, she couldn't do it to Trevor. There were real feelings between them.

"I've been trying to find you all day," he said, grinding to a halt at her side, emanating a frantic energy I'd never felt from him before.

I'd always worried my brother would be the one to break Belle's heart. But now, thanks to Elder fucking Monroe, I had to worry that it would be Belle who would destroy their relationship before it truly had a chance. Trevor hadn't let himself care before, moving through witches like they were free popcorn at the movies, but I had no doubt he was a complete goner over Belle.

"Can we talk, sweetness?" he whispered, but we all heard.

Belle's eyes briefly met mine, and I kept my expression completely blank. "Yes," she choked out, jumping to her feet and throwing herself into Trevor's arms. He held her close as she murmured over and over how much she missed him.

The entire scene broke my heart because there was no way Elder Monroe knew about this relationship, when he clearly hated our entire family line. I wasn't sure what would be stronger in the end: Belle's trust and loyalty to her father or her love for my brother.

Their bond, which had started to develop last year, had only grown stronger with time.

My worry exploded tenfold, and I prayed to the goddess that there was a way this could all work out. The happiness of my family was as important to me as my own, and I was determined that Belle and Trevor would have their time.

Even if I had to crush Elder Monroe to make it happen.

CHAPTER 22

My first week at Weatherstone lured me into a false sense of security. Classes hadn't been bad, and even with suppressed magic, I still made ground with my skills—in all areas except the one that differentiated me from my peers: my reaper abilities, which allowed me to draw on the souls of monsters from Purgatory. All necromancy was out of bounds for me, and I found myself lingering near the graveyard, even though I'd never voluntarily step foot in there again.

As the term progressed, classes got harder, and I ended up in the library most evenings, studying my ass off. Logan never let me skip dinner, though, and I slept in his room every night, even if half the time I was too exhausted to do more than pass out in his arms.

He kept the dreams away, just as he'd always done, but my fatigue continued to grow until I was barely able to keep my eyes open through the day.

It was late on a Wednesday morning when I heard the rasp of my name. It broke through sleep, but when I tried to open my eyes, I couldn't find the strength. I was just so tired. I wanted to fall back into the darkness hovering around my mind and lose myself. A jolt of energy slammed against my own, punching through the suppression potion and sending me shooting up like I'd been stabbed in the ass.

"Whoa," I cried, vision blurry at first until everything came into focus. Logan stood at the side of the bed, his eyes darker than I'd ever seen, his chest heaving.

"Paisley," he rasped. "Baby . . . Are you here with me?"

The fog remained around my brain, but I was no longer drowning in darkness. "Wh-what happened?"

Logan dropped to his knees beside the bed, reaching out to wrap his arms around me. "You were fading." His voice broke, and I would have done anything to erase that tone of devastation. "I felt your energy waning until your powers flickered and almost faded."

"Fading . . ." The opposite of a magical bloom, it usually happened right before death. I shook my head to clear the last of the fog. "How did you bring me back?"

He pulled me even closer, dragging me to the edge of the mattress. "Pure fucking power," he growled. "I jolted you with my energy, filling you up as much as I could through our bond."

A pure dose of spellcaster explained why I'd launched myself out of bed like I'd been struck by lightning. Clutching on to Logan, I felt the tremble in his arms. "What's wrong with me?" I asked against his throat, breathing in his soothing scent. "I've been so tired this year, and it's getting worse."

"I don't know, Precious," he whispered, and the ragged sound of his fear cut into my chest.

"Could it be the suppression potion?" I wondered, trying to work through the possibilities. "My exhaustion started late last year, which could have been part of the spell they cast over the school during the monster attacks. My magic might not like to be locked down . . . ." Panic simmered through my veins, adding to my confusion. "Maybe I should talk to Mom about it?"

"You were planning on heading home this weekend, right?" he said, pulling away to see my face. "Bring me with you, and we'll talk to her together."

"Okay, good idea. It's time for them to know about us anyway, and my issues will be a fantastic distraction from the fact that I'm sleeping with the enemy." My lame attempt at a joke fell flat. Logan's worried expression didn't ease up at all as I added, "I'll try not to exert too much energy over the next few days."

"I'll speak to your professors and get you excused today. You're not leaving this bed. You need to rest, and I'm going to be right here next to you."

Heat rose in my body, and I was relieved that there was enough energy within me to fuel my desire. For the first time, the slightest of smiles tilted his lips. "Not a chance, Precious. You're resting, and I'm catering to your every whim—"

I opened my mouth, and he chuckled. "Except that one."

"Orgasms give energy," I pouted, crossing my arms. "It's science."

With a shake of his head, he brushed his lips briefly across mine, pulling away before I could demand more. "We're not humans," he whispered. "Science isn't what drives us. It's magic, and yours needs to recharge."

"Hard-ass," I groaned, falling back into the pillows.

Logan stood, reaching down to brush my hair away from my face, the heat of his magic seeping into my essence. "You have no idea how much of a hard-ass I can be when it comes to you, Precious. I'd let the world burn around us as long as you were okay. I'm no hero except for when it comes to you."

I barely managed not to cry. "I love you," I whispered. I'd known this for a while now, and it had been said in more than words, but it was time to lay it out there. Give him this last piece of myself.

He jerked as if I'd been the one to strike him with power, and if I hadn't already been lying down, I'd have dropped at the look on his face. "Baby," he whispered, his expression burning.

Dragging on my meagre strength, I pushed to my knees, his shirt falling down my body. "I love you, Logan Kingston. I love you more than I thought I was capable of. I'm pretty sure I've loved you since I was four years old and forced you into a mate bond spell."

He was on me in seconds, gentle even as his big body slammed against mine and we crashed onto the mattress. "I fell at your feet the first time I saw your pretty little face, Paisley Hallistar. Even then I knew you were it for me. I love you too. I love you so fucking much that it's a delicious kind of pain I will crave for eternity."

He pressed his lips to mine, the kiss filled with fire as our powers clashed, and energy fueled me to the point that I couldn't remember being tired. Tears fell unabashedly down my cheeks, and Logan kissed across my face, his tongue swiping through my tears, all the while whispering his love for me.

Eventually he pulled me under the covers, and we stayed like that, wrapped up as tightly as we could get, until I drifted off to sleep surrounded by his love.

"Did you tell Mom and Dad you were bringing the enemy home?" Trevor asked, smirking when I arrived at Weatherstone's front gate with Logan. I'd made it through the last few days without fading, my fatigue a low ebb in my center, but power from Logan kept me from sinking into it.

"Nope," I said shortly. "I'm not giving them time to freak out about it. They'll just have to deal."

Jensen, who had a bag thrown over his shoulder, rubbed a

hand across his face. "This is going to be interesting. Jen and Alice are at home waiting for us as well, so you'll have the full house for this *surprise*."

Nerves assaulted me, but I couldn't back down now. It was time for everything to come out, a new plan to be made. The suppression wasn't working; my energy was fading along with my power, which meant we needed to pivot and figure out a new plan.

Logan stood silent at my side, dressed in faded denim jeans, a Henley, and black boots. He also had a backpack with changes of clothes, and I wasn't looking forward to telling Dad that we were staying in my room together.

But it wouldn't matter what he said.

Even if Logan's energy wasn't literally keeping me alive at this point, I was done living without him.

"Well, let's get this party started." Trevor's smirk was permanently in place, and it was nice to see him looking somewhat chipper. Belle being back had helped his snarly disposition, and now his joy was centered around the drama I was about to add to the day.

We left the gates and entered the booth already programmed to take us home. I'd requested the portal, so I pressed my hand against the panel and the power of the transport connected to my own. A few minutes later, we stepped onto the back porch to find Alice and Jenna waiting for us. Trevor, who had arrived first, blocked me from their view, but not even his size could block Logan. When I poked my head around, I wanted to laugh at the shock on the twins' faces, but the tension held me too tight. A gentle stroke down my spine loosened my muscles enough that I could step forward, debating if I should nudge up Jenna's slack jaw, or if that would get me a punch in the mouth. My older sister had quite the temper when riled.

"What the fuck?" she finally gasped. "What the fuck is happening here? I know there's not a fucking Kingston standing there with his hands on my baby sister."

Logan was such an intrinsic part of me now that it was hard for me to register her shock, to understand how this didn't feel as natural and essential to them as it did to me. Maybe I'd been better at hiding my feelings last year than I'd thought, because being around Logan but not *with him* had felt as if I'd carried a wound everywhere, dripping blood as I walked.

"We've got a lot to talk about," I said simply. "Are Mom and Dad home?"

Jenna shook her head, opening her mouth before slamming it shut again. Alice stepped in for her twin. "Is Logan the reason you've been shutting us out since Halloween?" She sounded hurt, and that killed me. I'd hated keeping secrets from them, and the truth finally coming out would be a relief for us all.

"Logan and I are not the issue," I said, looking between the two of them. "He's the reason I'm standing here today. He's saved me more times than I can even tell you." Meeting his gaze, I wondered how I'd ever thought his green eyes were icy when now they burned like fire.

"Oh," Jenna whispered. "Oh fuck. I've seen that look before on our parents. That's a true-bond kind of look."

It was.

"We're bonded with an ancient magic that wouldn't have worked unless we were true mates," I whispered, unable to look away from him. Logan brushed a finger down my cheek, leaving a fiery trail in its wake. "We bonded when we were kids, but the extent of it didn't truly emerge until my magic bloomed."

"Impossible." Jenna shook her head. "Kids can't access ancient magic or spells. There's no way."

Logan's expression hardened as he met her stare. "When you are true mates, you can. Most just haven't found the match to their power, but Paisley and my magic connected before it even bloomed. We've always been meant to be."

"They were unnaturally obsessed with each other as kids," Alice reminded us all.

Jenna shook her head, the shock holding her features fading into another. Hurt. "You never told us." She sniffled. "Don't you trust us?"

"I trust you with my life. Always. It was just . . . I was still fighting the part of me tied to Logan over the winter break, and that wasn't what I was keeping from you anyway. My distance was for another reason—I did it to protect you all, but . . . I can't keep it a secret any longer. Mom and Dad thought this was for the best, but it's not working, and we need a new plan."

Whatever was happening to me, we needed to deal with this as a family.

Just as we always did.

CHAPTER 23

The atmosphere in the house remained tense as we waited for Mom and Dad to get home. My brothers already knew the truth, and they tried to distract Jenna and Alice, but the twins spent most of their time eyeballing Logan and me.

I got why they were upset—I'd feel the same way if the situation were reversed. We didn't keep big secrets from each other, especially not when one of us was in trouble.

My actions had created this distance between us, and it was time to fix my fuckup.

The front door opened while we were chilling in the lounge, pretending to watch TV. Logan was sitting beside me, and when everyone jumped up, he helped me to my feet. Trevor's brow furrowed as he noticed my weakened state, and I forced myself to stand on my own, waving off his concern. He'd find out about our new issue soon enough.

"Kiddos," Mom called from the entrance. "We bought Chicken Larry's for lunch. We'll meet you in the dining room."

Chicken Larry's was a family favorite, with perfectly crisp Southern fried chicken pieces, crunchy fries, creamy mashed potatoes, and their secret-family-recipe gravy as the cherry on top. This conversation had better not ruin Larry's for us.

Logan swung his arm around me in support, and as much as I tried not to lean on him, I needed his strength. In more ways than just physical. "You got this, Precious," he whispered against my cheek, sending a shiver slowly down my spine.

"I love you," I replied softly. His thick, dark eyelashes shadowed his cheeks as he closed his eyes. He'd admitted to me that Rafael wasn't the sort of parent to hand out words of affection, not even when he was younger. He'd lost his mom when he was a child, and he'd felt alone ever since. No one had ever told Logan they loved him, and I was determined to say it every day we had together.

"I wish I'd been with you over the years," I said, trying not to fall apart; this wasn't about me. "The way we should have been."

"Me too, Precious. I only saw your life from the outside looking in, when I wanted to be right in the middle."

I paused, narrowing my eyes on him. "Wait . . . Did you literally watch me over the years, Stalker?"

His first real smile in days graced his lips. "When my magic bloomed, and I figured out how to use transport magic without checking in, I kept an eye on you. I had to make sure you were safe."

He was two years older than me, which meant he'd been watching me all that time and I'd never known. "Keeping my distance was the hardest fucking thing I've ever done," he promised me, "but I had to play Rafael's game for as long as possible. He wanted me to wait for you to bloom and then get close enough to give him updates on your magic."

"Are you sure he doesn't know about our bond?" Rafael had a plan, we were both sure of it, and it started with Logan watching over me at Weatherstone. But what was the next part?

Was he waiting to find out about my affinity?

Logan shook his head. "I don't know how he'd know

about the bond . . . I've never told him. He has been encouraging me to stay near you and elevate your magic. Fuck, he's half the reason I avoided you last year. If Rafael wanted us closer, then it couldn't be good for either of us."

"What made you change your mind?"

"Paisley!" Mom shouted from the dining room. "Lunch is getting cold."

"Coming, Mom," I replied, but I wasn't planning on moving until Logan answered my last question.

He knew it as well, his smile growing. "After what happened in the graveyard, when our magic combined and created pure power, I decided I was done hiding in the shadows. It was growing harder to keep you safe, and every time you were in danger, I'd lose my fucking mind. I was always near you, Precious. Your own personal stalker. The only difference is now you know about it."

My snort of laughter echoed around the room. "I can't tell if that's romantic or terrifying."

Logan shrugged. "No reason it can't be both."

Right. There was absolutely no reason.

He started to lead me toward the dining room, and I found myself asking a question that I immediately regretted. "What really killed your mom, Logan?"

As I finished speaking, Mom appeared in the doorway, her face drained of color. She'd heard my tasteless question. "Only one person can tell us that," Logan said shortly, watching Mom closely. "And she's standing right here."

"Paisley," Mom whispered, pale and shaking, "what's he doing here?"

If only she knew that my mate was the least of our problems. "We have a lot to talk about," I told her. "And Logan is, and always will be, part of my life and what's happening to me."

Her gaze flickered toward the dining room. "It's too dangerous for them to know," she said, her tone urgent.

"Half of them already know," I replied with a small cringe, hoping I hadn't doomed us all.

"And they're in danger either way," Logan said, always having my back. "Keeping them in the dark is limiting all the ways they can protect you and themselves. Not to mention they could unintentionally make it worse."

Mom wavered on her feet, but she got herself under control before she collapsed. She took a few more moments—looking between Logan and me—to decide where she fell on the situation. Not that it mattered, the choice had really been taken out of our hands. And she knew it. With a nod she croaked, "Okay, let's get this done."

We followed her into the dining room, and as Logan came into view, Dad shot to his feet. "What the Hel, Paisley?"

Mom waved him down, and his trust for her was so implicit, he didn't question the action, dropping back into his seat. "Logan's not our enemy today," she said, voice growing stronger with each word. "Paisley believes he's on her side, which means he's on our side."

"I will personally believe that when I see it," Jenna grumped. "He's probably playing games with her to enact whatever revenge plan Rafael has in the works."

Logan's growl shut the room down as he reminded everyone present that he was one of the most powerful warlocks in the world. "You can insult me all you want," he rumbled, words slow and biting, "but never question my feelings for Paisley. We're bonded by magic and love. She was it for me from the moment I met her, and just because she grew up with you doesn't change the fact that *she's mine*. I will kill and die for her. She's my mate. *Mine*."

His magic swirled, and all of us felt a subtle but powerful

slam against our own. Mine piped up like a puppy getting a treat. All excited and shit. As everyone stared open-mouthed, Logan pulled out a chair and gently deposited me in it. It was hard not to collapse, but I didn't want to reveal, just yet, the full extent of my fatigue.

Logan grabbed a plate and, ignoring everyone, asked me, "What do you want to eat, Precious?"

He cared for me in a way that we'd grown up watching Dad do with Mom, and I could feel the tension easing in the room. "I love everything from Larry's." I shot him a cheeky smile, and his chest swelled as he got to work dishing me up food. My family still hadn't moved, watching us closely, as if cataloging every movement.

When he placed my food before me and nudged it closer, without touching a piece for himself, the tension eased, and my family filled their plates as well.

Logan had given me so much that there was no way I could eat it all, so I grabbed an extra fork for him. "You can share with me," I said. "I won't eat half of this."

A familiar, stubborn expression crossed his face. "I'm not touching your food until you've eaten. Now go on, you need the energy."

That caught Mom's attention, her spoon of mashed potatoes hovering above her plate. "What is he talking about? Are you okay, Paisley?"

Logan ignored her completely, tapping his hand against my plate. I already knew from the last week at school that he wouldn't stop until I ate, so I rolled my eyes and grabbed my fork. "That's the reason we're here," I said as I spooned up some potatoes. "My magic is waning, and we're wondering if it could be the suppression potion."

Jenna's fork clattered to the table. "Why is she taking a suppression potion?"

Mom looked at me, then toward her eldest daughter. "We've been keeping you all in the dark about Paisley's affinity, and I want to apologize because it was my call. Your sister wanted to tell you all when everything blew up last year."

Jenna's hand shook as she grabbed her fork again. "You're going to tell us now, right?"

"Yes," I confirmed before Mom could. "I'm going to tell you everything."

Between bites of food, I started with the first monster appearances, and what had happened at the end of the year. "On All Hallows' Eve, when the blanket over Weatherstone lifted," I said softly, "my magic went haywire, and I called all the monsters. That's when I knew I was actually behind the attacks at Weatherstone."

My sisters didn't utter a word as I told them everything, including what we'd learned from the reaper book, the fact that we were called "night witches," and Gran's letters. After, Mom filled them in on the suppression potion we were using to keep my affinity a secret. We put it all on the table, and it felt right to have everyone know the truth.

By this stage, I'd eaten as much as I could, and Logan finished the rest of my plate in an orderly fashion. He ate the way he did everything in life, with methodical skill that accomplished his task in the fastest and most competent manner.

"What is your part in all of this, Logan?" Dad asked him. His expression was neutral, but we could see the flames in his eyes.

Logan didn't hold back. "My father hates your family. Since Mom's death, he's been building his wealth and power, all to take you down. He said that simply killing you all would be too easy. Too fast. He wants to watch you suffer the same way he has. He didn't tell me the exact plan, but I believe he hopes to start destroying this family one member at a time, until you're the only one left, Professor Hallistar—the best friend who didn't believe him when he said there was a dark magic aura around your wife. He blames you the most, and he wants you to suffer as much as he has."

The silence was heavy, broken only by a roar from Morris, who was outside. No doubt he was reacting to the devastation we could see on Jenna's face.

"He didn't tell me how he plans to achieve this goal," Logan continued, the deep baritone of his voice growing stronger. "I've tried to play the good, dutiful son to stay in the loop, but a part of him doesn't trust me. When he told me to go to Weatherstone last year to keep an eye on Paisley and report back what magic she has, I did exactly that, but I never told him my suspicion that she was involved in bringing the monsters into the school. Somehow, he knew, though, and on parents' weekend he broke through the blanket briefly and fed his energy into Paisley so her magic went haywire and temporarily brought dozens of monsters inside the barrier."

I jerked around to stare at him; he'd never told me that before. "So I didn't imagine them."

"Sorry, love," he said with a sad smile. "I felt his energy when I raced into your room, and knew it was involved, but I didn't know how. It wasn't until last month when he called me home and told me that you were from the night witch affinity, also known as a reaper, that it all made sense. He believes you had something to do with the monster who killed Mom."

I blinked. "Why hasn't he come after me, then? What's he waiting for in this plan to start killing us off, one by one?"

Logan's energy rattled through the room, his darkening

expression scary. "I can only guess that he's not ready to go up against me, not in a direct attack. But he'll have a plan, even if I'm at a loss of what it is."

The realization hit me all at once. "Logan, my weakness . . . what if . . . ?"

Dad shot to his feet, his power swirling until the room's temperature had us all baking. "What weakness? What's happening to your power, Paisley?"

I shook my head. "I have no idea, Dad. But I've been exhausted to the point that on Wednesday, Logan felt me fading." Swinging my gaze toward Mom, I asked again, "Could this suppression potion be weakening me? Draining my powers and energy until I'm in danger of fading away in darkness?"

She shook her head. "Not a chance, honey. It's not dark magic. It's very similar to the blanket magic over the school. To my knowledge, nothing but a very powerful curse can drain a witch's magic."

Logan snarled at this new possible cause of my waning magic. If anyone was going to conjure a curse, it would be his bastard of a father.

"I'm going to kill him," Dad raged, heat billowing from his skin.

Logan's rumble filled the room. "Not if I get to him first."

Two alpha males faced off, but for once we were all fighting on the same team. This was why I wanted everything on the table, because to beat someone as strong as Logan's father, it would take everything we had.

He'd been planning this for years. No way was he going to take us on without a plan B, C, and D. We just had to hope we could figure them all out before it was too late.

CHAPTER 24

"I'm going to see Rafael alone," Logan said, pushing to his feet. "I'm going to figure out what's happening to Paisley if I have to string that fucker up by his intestines to do it."

"No!" I shot to stand. "If he's kept you in the dark, he doesn't trust you. You can't just go in there demanding answers. Bring me . . . I'm sure he'll be dying to brag about how I'm cursed and it's going to take down my entire family."

Logan smirked, his answer already clear across his rigid features. "Cute that you think I'd take you anywhere near that asshole. Noah will be with me. Rafael might be blinded by hate, but I'm his only son. He won't kill me. And," he added when I opened my mouth to protest again, "even if he was ready to ditch the Kingston line, I'm strong enough to fight back."

Every part of me rebelled against what he wanted to do, but there was no real argument I could think of for me to be there. It was dangerous to deliver me directly to Rafael, but the thought of Logan going without me . . .

"For once, I agree with a Kingston," Dad said, using the tone that meant he would not be dissuaded. "You're not leaving this country to visit the psycho who wants to destroy our family. You've just told us that you're weak. Your magic is suppressed. There are a dozen reasons why this is a terrible idea."

"Logan going is a terrible idea," I bit out. "Angry and half-cocked. He's going to get himself killed." I faced him fully. "You're going to get yourself freaking killed."

As he shook his head, I squeezed my eyes closed, fighting to find a reason to stop him from leaving. I didn't trust Rafael not to hurt his son, or at minimum keep us apart until the curse ran its course and it was too late to halt anything.

"It's the only way," Logan said, his scent wrapping around me as he moved closer.

"I'm scared of what he will do to you," I whispered. "I don't have a good feeling about this."

Logan didn't look concerned, but as he was a powerful, arrogant spellcaster, I wasn't particularly surprised. He'd always been the strongest in the room, the predator that others feared, but his father was older and evil.

"How will we know you're okay?" Mom asked, and my magic hummed at the concern in her tone. "Paisley is your mate, and if this magical bond is as strong as it appears, she will break if anything happens to you. You have to think of her now when you make decisions."

Logan showed a level of calm in his response that was unexpected. "I think of her with every decision I make. My bond with your daughter is not a responsibility I take lightly. More than that, I love Paisley and would kill my father before I caused her an iota of pain."

No one could miss the truth in his words. "What if Logan wears a wire?" Dad said suddenly.

Everyone stared at him, including my siblings, who'd remained quiet during our discussion.

"A wire?" Trevor finally said with a shake of his head. "Like a human?"

Jenna sat straighter. "It makes sense. Rafael would never expect his son to use human technology. He's too strong to hide magic from, which makes a wire the perfect solution."

Logan looked between them, and through our connected magic I sensed his confusion. One day he wouldn't be surprised to be surrounded in support and comfort. "He could just call me and leave the phone in his pocket," I suggested with a smile. "No need to resort to anything too drastic." After all, phones were human technology that we all used in lieu of magic to easily communicate.

"That would work too," Dad said, his cheeks pinkening slightly. "When will you leave?"

Logan checked his watch. "It's the middle of the night there, so I'll leave early tomorrow."

The room grew silent as we considered what the next day could bring our way. For me, I hoped it was the truth, and a chance to move forward without the constant worry of my energy fading into nothing.

"Well, if this is our last day of normal," Trevor said, yawning and lifting his arms, shirt riding up on his tanned skin, "I vote for a movie afternoon."

"I'm in," Jenna said, sounding more like her old self.

"Me too." Alice popped to her feet and headed for the kitchen. "I'll grab snacks."

"Wait," I called, before everyone dispersed. "We never really discussed my affinity and what happened last year. Do any of you want to ask me anything, or maybe yell at me for keeping it a secret? Do you—" my voice broke, but I got it together fast "—hate me because I unintentionally got a student killed?"

I'd personally never forgive myself for what happened, but I had to move on with the knowledge that I'd never purposely hurt anyone. I wasn't a bad witch. I just lost control of magic that should have been explained to me upon my bloom.

"Paisley Jane Hallistar!" Jenna growled, pointing a finger at me. "You have to be kidding us. We would love you even if you turned out to be a serial killer. I mean, I wouldn't help you move dead bodies, because *ew*, but I'd never think less of you. I know you'd only murder evil assholes, and I'd trust you had a very good reason for it. You're the best of all of us, and that's saying something, because I'm an angel."

Trevor snorted and covered it with a cough when she glared at him. "Jenna is right," he said quickly. "There's nothing you could do that would make us turn against you. Hallistars stick together. And just as information to consider, I would personally help you hide the bodies, because I'm the better sibling."

Jenna flipped him off, and my heart flipped with it as a lightness infused my energy.

"Just never keep secrets from us again, sis," Jensen said, hopping up to wrap me in his strong arms. "Or I'll have to beat your ass."

Logan gently extracted me from Jensen's hold. "Threaten Paisley again, and the only ass getting beat around here will be yours." He shot my brother a feral smile that had Jensen backing up, hands in front of him.

My laughter was cathartic, especially when Logan's energy eased up and everyone clued in on the fact that he was teasing. *Mostly.* Having him here just felt right, and for the briefest of seconds I forgot the shit we were dealing with—that in a few short hours he'd be stepping into his father's evil lair to figure out what was happening to my energy.

After that, we threw ourselves into our favorite afternoon activity: family movie day. I sat on one of the softer couches with Logan, sinking against him. My energy wasn't as low as it had been—the support of my family was intrinsic to our familiar magical connection, and it was as important as my bond to my mate. I'd been neglecting that part of my energy, which hadn't helped the whole situation.

Logan held me close through the afternoon, both of us snacking on the popcorn and pizza Mom brought as no one wanted to leave the cozy room to cook. It was one of the best afternoons I'd had in a long time.

I fell asleep against Logan's chest halfway through our fifth movie, and when I woke very early the next morning, we were in my bedroom, my spellcaster wrapped around me. He was asleep, and I took a second to study his face in the low light from the rising sun outside my window. It was rare I had a chance to truly look at him like this, his dark hair a mess above a face completely unguarded, his all-seeing green gaze hidden behind closed lids and sooty lashes.

"Who's the stalker now, best friend?" he mumbled, sending goose bumps across my skin. "Watching me sleep like a creep."

"Like a real creep," I confirmed.

His smile was soft as he opened his eyes for me to sink into that endless green. "You slept well last night," he said in an attractive rasp, his hold across my back firming as he pulled me closer. "Your weakness has eased a little."

Letting my head rest against his chest, I listened to the steady thrum of his heartbeat. "I'm surprised my dad and brothers didn't try to drag you out of here."

His hand slid across my throat and tilted my chin up so he could kiss me. "They strongly encouraged me to leave," he said coolly. "But they conceded that it's my job to protect you, and for me to do that effectively, I need to be close at all times."

I shifted against him, desire rising like a tide inside me, until I was in danger of being washed away. Logan had been withholding sex due to my exhaustion, and it was the worst case of edging I'd ever experienced. I'd combust soon.

"Let me take care of you," he whispered against my skin, tasting my desire. "If you can stay quiet."

Goddess, there was no fucking way.

Logan slid down my stomach. "Use the pillow," he ordered, and before I could clarify what he meant, he buried his face in my pussy. As a groan was torn from me, I managed to yank the pillow over my face to muffle the sound. He devoured me until I was crying into the soft material, and when his mouth closed over my clit, I jerked. Logan slid one finger along my lower lips, through my arousal, before he pushed that thick digit inside me. I gasped as a second finger joined, the pair scissoring and pumping in and out. I was so slick that he moved with ease through my heat as he flattened his tongue against my clit once more.

At this point I was breathlessly crying into the pillow, hoping that no one was right outside my door. "Come for me, Precious," Logan growled, the speed of his tongue increasing as his fingers slammed inside me. "Now, baby."

Every muscle in my body tightened as I did exactly what he commanded, the walls of my pussy clenching around his fingers as he dragged out the pleasure until I was panting.

His hands traced down to wrap around my thighs. "You completely undo me, Paisley Hallistar. You're so fucking beautiful. Perfect." His voice lowered menacingly. "Whatever my father's plan is, I will make sure it ends today."

Drawing on my pathetic upper body strength, I lifted myself up toward him. The hard length of his cock was visible in his tight boxers, but when I reached for him, he moved away. "This morning was about your pleasure. You still need to rest until we know the exact reason for your magical malady." On occasion, Logan forgot he wasn't a warlock from the nineteenth century.

When I reached up to touch his face, he moved closer once more. "I love you and I trust you," I said, determined that when he left here today, he'd know exactly how much he meant to me. "Promise that no matter what you learn today, even if it's going to change my life, you tell me the truth. I don't ever want to go back to last year when you were a beautiful and scary stranger, keeping all your dark secrets."

Logan shook his head. "We're partners, Precious. I won't keep the truth from you, even if it's hard. You're mine."

"And you're mine."

Logan leaned over and brushed his lips against mine. "Always. I've been yours for most of my life. You know that."

I did know it.

Now we just had to hope that it wasn't too late to reverse whatever Rafael had done to me and my magic.

CHAPTER 25

Logan was showered and dressed in dark jeans and a hoodie. Noah had arrived too, and they were about to head to Italy, where the Kingston Enterprises head offices were located. "I'll call you soon," he promised as he pressed a kiss to my lips.

Noah gave me a quick hug and said, "I'll keep him safe."

Logan ignored his best friend, spending a few seconds opening the transport on the back deck. When they stepped through, my heart slammed in my chest, and I clutched my phone, waiting for his call. Mom and Dad guided me into the dining room, and we were soon joined by the rest of my siblings.

Everyone had put their life on hold to deal with my issue, and I couldn't be more grateful.

"Rafael didn't used to be a billionaire," Dad said as he sipped his coffee; he'd been attempting to joke me out of my nerves for fifteen minutes. "When I met him, he was a punk-ass kid building cars out of his garage, and computers out of his tiny bedroom. Always was brilliant with anything electronic or that contained an engine."

"He was brilliant," Mom agreed. "Isabel used to rave about how she wasn't good enough for him because he was so much smarter than her. But she was an earth witch, you know. One who reveled in nature and in the energy of the moon. She was never indoors, and yet she married this nerdy science warlock who would spend days tinkering with his computers."

"Yin and yang," Trevor said with a shrug. "There's a reason they say opposites attract. It's that lovely balance that keeps everything interesting."

His eyes met mine, and my heart ached at his pain hovering in the flames. Trevor was hurting. He hadn't mentioned Belle at all since we came home, but I knew she was on his mind. She'd be on mine more too if I weren't so stressed by my current malady—as Logan would say.

"When Isabel died, he broke," Dad said, his humor fading as the darker memories took over, "and I lost my oldest friend. It felt as if a part of my family died. It took me a long time to move forward without him. The second he enacted the blood oath against me, though, I put our past behind me and decided he was dead to me as well. A threat to me or mine was enough to cut the cord."

Mom toyed with her teacup, and I found myself asking one more time: "What actually happened that day in the forest, Mom? It's too late to worry about your theory disturbing our balance. We're already deep in it."

Dad lurched forward as if to intervene, but Mom answered before he could. "I truly don't know, but this theory . . . it's one that I've thought on ever since I read Mom's letters." She had all our attention, but she didn't lift her gaze from the delicate porcelain of her cup. "I think I did call a monster that day in the forest."

I tried to breathe through the tightness in my chest—Rafael hated our family because he believed Mom killed his wife, and . . . *he might be right.* "You told me that you don't have the same affinity as me," I whispered as my heart broke. "How could you have called a monster?"

She pressed her lips together. "I don't have your affinity, but I do think I might have tapped into it somehow. After you were born, I noticed a foreign strain of energy in my system. I could feel it, this weird, icy magic that didn't mesh with my elemental magic. It wasn't there before you were born."

"How could my birth trigger a magical share?" I asked, trying to recall if I'd ever learned anything like that in school.

"Your birth was quite traumatic." Mom tried to smile, but it didn't entirely hit the mark. "The most traumatic I had in all four pregnancies."

"She almost died. They had to do an emergency C-section," Dad added, his voice gruff.

Jensen looked between our parents. "You said Paisley's huge head almost cut you in half, but we didn't realize you nearly died."

This story wasn't a secret, but they'd clearly kept the full extent of the situation from us.

"Your sister's head was perfectly sized and shaped," Mom admonished Jensen. "It was just one of those births where everything went wrong. Mother and child in utero share blood and magic. A literal sharing of life. I can only assume that during either your development or maybe in the trauma of your birth, I took on more of your magic than I should have. A strain of reaper energy that could call a monster in the right circumstances."

My world ground to a halt, and it wasn't until Jensen wrapped an arm around me and said, "Breathe, Paisley. Breath, sis," that I felt the rattling of air in my lungs.

"My magic killed Logan's mom?" My rasps grew louder. "He's never going to forgive me."

Mom was around to my side of the table in seconds, her hands on my face, a lick of her power caressing my skin. "No! Paisley Hallistar, you will cease that line of thought immediately. Firstly, there's no fault with you. You were four years old, for goddess's sake. And secondly, magic is strange and volatile, and the elders should never have allowed an affinity as powerful as yours to be struck from our world. The fault lies with the magical community. Not those of us who were victims of their genocide centuries ago."

Dad stared at Mom and there was no mistaking the haze in his eyes. I'd never seen him cry, not that I could remember, but he was fighting back tears. "You're going to use your magic again, Beth." It wasn't a question.

Mom hugged me one last time, then straightened, stumbling until she fell into her husband's lap. He wrapped her up tightly, and I knew I wasn't the only uncomfortable one. If they got any closer . . . we'd all need a shit ton of therapy.

"I'm going to use my magic again," she confirmed, voice stronger than I'd heard in a long time. "I can't ask Paisley to be brave and strong if I don't show her the same in kind. I thought I was protecting everyone, but I understand now, I left us all at a disadvantage. One Hallistar short in our combined magical strength."

"Do you still contain a streak of my magic?" I asked her.

She shook her head. "No. I've never felt that magic again after that day I released it, but in the fear that it would return, I cut off all magic. That day in the forest we were spooked by a huge bear, that part wasn't a lie, and I reacted without thought. The power popped out of me, as if it were just waiting for the trigger to release. The shadowy creature was there for only a split second, long enough to slash through Isabel, who jumped between us, and then it was gone."

"When I first started seeing the creatures," I said, needing to explain even as my guilt weighed me down, "they flickered in and out of our plane before returning to Purgatory. My magic wasn't strong enough to keep them here. That would be what happened that day in the forest."

Mom straightened on Dad's lap. "This is not your fault, Paisley." It was the firmest tone I'd heard her use in a long time. "And Logan will not blame you."

My phone rang before I could have the breakdown hovering on the edge of my consciousness—Logan's name flashed across the screen. "Hey," I croaked as I answered it.

"Precious?" His voice held a note of concern. "You okay?"

"Yes—yes." I managed to sound almost normal. "Are you at his offices?"

There was a pause and it sounded as if he was walking. "Approaching now. I'm going to put you in my pocket for a second. Let me know if you can hear us okay."

Static sounded through the speaker, but it settled just as fast. Logan and Noah chatted quickly, as if in conversation, and while it was muffled, most of what they said was clear. Logan's voice came back stronger when he lifted the phone again. "All good?"

"All good," I confirmed. "Be careful."

"Always," he assured me, before he slid the phone back into his pocket. I hit the mute button on my phone, to ensure Rafael never picked up on our presence. It took a while for them to make it through the building, moving past multiple security checks, until I heard Logan say, "Hey, Lucille, is Dad ready for us?"

Lucille, who I could only assume was a receptionist or secretary, replied in what I would guess was Italian. Logan answered her in the same language, and I tried not to swoon at how sexy it was that he spoke multiple languages. Thank the goddess we weren't measuring the survivability of this relationship based on the skills we each brought to the table. Because I was woefully behind in that regard.

Logan and Noah remained quiet as they waited for Rafael, and it wasn't long before the voice I remembered from parents' weekend crackled over the line. "Son," he said, sounding thrilled to see Logan. "What brings you over here when you're supposed to be at school? Is your little band performing again?"

Little band. Condescending bastard.

"No gigs booked at the moment," Logan said, sounding bored and annoyed. It was a familiar tone I'd heard more than once last year, and as much as I hated it now, he was doing what was needed to play his part. "I'm here about Paisley."

Rafael scoffed. "What did that little traitor do? I told you not to trust her, son. Your job was to get close to her and report back on the family. I've been worried that your loyalty to *a child* would cloud your judgment of the adult."

Logan's laughter was hard and cynical. "You know my judgment is never clouded, *Dad*. You taught me that the hard way. To never lose sight of the end goal. To always play the fucking game. But the game has changed, and I need more answers if you want me to continue."

All of us leaned closer to the phone, not wanting to miss anything. "What changed with the game?" Rafael asked, and he wasn't as good at hiding his interest.

"Paisley is sick. She's collapsing at school, and when I'm close to her, her energy wanes. I didn't do anything to make her sick, so why is she exhausted with low magic? If you expect me to keep up with the plan, I need more information."

There was a terrifying moment of silence as I waited to hear my fate, and then Rafael laughed. That bastard actually laughed. "Ah, son. It appears that *you* were the one who changed the game, and we're finally closing in on the check and mate."

I exchanged a glance with Trevor, who wore the grimmest face I'd ever seen. "What are you talking about?" Logan growled. I heard Noah murmur, but his words were too low to make out through the muffled connection.

"You should take a seat," Rafael said. "This is going to be a bit of a story." The scraping of chairs sounded as Rafael continued. "It all started when Paisley was born. That was when I felt the change in Beth Hallistar's power. I mentioned it to her idiot of a husband, mostly in concern, but he dismissed me."

Mom's theory of what happened wasn't as big of a secret as we thought—Rafael believed the same truth. Which meant Logan was going to know.

He was going to know that it was my affinity that killed his mom, and despite my family's reassurances, I had no idea how he'd react.

"You think Paisley is the reason Mom died?" Logan wasn't a fool, and he didn't waste time with Rafael's dramatics. "You believe her magic infiltrated Beth's . . . Can the magic of a baby do that? She wasn't even bloomed."

Before bloom, we'd managed to form a magical bond usually reserved for true mates in control of their powers.

My affinity didn't follow the rules, and while Logan knew that, he continued to play his part well.

Rafael's next words snapped from him: "Just because we don't bloom young doesn't mean our innate magic isn't there. When that baby developed in the womb, her magic developed too. Beth got a taste of the monster."

"You can't know this," Noah said, harshly. "Maybe Beth has the same ability as Paisley."

"Nope. It was gone after that weekend," Rafael said, his voice breaking. "After it was too late, and Tom ignored me when I needed him to prove his goddess-be-damned loyalty."

Dad's face was dark as he breathed deeply through his nose.

"So, you decided to punish Paisley? Because it was her fault after all."

Logan's words slammed into my chest, and it was only the hand Jensen slipped over my mouth that kept my distressed noise slipping free; he must have forgotten the phone was on mute. My chest heaved as I attempted to breathe, all the while wondering if this was the point Logan stopped being *all in* with our bond.

This magical bond had existed last year, and he'd fought it. He could do that again.

Jensen dropped his other arm around me, holding me tight against his chest, offering the comfort he could.

"I'm still punishing Tom," Rafael said simply. "He was my brother and he ignored me, which destroyed my wife." Even through the phone I could feel the swell of his rage.

Across the table, Dad looked like he was about to start spewing lava, and deep in his eyes were flickers of pain and regret—he didn't count himself blameless here.

"Why the Hel is Paisley sick, then?" Logan's words were biting, his anger palpable. It simmered in my own energy as the metallic taste of Logan's rage coated my tongue.

Rafael's laugh this time was softer, less evil villain. "Nothing would destroy Tom faster than seeing his family fall. Paisley is just the first, but one by one, in reverse order of birth, the curse will take them all. Tom will be last, and he'll live long enough to feel the true pain of his loss."

Curse. Fuck. It had been mentioned earlier, but not with any real conviction because it was super dark and highly illegal magic.

"You cursed her? How? You have to place a curse personally, and in a way that the recipient is unaware you've had access to their magic."

Rafael's voice grew louder. Gleeful. "I didn't curse her, son. You did."

Jensen kept hold of me on the chair when my body jolted. I don't know why I even reacted, because I trusted Logan implicitly and his father not at all, but a sliver of worry that

I'd been played all along flickered through my subconscious. But why would Logan play me and then bring the phone in to reveal it all?

It didn't make sense. How did he curse me, then?

"What are you talking about?" There was genuine shock in Logan's reply, and I wished I could see his face.

"Why do you think I tried to throw you into her path so often?" Rafael sounded smug. "Even when you kept leaving her and observing from a distance, I kept pushing you to follow her around. She's a pretty girl, Logan. You have a connection to her and have since you were a child. Don't think I don't know why you've never dated anyone else. It was always that Hallistar bitch for you. Which came in handy."

Through our connection, in the swirls of our magic that had bonded us before we even understood why, I sensed Logan was about to lose his shit. His energy pulsed, and a crack rang through the speaker. In the scuffle, the phone was tossed around, and I panicked it was going to hang up in Logan's pocket.

"What did you do?" Logan was snarling, loud and angry, and thank the goddess we were still connected and I could hear him.

"The first time you slept with Paisley, you cursed her." Rafael sounded as if he was forcing words out through a hand around his throat. "Her magic is siphoning to my family line, draining her until eventually she'll die, and the curse will transfer to the next little shit in her family. We will gain all the power, and the Hallistar line will finally fucking end. It's been the hardest wait of my life for that last bitch to bloom, but it's all worth it now to experience Tom's true suffering."

I'd have been embarrassed that he'd outed my sex life to my family, but it was really the least of my worries. A curse was one of the deadliest, most difficult spells that could be enacted. They were rarely used due to how dark and destructive they were.

What the fuck was Rafael thinking?

Staring at the table, I couldn't look away from the phone as I waited for the next revelation. When Logan laughed, I almost fell out of my chair again.

Had he lost his damn mind? Or did he miss the part about a curse?

"You fool," Rafael said, clearly thinking the same. "Did you not hear what I just said? She's cursed and you did it."

Logan's laughter cut off abruptly. "There's a fatal flaw in your plan, old man."

Rafael didn't answer for so long I wondered if we'd lost the connection. "There's no flaw," he finally said. "This is exactly as I planned, from the years of research into the right curse, to waiting for Paisley's magic to bloom. I could have, of course, just killed them all years ago, but revenge is a dish best served cold and drawn out."

"Paisley and I bonded when we were children." It was a simple statement, and it fell into a silent room. "Through magic," Logan continued. "Your curse, it's affecting me as well. I'm weakening alongside her, and if that's the case, and it impacts family lines, guess who's next. You just set forth your own fucking downfall."

As I lurched up in my chair, Jensen once again kept me from face-planting as I panicked like an absolute pro. *Logan was weakening too!* He'd never said a damn word, and I hadn't noticed, but his power was so vast that it'd take a while to be obvious. In my own weakness, I'd missed his.

It was clear that he had been protecting me, but after our little conversation about not keeping secrets anymore, I was going to kick his ass.

"This can't be right," Rafael murmured, and it was low

enough that it sounded as if he was talking to himself. "I planned for every scenario. I had backup plans if you didn't sleep with her. There was another spellcaster under my control as well."

Another spellc— Fucking Hel. Was he talking about Marcus? He had Marcus there as a backup plan if I didn't sleep with Logan. No wonder that asshole offered me help over the winter break.

"How are you powering this curse?" Logan asked him, and I couldn't understand why he sounded so calm. This was bad. Big and super bad. We were all going to die.

"The spellcasters of Europe are pooling their power, causing trouble, and I'm siphoning off their magic." We'd guessed Rafael was behind that unrest, and he'd just confirmed it. "With a secondary purpose of keeping the council busy while I buy up their land and assets."

"What's your plan now, Dad? How do we end this curse before it takes us all down?"

It sounded as if Rafael was pacing across hard timber, a tap-tap-tap of shoes as he walked. "This is an ancient curse that took the power of many spellcasters to enact," he mumbled, still seemingly shocked by us being bonded, none of the usual bluster in his tone. "The path to breaking it is just as difficult, though without the same input of energy. It's the opposite, actually. You have to unravel it by using ingredients that oppose the original ones that cast it."

"What are the steps?" Logan pushed, still seemingly calm, though I felt tingles of his rage within my power.

Weatherstone College didn't have any classes on curses. All I knew was that they required immense power to create and were notoriously difficult to unravel.

As we were about to find out.

"There are only two steps, but they're not easy ones,"

Rafael said with a deep breath. "First, you need to gather these ingredients." There was silence for a moment, and I assumed he'd handed Logan a piece of paper. "Then you cast this spell. That starts the process."

"Is that all?"

Rafael's voice grew louder. "Did you look at the ingredients, son? You'll be lucky to get everything before she dies. And once she does, the rest of us will fall. The curse has to be stopped with Paisley."

"Should have fucking thought of that before you punished an innocent family for an accident."

The way my breath whooshed out of me would have been embarrassing, but I was too busy trying not to cry. *Logan wasn't angry with me.*

Rafael ignored Logan's recriminations. "I have to be there for that final step, as the one who initiated the curse. I believe it'll take my blood to end this." His voice grew even louder. "Do not sleep with her again. Every time you do, you are weakening her further and strengthening the curse."

My family were absolutely staring at me now, and I ignored the heat rising in my cheeks.

"How long does she have before the curse will kill her?" Noah asked.

"There's no time frame. It depends on the power of the magical being, but it was a guarantee that each death would be slow and drawn out. That was the only way I could ensure Tom truly suffered."

Logan and I had first slept together last year, only once though. Clearly, our recent activities had sped up the process.

"Just know, Father," Logan said, the rumble of his voice vibrating through the phone. "The only reason you're still alive right now is that we might need you to break this curse. But when I'm done saving her—my fucking soulmate you tried to murder—I'm coming back for you. I will destroy you and take everything you've worked for."

Rafael's sigh was extended. "I would expect nothing less from you. I look forward to our battle, but for now, you have a much larger fight on your hands."

There were no more words, just the sound of heavy boots slamming against the floor as Logan raged his way out of his father's office. My hand trembled as I reached out and grasped the phone, pulling it closer, my head a mess as I freaked out.

"It's going to be okay, Paisley," Dad whispered. "I promise. Whatever you need to reverse this curse, we're going to work together to get it done. I won't let Rafael win this battle. I won't lose any of you."

A single tear slid down my cheek, and I fought the rest, knowing this wasn't the time to fall apart. "I know, Dad," I replied, just as softly. "I won't stop fighting while there's any magic left in my body."

Not when I had everything to live for. Sure, my affinity was an issue that could get me killed as well, but there was no chance to fight past prejudices if this curse took me out first.

I jumped when Logan's voice came through the phone again. "Precious," he rasped. This was followed by what sounded like an explosion, and I fumbled with the phone to hit the unmute button.

"Logan," I called, terrified that Rafael had followed him.

A thrum of pure power shot through our bond, and I turned my panicked gaze on my family.

"What's happening?" Dad asked with urgency.

I had no idea as I shook my head roughly. A beat later Noah's voice echoed through the phone. "Paisley, are you there?"

"I'm here. What's going on with Logan?" I said in a rush.

"He just leveled the entire block around his father's building," he said, sounding tense. "He's not dealing so well with the knowledge that the curse originated with him. Give me a few minutes to calm him down and he'll call you back."

The line went dead, and I tried not to bite straight through my lip as my teeth pressed down hard. "It's not Logan's fault," I whispered. "This all rests with Rafael."

Mom offered me her most comforting hug, and I fell into it for many minutes, only emerging when my phone rang. Jumping back, I answered before it could ring again. "Logan!" I gasped.

"I'm so fucking sorry," he said, barely getting the words out. "This is all my fault."

"Logan Kingston, don't you ever say that again. This is Rafael the evil bastard's fault. End of story." His breathing was harsh, and when he didn't answer, I softened my tone. "Come home to me so we can figure out how to stop the curse and save everyone's lives."

We were already running out of time. This curse would drain my magic until death, and then it would take my entire family.

We couldn't let that happen.

"I'll be home shortly," he promised, the gravel in his voice more pronounced than ever. "I won't let this curse take you—even if I have to burn the fucking world down to stop it."

With that, the phone went dead, and I clutched it until my hand ached. For a scary second, I knew I'd let the world burn if it meant saving my family and Logan.

Fuck, I'd burn it myself.

Starting with Rafael.

CHAPTER 27

I waited on the back porch for him. My family remained inside, including the twins, who were supposed to be with their coven, settling into their new roles.

But we were processing what we'd learned.

For me, I couldn't deal with anything until I saw Logan.

I needed a moment with my mate before our world turned to shit. Okay, it was already shit, but it'd feel less so once we were reunited.

When transport magic tingled across my skin, I stepped back to give them room. Logan was first through, his arms around me in the next heartbeat. My feet left the ground as he lifted me higher, burying his face in my hair, his chest rumbling in hard, jagged sounds.

He was unraveling.

"I'm so sorry," he said, over and over.

Pulling him closer, I ran my hands up and down his back in what I hoped was a soothing motion. "This is not your fault," I murmured forcibly. "If you don't blame me for your mother's death, I certainly don't blame you for what Rafael did."

He released another wounded sound, continuing to hold me like he'd crumble if he let go. Footsteps behind him had me lifting my head to find that he'd returned with more than Noah. Tobias, Sara, and Haley also stepped through. "You brought everyone?" I asked against his shoulder, and when he finally released me enough to see his face, my heart skipped at the exhaustion dragging his features. This curse had its hooks in his power too.

"We're going to need everyone if we have a chance of gathering the ingredients for this curse reversal in time," he said, staring down at me as if he wanted to memorize my features. "I'm so fucking sorry, Paisley."

"It's not your fault." I'd repeat this until he believed me. I pressed my lips to his—we might not be able to have sex, but I would kiss my mate every chance I got. "This is a screwed-up fate we're fighting against, and I don't care what it takes, *we will win*. We have too much to live for."

"We have everything to live for," he said, and I was relieved to finally feel the anger riding his magic lessening.

When he pulled me to his side, I smiled at our friends. "Thank you all for being here. I didn't want to drag you all into this, but with our lives on the line, we need all the help we can get."

"Logan told us everything when he grabbed us from Weatherstone," Sara said, stepping forward to hug me—and Logan because he wasn't letting go. "We're here for you both. Whatever you need, we're ready and willing to fight."

"And I love you for it," I said as warmth swelled in my tired body. "No Belle though . . ." I noted with a sad huff. Not that I'd have expected her, but it hurt nonetheless.

Sara and Haley exchanged a glance. "I heard her on the phone last night with her dad," Haley said, lowering her voice. "She was updating him on your absence from school this weekend. She's spying on you, Pais. There's no other explanation."

I'd suspected that was part of the reason she was both back and still hanging on the periphery of our group.

"She probably has no choice," I said, trying to shrug off the hurt.

"She definitely doesn't have a choice," Trevor grumbled from behind us, and I turned to find my family had gathered in the doorway. "Don't give up on her, Pais. She's going to need you after we deal with her father."

Noah snorted, crossing his huge arms. "Belle and her evil father are barely even a blip on our worry meter at the moment. This fucking list of ingredients we need to break this curse is half a page long, and most won't be sitting around waiting for us to find them. It's going to take time to get it all together."

"Between us we can handle this," Mom said in a strong, unwavering voice as she stepped out onto the front porch. "We have all the affinities covered, especially with Logan."

That reminded me that my family hadn't met everyone here. "This is Noah and Tobias," I said, waving toward Logan's best friends. "They're Logan's family."

Mom shot them both a smile. "Please call me Beth, and my husband is Tom. We're so thankful that you're here to help our family. If you ever need anything from us, please don't hesitate to ask."

The guys shook her hand, and then Dad's, as he remained protectively by his wife's side.

"The honor is ours. Paisley is part of our family, which means you all are too," Tobias said, sounding very much the aristocrat. Noah nodded his agreement.

Mom beamed, and I pushed down the flutter of warmth that followed his declaration. I'd always had an amazing family behind me, but it felt so much more complete now. Along with Sara and Haley.

When Logan brushed his finger down my cheek, in what was absolutely his signature move, I looked up at him, concern filling my mind. "How's your magic? You said you felt weaker?"

He shrugged. "A mere drop in a million drops, Precious. I can handle whatever is required to gather our ingredients."

"Which are what exactly?" Jenna asked, looking between Logan and Noah.

Logan pulled the list from his pocket. "Rafael wrote it out for us, and it matches up with the original curse he showed us. This is not going to be easy."

He handed it to me so I could skim it quickly. "Fuck me," I grumbled.

1. Grains of paradise from West Africa
2. Silphium grown in the Lombardy region of Italy
3. Belladonna berries from Asia
4. Frankincense
5. Deep-sea urchin venom
6. Mandrake root
7. Black pepper standard
8. Amanita nouhrae mushroom from Chile
9. Two everlasting candles
10. Lava from an active volcano
11. The essence of the dead
12. A finger bone of a reaper witch
13. Blood of a spellcaster
14. Venom of a western taipan from Australia
15. A purification herbal mix

This was a mammoth and near impossible task—especially the essence of the dead, since we didn't have a necro on our team, and spellcasters couldn't access the dead.

Only I could.

"I'm going off my suppression potion," I said to Mom, handing the list over to her. She read quickly and passed it on. "You're going to need my power for a few of these items." If my magic held out long enough.

"Where do we start?" Sara said quickly, her pupils moving as she read over the items. "We should split the items up and tackle them all over the next few days."

She returned the list to Logan, and I forced myself not to slouch into my exhaustion. It'd been a long, stressful day, and my body was ready to crash.

"We'll start tomorrow," Logan said shortly as he discreetly took my weight. "We'll start tomorrow and divide the list according to our skills and affinities."

Mom clapped her hands together. "Perfect. I'm going to find places for everyone to sleep, then we'll order food." She disappeared inside, Dad right behind her.

Logan linked our fingers, the motion pulling at my insides and sending butterflies through my chest. He led me to the living room and sat on the couch before pulling me onto his lap. I didn't move for the rest of the evening, my head resting against his chest. By the time we'd eaten our pizza, watched movies, and he half carried me to bed, I found that I wasn't as drained as usual. This was a normal sort of tired.

Our bond might have passed the curse back to Logan, but it was also fighting the drain.

"How are you being affected by the curse?" I asked as we snuggled under my covers, completely clothed to keep ourselves from accidentally accelerating my death through sheer horniness. "Because it feels as if our bond has kept me alive far longer than I would have otherwise."

Logan dragged his fingers down my arm, finding slivers

of bare skin, his calluses from years of guitar sending tingles through my body. Clothes were definitely the right idea.

"I haven't had enough time to research exactly what's happening to us," he said, his voice as rough as his touch. "But it really doesn't matter. We're going to fight, and you will fucking live." He rolled onto his side to bring us even closer. "And on the very slim chance we fail, I'll happily follow you. Our souls are bound, Precious. That means not even death parts us."

The thought of Logan not existing in this world broke a fundamental part of me. Cracked it right down the middle until my insides seeped from my body. "Don't even say it," I whispered. "We're stronger than Rafael believes. He's not going to win."

Logan's lips pressed against my forehead, lingering for a few tantalizing seconds. "That's the spirit, Precious. We have the counter-curse, and he has no choice but to provide his blood to reverse the spell. It's as if the Fates themselves don't want our deaths, as if they've given us every weapon to fight back."

I snuggled into him. "I'd never ask you to hurt your dad for me."

His hands flexed against my back. "Baby, I'd rip his heart out with my bare hands and present it to you as a gift. He's nothing to me, and you are fucking everything. There's not a single being in existence I would choose over you, and there's not a single one safe from my wrath if they hurt you. That's a promise I can easily make."

Goddess above, he was destruction wrapped in a beautiful package. A destruction I was happily signing up for. "Fuck, I love you," I said against his chest. "So much."

"I love you, Precious. And now it's time to sleep. You need to rest."

With my head filled by fifteen—very difficult to procure—ingredients, I didn't expect to drift off, but Logan's touch eventually lulled me into a restless sleep, and I didn't rouse until the sun peeked through my curtains the next morning.

When I opened my eyes, I was alone in bed, and Logan's side was cold. He'd been gone for a while, and I wondered what I'd missed. As I sat up and swung my legs over the side of the bed, I was relieved to feel no worse than yesterday.

I gathered up clothes to change into and headed to the bathroom. By the time I'd showered, dressed in jeans and a long-sleeved shirt, with my hair pulled back in a ponytail, my stomach was growling at me. In the kitchen Mom was already cooking up a storm for the group gathered in the living room. "Morning, honey," she said, shooting me a smile. She looked pale and worn-out, as if she'd barely managed any sleep last night.

Wrapping my arms around her from behind, I breathed in her familiar lavender scent and let it calm the ragged edges of my magic. "Morning, Mom. Is everyone planning out how we're dividing the items?"

"Yep. Go and join them in the living room." She shooed me away. "I'll get all the food out in a minute."

Ignoring her dismissal, I moved to her side. "Let me help you. There's a lot of mouths to feed out there."

She shot me her famous *Are you sassing me, young lady?* look. The one that suggested it was not in my best interest to prod a momma bear when she was in worried and protective mode. "You need to be resting every second you're not required to participate in this curse reversal. If it wasn't for the fact that we have no necromancer in our team so at least one of those items will require your skills, I'd have you locked in your room."

A genuine laugh escaped me, and I leaned forward and

pressed a kiss to her cheek. "I love you too, Mom. But I'm fine—" Her eyes narrowed to slits, and I barely managed not to laugh again. "Okay, okay. I'll go and rest. Call if you need help. As far as I'm aware, Trevor's a few rungs down the curse list, so he should be fine to carry everything in."

"I heard that," my brother shouted, but he was smiling as I entered the living area. My heart felt weirdly full, my magic swirling at the sight of all the people I cared about in one room. Curses might be dark, scary magic, but I felt blessed all the same.

I'd always had a lot to lose, but now . . . Now I had everything.

CHAPTER 28

By the time breakfast was done, and everyone was sipping coffee or tea, the list had been divided by affinities. "I'll take all the herbs," Mom said, ticking them off. "I have a lot of them here already, and I can have the equipment to ensure they're purified and set up for the spell."

"I'll go with her to find the few we don't already possess," Dad said, taking a large gulp of his black coffee. He appeared to have slept as little as Mom. "We'll have them all back here by the time you all return."

"Jensen and I will find the deep-sea urchin," Mom added. "You need a strong water affinity to go that deep."

"I'm handling lava," Trevor rumbled, sounding tired. "Dad's going to be busy helping Mom with all the rest."

Dad pointed his finger at his son. "You call me if you have any issue. You haven't graduated yet."

"I'll go with him," offered Tobias, who was also a fire elemental.

"I think it's best no one goes alone," I suggested, pushing myself forward on the couch.

"Agreed," Jenna said quickly. "Alice and I will go after the snake. There's one at the reptile house in Chicago, so we don't even have to leave the country."

"We'll get the candles and plants," Noah and Haley said together. Noah added: "Most can be found at Weatherstone, and the others will be in the Kingston private stores."

And Rafael Kingston wouldn't stop them when his life was on the line.

"Leaving Logan and me to deal with the essence of the dead, a finger bone of a reaper witch, and, of course, the blood of a spellcaster." I exchanged a glance with my mate. "That one will at least be easy."

Logan's smile almost did me in. "I'd happily bleed for you, Precious."

Good-natured groans rang out around the room, but they all knew better than to give him too much shit about how soft he was for me. Though I did think I heard *simp* from Tobias as he grinned at his friend.

Logan sent him skidding across the floor with a little blast of power, before leaning back casually. "Not that we will need my blood. It'll come from Rafael, since he's the one who set this curse in motion." Karma was knocking on that asshole's door, and I couldn't be happier about it.

"Everyone stays updated in the group chat," Dad said, pocketing his phone and his part of the list. "We should aim to all be back with our items by the end of the day. Let us know if anyone has a problem with that."

Mom spoke up quickly. "Wait, the suppression potion will take at least a week to release Paisley's power."

Logan's expression was worrying as he leaned forward. "I have a plan to cleanse it from her essence quickly, once I con-firm it won't worsen the curse. If it's not possible, then we'll find a necromancer to help us. Headmaster Gregor owes me more than one favor. It's not ideal, because we don't want to bring attention to Paisley and her affinity, but we can't delay with this curse worsening."

I wasn't surprised the headmaster owed him favors . . . It felt like a normal day when you were mated to a powerful spellcaster. Even if he was only two years older than me, Logan had lived a *Hel of a lot more life.*

"How will you procure the bones of a reaper?" Jensen asked.

Mom's face fell, but she didn't cry. "I know that your gran would want us to save Paisley. She's buried in the family crypt. You'll find the bone you need there."

Taking the bones of a witch or warlock wasn't as easy as it sounded. Essences of the magic that bound us in life would linger in death. Unless she released her bone to us, we'd never be able to steal its power. We'd have to wait and see how Gran felt about us taking her bones when we got to her crypt.

"It's settled, then," Dad said, looking around the room. "Those of us with the ability to open transports can collect the ones who can't, and we'll all meet back here tonight. If someone doesn't show up or check in, we'll track them down and make sure they're okay."

"Good luck," Logan said.

"And thank you," I added. "I can't tell you how much I appreciate every single one of you in this room. You're the best family and friends I could have hoped for."

I gasped as Tobias barreled into me for a hug, holding me against his hard chest as he rocked back and forth. "If you knew my actual family, you'd understand why I'm so happy to be part of this one," he said with a fake sniffle. At least I assumed it was fake.

Logan nudged him away. "Hands off, Tobes. If you want to keep them."

Tobias and Noah exchanged an amused glance. "Jealous Logan is my favorite," Noah said. "It's nice to see him flustered for once." Logan simply leveled him with a glare, and Noah laughed, unconcerned.

"He simps only for her, remember," Tobias added, exaggeratedly serious. "Let's not get our asses fried."

My heart fluttered when Logan didn't deny that comment. That flutter turned into a hurricane as his hand slid down my back and cupped my ass. I spent a good few seconds reminding myself that there was no sex *at all* until this shit was over. Which was almost as much incentive as the whole *going to die from this curse* part.

As Dad and Logan headed out to the porch to set up the transport magic needed to start moving us around, Mom pressed a kiss to my cheek. "We'll see you soon, honey," she said. "Stay safe."

"Love you," I replied, throwing my arms around her and holding on tight.

Everyone else gave me a hug as they left, until it was only Logan and me in the house.

He took my hand, leading me back into the living room. "We need to try to cleanse you of the suppression potion first," he said. "But there are a few risks."

Magic was all about balance, and I was more than ready for the payment. "What are the risks?"

"Firstly, I could trigger the curse and move our timeline up much faster. If it looks like that's happening, I'll stop what I'm doing. We can't risk sending you into a downward spiral of dark energy, or pushing the curse past the point of reversal."

I nodded. "What else?"

"I could trigger your affinity and unlock the magic completely. You have no idea how to control it, and we're in no magical position to banish dozens of monsters like we did on All Hallows'."

This worried me more than hastening the curse. "If I stay calm and keep my emotions and magic level, I shouldn't call monsters." I wasn't sure who I was trying to convince with my confidence. "Any other magical issues we need to concern ourselves with?"

Logan pressed in closer; my breath caught in my chest as he leaned down and skimmed his lips along the edge of my jaw, breathing me in. "None as concerning as those two. Are you ready, Paisley Jane Hallistar?"

"Full name, hey?" I was breathless, fighting for composure. "Must be serious."

His huge hands slid around my waist, pulling me against his body until there was no distance between us. "The forever kind of serious," he whispered, and then his power rose, hotter than I'd ever felt from him, and I wondered if the plan was to burn the spell from my essence.

As the heat built, so did the bite of flames, and I cried out as Logan's lips closed around mine. His attempt to scorch the suppression potion from me was forgotten as I tasted his power, mint and evergreen surrounding me. His magic bit into my skin and body, colliding with the shield around my magic.

At first, Gran's spell fought back, but Logan's magic found a few chinks in the shield, destroying the energy. By the time he cracked the first few layers, I was panting, locked in the sensation of skin charring from my bones. I wanted to rage at him for not telling me exactly how painful this would be, but I should have guessed after he told me there'd be a price.

"Breathe, baby," he whispered against my lips, voice rasping across scorched nerves. He didn't sound happy about the pain as he kissed me to take as much as he could.

"It h-has to be done," I managed to choke out. "Hit me with every-everything, mate."

Logan's eyes darkened as his power swelled. I tasted fire and ice, earth and metal, as elemental air swirled around us. The earthiness increased as he tapped harder into his spellcaster side, a hint of rosemary and mint dancing across my tongue.

When he shattered the next layer of the spell, he quenched the burn with water droplets, steam sizzling off us. That was when my legs gave out, but Logan held me upright. His gaze never left mine as I sank into the pain, and I almost let it take me over.

"Last layer," Logan growled, sweat beading his forehead. "Your gran's spell is strong, and your mom is quite the adept weaver, which is unfortunate today."

She'd spent decades honing that side of her abilities while ignoring her innate magic. She was the best. Gripping his shoulders, my nails dug into his skin, but he didn't even wince. I attempted to loosen my grip when I sensed I was cutting into him, but it was as if he was the tether keeping me grounded to this world.

"Don't let go, Precious," he encouraged, as if hearing my thoughts. "I'm going to jolt that final layer hard, and I want you to hold on to your magic. Don't let it go."

We'd practiced this in general magic classes last year—how to contain your magic and prevent it from seeping out into the world. There were times the energy needed freedom, and others when it had to be locked down. Logan wanted me to lock mine down.

I just hoped I had the strength to do it.

The heat rose another few degrees until we were burning in Hel. A burn I'd endure all day every day if it saved Logan and my family.

When his final storm of power crashed into me, a scream ripped from my throat, followed by vomit, and I turned my head to avoid hitting Logan in the face.

The expulsion of the suppression potion was audible, my magic exploding from within my thinly held grasp. It had been held captive for too long, needing freedom from its cage. For a second I thought it was all over, that the monsters would come and I'd be too weak to drag them back. Logan's energy slipped inside me at the last second, stitching our powers together to keep my magic contained.

The fire died, along with the need to spew power and the contents of my stomach across the living room. "It's done," I whispered, breathing heavily as I tilted my head back to meet Logan's fiery gaze.

His eyes were piercing, but he was paler than I'd ever seen, having expelled a ton of his power. "Are you okay?" I asked, concern filtering through me when he didn't reply. "Logan? Babe?"

"Don't move, Precious," he murmured as he lowered his head right near my ear.

That small shift from the spellcaster still set off a scuffle behind us, and faster than I'd ever moved before, I spun and placed myself between Logan and the scuffle.

Because I knew exactly what was behind us.

Logan hadn't contained my magic quickly enough and I'd called a monster. The creature shuffled in from the kitchen, and it was the smallest of any I'd seen. Only standing a few inches taller than me, looking like a giant, black-furred field mouse on two legs. Beady eyes observed us as it sniffed around.

"Don't move," Logan rasped again, and I hated how drained he sounded. "Let me deal with it."

"I need to learn to control them," I said softly, not turning away from the creature. "I can't keep running from my magic. If I don't learn my affinity, there's no point worrying about the curse—the council will kill me anyway."

Logan's hands tightened on my shoulders, and I had no doubt he was about two seconds from shoving me behind him. His first instinct was always to place himself between me and danger, but today I was the protector. "Trust me," I whispered. "I can do this." I had to do this.

His hands flexed again as his chest rumbled, but he didn't move. "You've got two minutes, Precious. If you don't deal with it by then, I will."

This was my monster, and I was no longer letting the affinity control me.

I was in control.

CHAPTER 29

At first the creature sniffed around the room like an actual mouse, getting down on all fours near the couches and gnawing on empty space, chomping its teeth and swallowing as if it had found food.

"How are you going to control it?" Logan asked me.

"I know where the power to draw it comes from now," I said, feeling those icy tendrils inside. "When I finally realized in the graveyard that I was calling the monsters, I felt where the power stemmed from. Weirdly, my training last year was preparing me for this moment, for when my magic would be free and fully infiltrated into my essence. I've got this."

Previously, when faced with a monster, I'd tried to blast it away—like a wrecking ball smashing against an object. This time, I used that cold tendril, recognizing the sensation of necromancy, which used to give me chills but now felt like coming home.

I sent out the icy tendril toward the monster it had called, and to my surprise, the creature jerked to a halt and lifted its head to stare at me with black eyes.

Recognition passed between us, and I stepped closer.

Logan stayed right on my ass, and I could feel him readying himself for a fight; he was a blast of heat against my icy magic.

"Come to me," I murmured, holding my hand out. I was sure that I'd tethered the monster, but it didn't move from the spot. *Come.* I used more magic, sending it along that arctic tether in my mind's eye. The mouse-monster shuffled forward, and sulfur filled my nose, drowning out every other scent. The tendril started to fray, and I had to reinforce it with more magic. The monster wasn't fighting me, but its energy ate away at my magic because it wasn't supposed to exist on this plane. At least not permanently.

"You don't belong here," I whispered.

Drawing on my memories from necromancy classes last year, I let my magic seep through the planes of existence. None of them were blocked to me, outside of the Eternal Lands, where the blessed rested their souls. It was easy to find the layer the monsters hailed from: Purgatory. Their slimy, icy energy felt like this plane, and when my power stopped there, I added another tether to my magic so there was one connected to the mouse-monster and another to Purgatory.

With me the conduit between the pair.

I dragged in a deep breath and forced my will onto the creature. "Return to your home," I told it. "You can't be here."

Instinct rode me hard as I embraced the ancient magic inside me. Trusting in what I had to do. "Next time, I won't bring you here without a tether to keep you from hurting others," I said, my voice swelling until it thundered. The monster sniffed one last time, and I swore that my vision briefly crossed over to highlight layers of darkness in my house, before the creature slipped along the other tether and returned home.

My vision reverted to normal, and I released my hold on

that frozen plane and its inhabitants. The reaper magic sank back inside me, and I was secure in the knowledge that I could pull from it again whenever I needed.

A quick glance around eased the panic I'd been brewing—I hadn't accidentally opened a doorway to usher in a million dark creatures to the world. I'd done exactly what I hoped, trusting instinct and my magic, and I'd sent the mouse home.

"You're incredible," Logan said with a whoop, his excitement spilling over. "I could feel that frosty necro magic through our bond, and the power . . . I've never experienced anything like it before in my life. Not even when my father channeled other spellcasters to do his bidding."

"It was all instinct," I said, unable to explain it any other way. I had never been specifically trained as a reaper, but the knowledge was there within me. Almost as if I'd inherited it. "It doesn't feel as if there's any training that could teach me what my magic innately knows. This is ancient magic, Logan, and the council and elders just wiped it from existence."

The excitement he'd been expressing faded slowly. "I won't let that happen to you, Precious. We'll be so powerful by the time they find out that no one can come for us. Even if I have to build an army to make it happen."

Letting my head fall against his chest, I just breathed him in until the scent of sulfur was completely gone. "I'd like to show them I'm not a threat," I said, revealing my deepest hope. "I don't want to battle to stay alive for the rest of my life. This magic should exist in the world. There must be repercussions for wiping out an affinity. I will figure out what they are and show them that reapers are needed."

Logan held me tighter, and I was relieved to feel his magic connect to mine with the same strength as always. "How are you feeling?" I asked. "Do you need the night to recharge?"

"Your power refueled mine as if I was struck by an energy source," he admitted against my throat. "I'm more than ready to start our mission and get these ingredien—"

The chiming of our phones interrupted, and I pulled mine out to see a message in the group chat.

Noah: You can cross two everlasting candles off the list. We're heading for Weatherstone now to gather the plants.

There was another from Alice that we must have missed earlier:

Alice: Snake venom procured. Lucky our magic worked to calm it because they're vicious little biters.

My fingers flew over the letters as I replied.

Paisley: Great job! You're killing it. Logan just cleansed my energy of the suppression potion. It was tough, but all good here. We're about to head for the crypt.

"Looks like the rest of them are working fast," I said. "We need to do the same."

"Let's get to the family crypt, then," he said, pocketing his phone. "Your mom said we'd have to drive because there's magic preventing transport pockets all over the area."

The family crypt was about two hours from Spokane. It was where my mom's family had been buried for generations—we owned a private burial ground, which was heavily protected by magic and wards.

When we reached the garage, I grabbed the keys to Mom's Jeep. It was ten years old but ran well enough for this trip.

Logan held his hand out. "Want me to drive so you can play passenger princess?"

I snorted. "Look, this princess throws hands, but I won't fight you if you want to drive."

Logan's energy wrapped around my body, drawing me to a halt. "I want to take care of you," he corrected. "I protect what's mine."

"I protect what's mine too." I had a stupid grin on my face as I released my hold on the keys. "Let's go, mate."

Logan's eyes darkened. "I'll never grow tired of hearing that, *soul*mate."

He opened the door for me, lifted me into the seat, and clipped my seat belt on, all before I got myself together. *Soulmate.* That hit me hard enough to leave a permanent mark.

One I was proud to wear.

Once Logan was in the driver's seat, he opened the garage door and started the car. Silence descended between us as we left Spokane, the navigation system directing Logan toward the freeway. His large palm rested possessively on my thigh, while his thumb ran along my jeans. It was a relief to feel the strong beat of his magic against mine, his energy already back to full strength.

There was no ice in our bond, my reaper side dormant until needed, and I wondered if there were more reapers out there, hiding their gifts the way Gran had hidden hers. Families who passed on this secrecy to their offspring, leaving us alone and broken, unable to access our magic as we should.

"Now that my magic is unlocked again, do you think the council will track me through my energy?"

Logan took his eyes off the road to level his green gaze on me. "Yes."

I jolted at the prospect, and he tightened his hold on my thigh, sending soothing heat through our bond. "Your power is strong and feels unlike any of the other affinities. We won't be able to hide you for long, especially once the curse is broken. It's still sapping your strength at the moment."

I could feel it inside, like a tapeworm eating through my magic, one chomp at a time. I had power still, but it would be gone within a few weeks at this rate. Maybe less.

"We need a plan for how to deal with the council by the time we break the curse," I said with a huff, dropping my head back against the seat. "Even if that plan is for me to go back on the suppression potion."

Logan didn't look particularly happy at the prospect of suppressing my magic again. "One step at a time, Precious," he said, eyes on the road as he navigated a pocket of traffic. "First, we save our lives. Second, we destroy my father. Third, we bring the magical world to its knees. They will accept your affinity, and if they don't, I'll make my father's mission for the last twenty years appear like a charity run." His voice grew harsher with each statement, and I feared what might happen to him if he had to make the choice to fight his father or the council.

CHAPTER 30

I hadn't been to the burial grounds for years. The last was when I was ten and we'd gone to share magic with our ancestors.

Dad's family graveyard was halfway across the country, and we traveled out every few years to visit. Now that my magic had bloomed, it was my responsibility to commune with our ancestors.

Logan pulled onto a patch of ragged brown grass leading to the ancient burial grounds. I could feel the energy of my ancestors even before I neared the old stone wall, which stood no higher than my thighs, surrounding the parcel of land. There were no human dwellings nearby; magic and wards kept them out of this area. We weren't the only private burial grounds in the vicinity, with other magic users having purchased parcels over the years.

"Do you know where your gran is entombed?" Logan asked, scanning for danger.

My magic pulsed as I closed in on the arched, gateless entrance. There was no need for a barrier, with the warding keeping out those not of blood. As my bonded mate, Logan should be able to enter with me—this would be the first real test of our magical connection.

"Yeah, I was here with Mom when I was younger. I know the way."

Reaching out, I grasped his hand, heat unfurling through me as he laced our fingers together. "You know how to release your magic now, don't you," Logan said. "Those blocks I used to have to break through are all but gone."

I nod. "Yeah, it's because my affinity should be used in conjunction with other reapers."

I'd never be as strong without others of my affinity, but I also wasn't a complete dud now that I'd figured out how to tap into the reaper side.

Logan captured me in a fierce kiss, and I was breathless when he released me. "If there are others of your kind out there, we will find them," he promised in his intense way. "You don't have to be alone. You'll never be alone with me."

"You're more than enough to fill that void in my magical soul," I told him, meaning every word.

We reached the arch, ancestral magic wrapping around us. "There's true power in your family line," Logan said huskily. "How many others do you think were reapers?"

"I have no idea." I was sad not to have this knowledge. "Gran would have known. It's so unfair that she was lost to us before I was born."

Logan tugged gently on my arm. "Come on, Precious."

I drew him to a halt. "You're not worried about the wards blasting you to pieces?"

His chuckle contained exactly zero worries. "You know our bond will stand up to the protection spells of your family."

"At least we're in a good place for your burial if it doesn't work," I muttered, and his grin kicked up a notch. Cocky bastard.

Familiar energy caressed my skin like a warm hug as I stepped through, and Logan showed no sign of discomfort as he followed me past the warding and into our burial grounds. The magic here was strong, with many goddess blessings bestowed on our magical line over the years.

"Your maternal family line is *really* powerful," Logan noted without any real surprise.

"I'm sure your dad's is strong," I said as we walked through the front lot. "I hear there are many spellcasters in your family line."

"Almost all of them," he said with a shrug. "Most who didn't deserve the power they were gifted."

Logan's family line, if one looked at pure power, was the crème de la crème of the magical world. Sure, there were a few crooked branches in the tree, but for the most part it was still hard to comprehend that we were fated mates. If that magical spell hadn't worked at an age when it *should* have been impossible, I'd never have believed it.

When we were past the first headstones, Logan released me. "It's time for you to flex your magic, baby," he said. "Can you tap into your elemental side?"

A snort escaped me. "Are you back to kicking my ass in training? If you pull out a set of weights, I'll beat you over the head with them."

Logan laughed so hard his head dropped back, the strong lines of his throat drawing my attention. It was a captivating sight, but I managed to keep myself under control and not jump his sexy ass.

"You show more fear of weights than you do of my deranged father," he finally said. *Fucking truth.* "Don't stress yourself, love. I'll do the heavy lifting when the time comes, but you still need to flex your magical muscle. You've spent the year since your magic bloomed locked down in one way or another. It's time to let the energy free."

The very thought sent a flutter of lightness through the tendrils of exhaustion from the curse.

I'd sat through enough classes to know how to draw the elements to me. I built it in layers as I'd practiced countless times, swirling the wind around us until it felt strong enough to lift us. Pulling more power, I sent us zooming over the rows of graves, tombs, and crypts, slowing only when I recognized the crypt where Gran was buried.

I'd had no practice with gentle stops, and if Logan hadn't used his own control over air to help, we'd have gone splat against the side of the crypt. "Whoops," I huffed with a spurt of laughter. "Overshot."

Logan looked thrilled by my effort. "You're perfect. You fucking nailed that."

Wanting to preen like a damn peacock who'd been told they had a pretty tail, I forced myself to focus on our task. "Gran rests here," I said, pointing to the small entrance, which was a roughly hewn stone doorway surrounded by a weathered exterior.

"How many others does it hold?" Logan asked as we approached the door.

"Gran's crypt contains three witches, from what I remember. Her maternal line . . ."

It was our choice where we resided in death, with our maternal or paternal line. For some, it was an easy choice, especially when they were tied closer to one parent over the other. True bonded mates resided together, with one side of their families, or started their own site completely.

I'd never given it much thought, but now that I had Logan, it was a discussion we needed to have. Our wishes would be cast into a magical will that would release upon death.

"Where would you choose to reside?" I asked Logan.

"With you, of course," he said as he opened the crypt door, the heavy stone taking effort to shift. Strong magic slammed against us as we stepped into the darkness, lanterns lighting along the walls and down the set of stairs. "We're joined in life and death, Precious. When we return for our next journey, we'll find each other again. Again and again, until there's no more existence." I was still in the entrance, my heart racing.

"Paisley," he said, turning back. "You okay?"

He must have felt the surge of my emotions as he tracked back toward me. "One day," he whispered, pressing his lips to the sensitive spot behind my ear, "you won't question the depths of my devotion to you. One day, you'll *expect* me to choose you, because you'll understand that I don't exist without you. One day—" another kiss "—the depth of my love will feel as natural to you as magic and breathing. Until then, though, you can trust my word. We're eternal."

I threw myself into his arms, desperate to breathe him in and bathe in his love. "I love you," I managed to say. "So fucking much. I don't care where we reside in life or death, as long as we're together."

"Come on," he said, tucking me against his side. "I'm not ready for the death part yet, so let's ask your gran if she can help save our lives."

My heart told me that we'd be fine, but the truth was, if Gran refused our call, we'd have to find another reaper. And hope they would be more giving.

CHAPTER 31

"Hello, Gran," I said, staring at the plaque on the wall hiding her body which lay at rest. Her soul would be in the Eternal Lands, with most of her magic, but the bones would always hold echoes of her affinity. *My affinity.* "I know it's been a long time, and I have a lot to tell you."

Even though we were in a freezing underground tomb with at least three of my ancestors' bodies, a warm breeze washed around us.

"That's a new touch of magic," Logan said, sounding unsurprised. He stood close but was careful that we didn't touch. Gran was my ancestor, and I had to be the one to take from her. "Her presence is strong."

It was strong. More than I'd ever felt before in this crypt, and I wondered if it was to do with my magical bloom. "I need your help, Gran." I reached out to press my hand against the stone hiding her from view. There were no words written on it, but there was an image of a scythe. I'd never understood why until now. We were reapers.

Able to move souls between the realms.

"I need your magic, Gran," I continued. More of that heated air swirled against me, sending my magic into a frenzy. "I've been cursed, and it's going to destroy our entire family line. And my mate. I would never ask unless it was life and death, but would you share your magic with a finger bone?" The air turned downright sweltering, and with it, I felt a single sliver of icy reaper energy.

The stone sealing her tomb popped open, and I barely managed to stifle my gasp as Gran's body came into view. She'd been perfectly preserved with magic, and if it wasn't for the waxy gray skin, she might look like she was sleeping.

"Hi, Gran." My voice swelled with reverence. Exhaustion was my constant companion these days, but with Gran's magic washing over me, I felt rejuvenated. "I'm sorry that we have to ask this of you, but thank you for your gift. We miss you."

I might never have met her, but in my essence, I mourned her loss. A witch who should have been here to nurture our magic. There was enough space in her tomb for me to lean forward and grasp one of her hands which were rested against her chest. The heated air eased until it was a mere trickle against my cheek, and I closed my eyes at the loving sensation.

It told me that Gran knew me, even if I didn't know her. She'd been watching over me from the Eternal Lands, and it broke my heart that it was the one plane off-limits to me. I'd have loved to truly feel her soul, or even talk to her, if for only a few minutes.

"I love you," I whispered, trembling as I wrapped my hand around her right pointer finger, my magic swirling inside me. "How do I sever it cleanly?" I asked Logan, who remained close to my back.

"Use fire," he said quickly. "If you burn hot enough and keep it closely contained, it can act as a laser, severing the bone cleanly."

I wasn't sure if my control was good enough, but we were running out of time.

"Or you can just snap her bone," Logan added.

My head was shaking before I even considered it. Gran deserved better than that. She deserved me to control my elemental magic and respect her gift.

"Can you call a flame without assistance?" Logan asked, moving close enough that our magic mingled happily.

"Yes, but only recently." As in *the last few elemental classes* recently.

Heat built in my center as I tapped into my connection with fire. A flame popped into my hands, and I fought to keep it low and controlled. My newly freed magic felt natural, reminding me that I'd been living with half of myself locked down for most of my bloomed life.

"Send that fire internally, until your finger is filled with heat." Logan was still my most frustrating and successful professor. "That's how you'll contain the flame."

This took effort and concentration, but Logan didn't pressure me. He was all reassurances and advice until I achieved my goal. I touched Gran's hand, pressing the burning tip of my finger to her index finger, and in less than a second, I'd completed my task.

With a lump in my throat, I cradled the finger in my hands. "Thank you," I whispered, stepping back from the crypt as I doused the fire inside me.

Logan didn't touch it, but he did weave air magic around the length and levitate it from my grasp. "When we leave the graveyard, I'll be able to send it back to your house."

"Thank you," I repeated for him this time, my voice rough with overwhelming emotions. It had been another long day, and I was ready to crawl back into bed.

Logan swept us through the graveyard this time, his winds gentle as they cradled me and deposited us by the car. With another flash of his impressive energy, Gran's finger bone was safely on its way to the house. To be deposited behind the wards of my home, safe and sound. Logan grasped my hands, a cool wash of water erupting from his palm to cleanse them. He'd sensed through the bond that I was feeling a little ick at handling Gran's dead body. "Thank you," I repeated around a yawn. "You take such good care of me."

"I will always take care of you, Precious," he said, lifting me into his arms.

I'd have normally protested, but today I let him deposit me gently in the seat and click my seat belt into place. His magic cushioned my head as the door gently closed, and I slumped against it. My eyes were closed by the time he got in the driver's side.

"Sleep, baby," he murmured, and I felt a featherlight touch against my cheek. "I'll keep the monsters away."

I could handle my own monsters these days, but it was nice to know that I didn't always have to. "I'll protect you too," I mumbled, almost gone.

I was asleep before I heard his reply, and didn't wake until we pulled into the driveway of my parents' house. Logan's face was calm when he opened my door, but there was a darkness simmering in the depths of those green eyes. His energy felt tumultuous through our bond, and I got the impression he'd spent the drive worrying. I wanted to alleviate those concerns, but I couldn't. *The curse is progressing.* I felt it in my essence as it ate away at both my magic and my life-force.

"A few of the others are inside," he told me, his voice deeper than usual. "Let's go and see what they've managed to procure from the list."

He held out a hand for me to take, and as I stumbled, he hoisted me into his arms, pulling me gently against his chest. With a wave of his hand, he closed the car door and then strode into the house, carrying me all the way. We entered via the front door to find Mom and Dad, Trevor and Jensen inside.

"Paisley . . ." Mom sounded panicked, and she rushed toward me before we were through the entry.

"I'm okay," I said, my voice stronger than I felt. "I'm just drained, but we got Gran's finger bone. How did it go with all your items?"

Mom fussed about me for a second, before she settled down and pulled out her list. "Okay, we got the grains of paradise, frankincense, black pepper, and the purification herbal mix. Trevor got the lava, and Jensen found the urchin venom. Your sisters dropped off the snake venom and they're heading to the coven to see if we can borrow one of their spellcasting rooms. We don't have the facilities here to create an anti-curse this strong."

"There's no need for that," Logan reminded them as he settled on the couch with me on his lap. "Rafael cast the curse, and he has to be the one to lift it."

Mom nodded. "Right. Right. I'll let the girls know." She grabbed her phone to message the twins, and I pulled the list of ingredients from my pocket and crossed out what had been found.

1. ~~Grains of paradise from West Africa~~
2. Silphium grown in the Lombardy region of Italy
3. Belladonna berries from Asia
4. ~~Frankincense~~
5. ~~Deep-sea urchin venom~~
6. Mandrake root

7. ~~Black pepper standard~~
8. Amanita nouhrae mushroom from Chile
9. ~~Two everlasting candles~~
10. ~~Lava from an active volcano~~
11. The essence of the dead
12. ~~A finger bone of a reaper witch~~
13. ~~Blood of a spellcaster~~
14. ~~Venom of a western taipan from Australia~~
15. ~~A purification herbal mix~~

"We're getting close," I told Logan, holding the paper out to him.

He didn't even look at the list, his dark gaze locked on my face. I had no idea what I looked like, but his expression told me it wasn't good. Thankfully, he was distracted when the rest of our friends returned, and between Noah, Tobias, Sara, and Haley, they'd managed to gather up every other item on the list, except the essence of the dead.

Pulling myself off Logan's lap, I stood and glanced around the group. "I've never covered this in class. Does anyone know how I gather the essence of the dead? I can feel the planes now, and I know I need to call it from the dead zone, where the souls haven't been judged or moved on to Hel or the Eternal Lands yet, but how do I contain it?"

"You need a magical seal," Dad told me. "It has to be formed of your energy, and it'll hold the essence—or energy, really—of the dead you'll call."

"You'll be able to find that soul again," Logan added. "You can call on their essence whenever you need."

I jerked at the abhorrent thought. "There are necros who continually drain a soul's essence? Surely if you keep calling for their essence, you'll eventually destroy their energy completely."

"No, it doesn't work like that," Logan told me. "You're essentially draining their magic, and like ours, it will regenerate. Magic is eternal and spans the planes, so you're free to have what is the equivalent of a soul familiar."

A dead familiar. Amazing.

"I think I'll stick with my plans to get a cat," I said, shaking my head as my stomach flipped. "No other familiar required."

Logan smiled for the first time since I'd woken in the car. "Misti will be pleased to hear that." His smile faded quickly. "Are you sure you have the strength for this final item? I can find another necro."

"It should be tied to me," I said with a shake of my head. "I'm the initiation of the curse, which will make the counter-curse more effective if I call the energy."

"Maybe we should wait until the morning?" Mom said, wringing her hands as she watched me. Fuck, I must look terrible, since they all wore expressions like I had one foot in the grave.

"Great idea," Logan said, on his feet in a single leap. "We can wait until tomorrow." He hoisted me into his arms before I could protest, heading for the stairs to a chorus of "bye" and "see you in the morning." This was a case of choosing your battles, and I decided that sleep before calling the dead couldn't be a bad idea.

Tomorrow it would all be over, one way or another.

CHAPTER 32

"You ready, Precious?"

Logan's concerned expression hadn't left me all morning. Not when I woke up feeling like crap, or when he joined me in the shower—not for fun times, but to ensure I didn't slip and crack my head—or when he guided me through calling on the essence of the dead.

I now had a magical seal, which resembled a pouch formed by air and water, attached to me and invisible to everyone else. It trailed behind me, tethered to my magic.

It had been the weirdest sensation, dragging a magical essence between the planes. I'd lost control of the first two, but by the third attempt I managed to keep and trap the power in the seal. My icy brush with the dead still filled my center, even as Logan's heated power wove through mine.

We were now standing in the doorway of Rafael's headquarters. Businessmen and women bustled around us, without the knowledge that we were about to break a deadly curse. Logan held all the items required for the counter-curse in his own pocket of magic, carrying it because I could barely manage to keep myself upright. I'd avoided mirrors this morning, but the gray pallor of my hands told me all I needed to know.

I was on borrowed time.

We had to end this curse today, or it'd be too late.

Logan didn't address anyone as we strode inside. There were multiple reception desks between the entrance and the top floor, where Rafael's office resided. None of the beautiful women behind those desks said a word as Logan marched through the building. The look on his face would deter any but the strongest . . . or most foolish.

Rafael apparently didn't hire either, so we made it to the impressive double doors without interference. Logan's power slammed them open, and Rafael, who was seated at his desk, shot to his feet. He didn't look surprised to see us, since there were undoubtedly multiple security cameras all over this place. Not that a spellcaster needed such means to feel Logan's rage.

Still, he did look mildly affronted by Logan's aggression. "Son," he said softly, shaking his head, "we are not alone here."

Except for the pretty redhead assistant outside his office, there was no one else to notice us. "Fix your fucking curse now," Logan snarled.

Rafael finally glanced my way, his lips twisting into a cruel smirk. "She doesn't look very good, does she? We might be too late already."

Logan crossed his arms. "Then we all die, and I'll be reunited with her in the Eternal Lands, while you live forever in Purgatory or Hel, because I'll never let you cross into any plane that offers you peace."

Rafael's face darkened, his cheeks mottled with his anger, but Logan didn't give a fuck. He dumped the invisible bag on the heavy mahogany desk, releasing his power over it to reveal the items within. "We collected what you require. Now break the curse before it's too late."

The doors to Rafael's office closed suddenly and he waved a hand to lift the items off his desk. I kept the essence of the dead with me for now. He strolled toward a large bookcase along the back wall and pulled out a book. The shelf popped open to reveal a door, and I cursed at this evil villain getting a cool hidden lair. An excellent use of his billions, but entirely unfair when he was an asshole and deserved nothing.

Logan grasped my hand and I leaned on his strength to move forward and follow *my* spellcaster down a set of metal stairs spiraling into a well-lit room. It was lined in iron, the usual to contain elemental and spellwork. Tables sat in a long row down the middle of the room, with pentacles, candles, and a multitude of other equipment neatly filling the shelves below.

Damn him. I wanted one of these secret spell room beauties.

New plan: kill the spellcaster and steal his lair.

Logan led me to the opposite side of the tables from Rafael, his expression thunderous. "Start," he snarled. My mate was losing control, and if his power was weakening from the curse, there was no indication today.

It was in his dad's best interest to get moving and fast.

"You're missing an ingredient," the asshole said.

Logan's touch was gentle as he wrapped it around my wrist. "Release the essence, Precious." His thumb rubbed gently across my pulse point, soothing me.

Taking hold of the tether, I released it, and Logan guided the pouch toward his father. "It's good that you didn't touch this, son," Rafael said as he wrapped air around the pocket. "Only those who cast and initiated the curse should have a hand in essences."

One could argue that Logan and I had initiated the curse together, but this wasn't the time for arguing. My legs buckled briefly, but I caught myself before anyone noticed. Or at least I thought I had.

Logan's chest rumbled as he wrapped his arm around my waist.

Rafael, who appeared to also notice, started moving faster. Pulling forth a medium-sized cauldron, he began the complex counter-curse. For a few of the steps, Logan had to assist, ensuring that no one screwed up the order of ingredients or the blessings required to power the spell.

When it was time to add Gran's bone, Rafael's face morphed into a mask of rage, tainting him in darkness. "This is the evil energy of your kind," he spat at me. "You killed my wife, and you're going to pay. I've decided that as long as I destroy all reapers from this world, it's a fair exchange. Mark my words, Paisley Hallistar. I will break this curse, and then I'll break you."

I didn't even bother to reply, because his threats meant nothing when I was hours from death anyway. Logan also managed to retain his own anger, at least on the surface, but I felt the tumult of his magic through our bond.

We'd already discussed how we'd fight once the curse was broken, and I'd decided that I'd call on the entire monster world in Purgatory to keep Logan safe.

When the finger bone landed in the dark mist of the spell, there was a hiss and sparks emerged. The icy magic of reapers buzzed down my spine, sending tingles to my fingertips.

It felt as if I stood with Gran in this room, surrounded by ancestral magic.

The candles Rafael had lit around the pentacle sparked higher. "Essence is last," he said, meeting Logan's gaze. "And the blood of a spellcaster. I will bleed for this because I bled to start it, binding me to your pretty mate for the rest of her life. Which won't be long."

Logan's fists clenched as a low growl ripped from his throat, but he didn't attack. We needed the spell finished first.

Rafael swirled the essence a dozen times clockwise and two times counterclockwise. When it finally settled with the other ingredients, power swelled in the room until it pressed against my chest and I struggled to breathe. Oiliness coated my skin, and I could taste the darkness on my tongue. Curses did not gel with our energy, working against natural magic.

A counter-curse was the opposite. The yang to the yin.

"Maybe we should use your blood," I whispered to Logan.

He jerked forward just as Rafael went to slice his hand, halting his father. "It should be the yang to the yin," I repeated my thought with surety. "You need the light to break the darkness."

Without a single question asked, Logan sliced his palm with magic. "Three drops," his father shouted, and Logan controlled the fall of his blood, allowing only three drops to hit the surface.

There was a pause, and I held my breath, hoping I hadn't fucked it up.

"Revertasia conquestila murdae formin abala. Castisa forrina forla. Paisley Hallistar. Breakista ghilina." Rafael started to chant, repeating the phrase over and over. Air moved through the room, sending our hair into disarray as the curse fought against its counter.

Dizziness swept over me, and I fell against Logan. He wrapped his hands around my waist, keeping me upright. My weakened energy pulsed against the dark tendrils of the curse rooted within my essence. It was deep and insidious, feeding on my power.

Rafael's voice rose up, those unnatural winds buffeting us with enough force to almost send us sprawling. The curse smashed against the counter-curse, dark and light, two opposing sides battling it out.

"It won't let her go," Rafael shouted. "We're too fucking late." A chill raced through my limbs at his defeated tone.

Logan's energy bolstered my own, our connection strong even among the hailstorm of elements and magic. "Don't stop fighting, Precious," he roared, and I doubled down on my effort to pry the curse from my soul.

"You should have used my blood." Rafael snarled at us. "It's not sated."

"Sounds like a plan," Logan shot back, and I gasped when his power slashed across his father's chest, cutting so deep I saw bone. "You can bleed, asshole."

Rafael never saw the attack coming and he gasped. Then there was another icy brush of magic, and another slice, this one severing his throat. As the evil spellcaster grasped his neck in a failed attempt to prevent his lifeforce from exiting his body, I jerked around to stare at Logan.

He shook his head, visibly blanching. "That second cut wasn't me. The curse took its pound of flesh and magic from the one who dabbled in the darker arts."

Rafael slumped forward over the cauldron, his blood seeping into the spell, until we were surrounded by a metallic-scented wind. There was an explosion, and Logan and I hit the floor hard, my mate covering my body with his own, before everything went dark.

CHAPTER 33

Rumbly voices roused me from the darkness, but when I tried to open my eyes, I couldn't manage to pry my heavy lids up. I wasn't ready to step back into full consciousness, where pain and fatigue awaited me.

I preferred this dark abyss, just out of reach.

"What the fuck happened?" Noah sounded far away.

Logan's heat surrounded me, and as light filtered into my consciousness, I knew he was holding me close. Logan's voice was rough: "The curse is broken . . . and with it, the drain on her power is gone."

"Bloody Hel, mate." Tobias sounded impressed. "And what happened to your cock tosser of a father?"

Logan's chest rose sharply beneath me. "He signed his own death warrant when he messed with curses. Dark magic requires a price, and I was hoping he'd be the one who had to pay."

"I'm sorry, brother," Noah said as I once again attempted to force my eyes open. "Rafael needed to die, but I never wanted you to make that choice."

"Me neither," I rasped as I finally lifted eyelids that weighed a hundred pounds.

As Logan came into gritty focus, I found myself cradled

on his lap on the floor, Noah and Tobias standing above us. We were still in Rafael's secret, *awesome* spell room.

"Precious," Logan groaned, his gaze frantic as he took me in. He dropped his head to my neck, running his nose along the skin as he breathed deeply. "You're awake. You're okay."

My arms were weighed down too, but I managed to lift my right hand and cup the back of Logan's neck, rubbing my fingers across his skin. "What happened?"

"The curse was embedded deep in your essence," he said, his hands tracing up and down my spine, slipping under my shirt to graze bare skin, sending sparks of magic into me. "The counter-curse wouldn't work without blood and magical sacrifice. Rafael didn't expect me to make the choice between the three of us so easily, but it wouldn't have mattered who else was in the room. He was always going to be the sacrifice."

Logan lifted his head, and my heart clenched at the hurt dancing in the depths of his beautiful eyes. There was an innate pain in taking the life of a parent, even if that parent was an evil asshole. "I'm so sorry, baby," I whispered.

His eyes closed briefly, thick dark lashes swiping against his cheeks. "I love you," he breathed, leaning down to press his lips to mine. "I'll always choose you."

My magic swirled to connect with his in a way I'd never felt before. It was a clash of our power, the surge of energy between us strong enough to decimate the building. Thankfully, after years of being a badass spellcaster, Logan was better at controlling immense power, and he kept it contained in our bond.

"Uh, Logan . . ." Noah's voice was both tentative and laced in humor. "Did you forget our extra little problem?"

"What extra problem?" I asked, pushing myself higher on his lap.

For the first time since opening my eyes, I wasn't staring at Logan's face or chest, and I finally noticed what was happening in the room.

Oh. OH.

I lurched to my feet, legs taking a beat before they supported me. "What the actual fuck?" I whipped my head around so fast that my neck ached. "Am . . . am I dreaming?"

The room was *filled* with monsters. They stood everywhere, except in a small circle around us.

"They're not attacking," I noted, confusion crashing into me.

"You called them when your magic was freed from the curse." Logan was on his feet as well.

By instinct, I moved toward the first creature. It was the praying mantis, similar to the one from the hallway in Weatherstone, just a little smaller. As I approached it, my magic started to hum in my chest, and I expanded my sight to beyond what was before me until I felt the icy tether between the monster and me.

Logan pressed in close to my back. "Your magic isn't locked down any longer. You tethered them all and there's no strain on your energy. I've never seen anything like it."

Tobias and Noah followed us, everyone staying close to the monster wrangler. *Me.*

"Can you control them?" Noah asked, looking about as nervous as I'd ever seen the big guy.

"More importantly, can you send them back?" Tobias added with a strained laugh.

"Yes."

It was a truth I felt deep in my magic. The suppression potion and curse had impacted my control, but I was now free of both. I held the tethers to these monsters, and if I tugged on them, they would move.

Return home.

I used my energy to guide each monster through the planes, and I didn't even have to close my eyes. Frost filled the air, my magic spinning on flakes and flurries as we watched the creatures fade away back to their realm. It was the same as the first time I'd—unknowingly—called the monsters. I'd sent the ones in the lake and graveyard away, having no idea that I'd returned them to their plane.

Tobias swung around to face me, eyes wide and glassy. "Well, butter my toast and call me breakfast. You're unbelievable, Paisley." He thrusted his thumb toward Logan. "Are you sure you want to shag this arsehole for the rest of eternity? I swear, my cock is much—" He didn't get to finish because he was tackled against the metal wall. Tobias's laughter turned breathless when Logan's forearm lodged against his throat. "Don't get your knickers in a twist, mate. I w-was . . . kidding."

Logan's response was a growl. Then he pulled back enough to slam Tobias against the wall again. When he stepped away, he let the warlock slide to the ground.

"You asked for that," Noah said, crossing his arms and shaking his head.

Another growling series of curses came from the spellcaster, and then I was in his arms. He opened a transport doorway in the next breath, taking us both through.

"See you at Weatherstone tomorrow, you cranky sod," Tobias called cheerily. "We'll deal with your father's body and let Paisley's family know you're going to live. You're welcome."

"Fucker," Logan grumbled, just as he closed the transport, leaving us standing alone in front of his farmhouse gates. My heart lifted at the sight, and I sucked in a long, slow breath, the scent of lavender filling my lungs. How a place I'd been to once could smell like home, I had no idea, but here we were. "Call your parents," Logan said softly, handing me his phone. "Noah and Tobias will give them more details, but they should hear from you first."

He was right, and I quickly dialed Mom's number, relieved when she answered immediately.

"Mom, we broke the curse," I said, no preamble. "I'm going to be okay."

The relieved sob she let out told me how close to a breakdown she was. "Thank Selene," she murmured, her words husky.

I spent a few more minutes quickly filling her in on what had happened, before adding that Noah and Tobias would be by soon with more information.

"We love you, Little Gem," she said as we wrapped up the conversation.

Hearing Dad's nickname for me had my throat so tight I could barely get words out. "I love you all too. Thank you. I'll see you soon."

When I hung up and handed Logan his phone back, he slid it into his pocket and cupped the back of my head. Our first kiss was heated, pent-up emotions spilling from me. By the time we pulled apart, my breaths were staggered and heavy.

"Come on, Precious," he said, turning me toward the gate. "Let's go home."

To no one's surprise, he knew exactly how I felt about this place. "I love this farm," I said, reaching out to brush the gate. It opened at my touch, and I jumped back to look at Logan. "Did you open it?"

He shook his head. "It belongs to both of us. It's been keyed to your magic since the moment you bloomed."

My lips twitched, even as heat burned my eyes. "Stalker."

He leaned over and kissed me again, harder, his fingers

sliding under my hair as he possessively wrapped a hand around the back of my neck and pulled me closer. "For you, baby, always."

We stumbled up the front path, kissing and touching, unable to keep our hands to ourselves.

"Fuck, Paisley," Logan growled and hauled me into his arms, storming up to the porch and through the front door. Our lips met in another desperate kiss, our movements frantic as we drowned in each other. I clawed at his shirt, needing bare skin under my touch.

We didn't make it upstairs to his room. Logan pressed me against the entrance wall, his magic disintegrating our clothes. As our bare skin slid together, the heat between us intensified until I ached. I thrust my hips on a sob against the hard planes of Logan's stomach, my legs settling around his waist. Logan shifted my position higher to trace a burning path of kisses down my throat and across my tits. His tongue caressed my right nipple, biting into the sensitive peak. When I cried out, he made a satisfied sound that came deep from his chest. He moved on to the left, tormenting and teasing it too. When he bit down again, a ragged scream left me. "Please," I begged. I had no idea what I was begging for, but I needed *more*.

"You taste like the Eternal Lands. Like forever," Logan growled as his hand slipped between us and pressed against my clit. His thumb slid hard over the swollen bud and I was panting—fucking panting at the sensation. Slowly, destroying me with each stroke, he slid one finger through my dripping slit and inside. He added a second finger, fucking me harder. All the while, his thumb's assault on my clit never eased.

I was lost to the sensation as our magic burned, and when his teeth closed around my nipple again, the pleasure exploded, and I came, screaming his name.

Power detonated from me, but Logan contained it, drawing the energy back into the heat between us. The walls of my pussy clamped around his fingers as I rode out the last of my orgasm, and I almost cried when he withdrew them—until he changed the angle of his hips and thrust into my center. The thick head of his cock slid in first, stretching me with a pleasurable burn.

Logan usually gave me a second to adjust, but he was too far gone today, thrusting again until he was seated balls-deep. It was almost too much to take, but as the pleasure edged out the pain, I decided I didn't care. With Logan, pain amplified pleasure until I felt like I'd die from the sensation.

He started to slam into me, my back hitting the wall with each thrust. I groaned when he lifted his hand and licked his fingers that had been buried inside me a moment ago. "Fuck, spellcaster," I cried out, the muscles of my pussy clenching around him.

"You taste delicious, baby," he purred, his eyelids heavy as he stared into my soul.

When he had the use of both hands again, he gripped my hips and pulled back from the wall, taking my full weight. He lifted me higher to adjust his angle, giving himself the leverage to slam up into me. "You're gushing all over my cock, Precious." His voice was strained. "You're the hottest fucking witch I've ever seen in my life. I'm one lucky asshole to have a mate as perfect as you."

If I'd been gushing before, I was a fucking waterfall now.

"Don't come yet," Logan growled. "Wait for me, perfect girl. I want us to fall together."

I panted out a response. "I can't—control—it."

Logan growled again, the deepest rumble filling his chest as he moved harder and faster, losing control. "Wait for me . . . wait for me. That's my good girl. You're doing so well, baby."

Mewling little cries spilled from me as I tried to hold back, and with each thrust, the need and want grew stronger until I wasn't sure I'd survive the fallout. "Now, baby," he said, our lips meeting in a biting kiss. "Come with me."

My head slammed back as my body detonated, and I was screaming loud enough that if there'd been neighbors close by, they'd be calling the cops and reporting a murder.

Only there was no pain as the orgasm ripped through me, Logan's following until I was filled with the heat of his release. The connection that had always existed between us, even when we were ignoring it, exploded, and I felt the bonds of our magic fusing together. I sensed Logan in a way I never had before, and my heart swelled at the depth of his emotion.

It was beyond anything I'd ever expected. His love for me raged through my soul and left an indelible mark on it.

Logan. The whisper of his name was as instinctive as breathing.

Precious.

It wasn't as if we were suddenly in each other's heads, but we were in each other's souls. I felt his magic, and the bond, and the immense world-shattering love that ebbed between us, which was no longer restricted by curses or magical suppression.

The only existence was us and our bond.

It was everything.

CHAPTER 34

My stomach rumbled as I rested my head on Logan's chest. We'd made love through every room of the house, and when I was too tired to keep my eyes open, we ended up in his bed. The aim had been to sleep, but we'd gotten sidetracked—again.

Logan laughed as my stomach made another angry sound. "I better feed my mate," he said.

A burst of magic filled me, the energy moving freely between us, and it was hard to tell if it was mine or Logan's at this point. We'd indelibly intertwined our magic through copious amounts of sex and bonding.

"You've fed me plenty," I rasped. "It was mostly your magic dick, but it counts."

I had almost no experience sucking cock before Logan, but I was going to classify myself an expert after the last twenty-four hours. This time he laughed so hard that I found myself smiling at how perfect this moment felt.

Outside of a few quick phone calls to my family, double reassuring them I was okay and would be home soon, we'd been in a lovely love-filled bubble.

Why did we have to leave?

Here, there were no curses, deaths, or prohibited affinities.

Here, there was only us and our bond, and it was everything.

Logan kissed me, before slapping my ass and rubbing the sting away with a gentle pat. "Come on, baby." He wedged his arms under my torso and lifted me from the bed. "You shower and I'll get us food."

We were well aware that if we showered together, there'd be no food, so I reluctantly parted from him and entered his gorgeous bathroom. With its multiple showerheads, steam bar, and array of expensive bodywashes, shampoos, and conditioners, his shower was a gift from the goddess.

There'd been so much drama in our relatively short relationship that it hadn't fully occurred to me that Logan was rich. No, *not rich*—absolutely loaded. With Rafael's death, he would inherit everything in the Kingston portfolio.

We'd had no issue with Rafael's death so far. Noah had called a few hours ago to explain that the council had investigated and decided that Rafael had been dealing in dark curses and manipulating other spellcasters—causing the battles across Europe—and that he'd been his own downfall.

Which was the truth. The magical will had gone into effect straight after, leaving Logan in charge of the company, the magical objects his father had possessed, and all their properties.

The sheer scale of money and assets he now controlled was so far beyond me, I kept pretending it wasn't happening—the best way to keep feelings of inadequacy at bay, no matter how ridiculous they were in our magically blessed bond.

I knew the truth: Even if we lived in a tent on the streets, I'd be happy as long as I had Logan.

This shower was a nice bonus though.

When I finished and had dried off, I applied a delicious lemon-scented body butter to my skin. Upon entering Logan's walk-in closet, I paused at the new selection of women's clothes. A quick glance told me that everything was brand-new and my size. He'd also cleared out a few of his drawers for bras and panties, along with an array of soft pajamas.

"What the Hel?" I gawked, trying to figure out when he'd had the time to set this up.

Slipping on a matching set of lacy black panties and bra, I grabbed light blue jeans with rips across the thighs and teamed them with a black slouchy shirt that hung off one shoulder.

The house was warm thanks to Logan's magic powering through it, so I padded barefoot down to the kitchen. Logan had pulled on a pair of gray sweats, and I paused in the doorway, enjoying the view of him flipping pancakes and pouring juice.

His magic wrapped around me as he opened the huge industrial fridge and pulled out a bowl of already diced fruit. The play of golden muscles in his back kept me mesmerized until he shot a smirk over his shoulder. "Feeling a little objectified, Precious. My eyes are up here."

A snort escaped me, and I strolled to him, pressing my hands against his back. "Aw, baby. Don't you like being my sex toy?"

His smirk faded as he dropped the fruit on the bench and hauled me up next to it, pressing his big body between my legs. His magic handled the pancakes and bacon as he dragged his hand across the bare skin of my exposed shoulder. "The only reason you're not naked and screaming under my mouth, Paisley Hallistar," he whispered, grazing his lips across my throat, "is that I promised to feed you first. But don't tempt me."

My core clenched as I dug my nails into his arms. Logan's eyes darkened, and I swear that even I could scent my arousal. "Shit," I gasped, pushing him back so I could slip off the bench and race around to the other side.

He'd already set a place for me with juice and toast, so I slid onto the stool and tried to regulate my breathing. Logan's laughter followed, but he stayed on his side to finish cooking. When he was done, he set an overflowing plate in front of me, before joining me with his own.

The pancakes were fluffy, the eggs light and mildly spiced, the bacon crispy, and the juice sweet and fresh. "I had a moment upstairs thinking about how stupidly rich you are," I said around a bite of perfect eggs. "It's an imbalance between us, which bothers me. But I really should have freaked out about how well you cook. That was the one skill I thought I could bring to the table."

Logan's expression was soft as he stared at me for an extra-long moment. "Baby, there's no imbalance between us. If anything, you're too perfect for an asshole like me. But I can't let you go. I tried, and I couldn't do it, so . . . I'm keeping you. I'll always cook if you want me to, and my money is yours, so you're stupidly rich now too. There's nothing in this world, or the other planes, that I won't give to you, because you've given me everything."

Tears slipped down my cheeks, the saltiness catching on my lips. Logan dragged his fingers across the wet paths on my skin and leaned in to taste their saltiness. "I love you," he said, looking more serious than I'd seen before. "I love you. So much."

"I love you too." More than I'd ever fathomed being able to love another.

Even the love I had for my family, while unbreakable and deep, wasn't the same as what existed between Logan and me. "I don't know if the right path for us is returning to Weatherstone," I admitted as he held me close. "I've been so desperate for college, to find my place in the magical world. But . . . my affinity will never fit into their mold, and I'll always be an outsider even when I try to conform."

Logan ran his hands over my back, his touch both soothing and arousing. "You don't have to go back, baby. I'll never join a coven. Spellcasters rarely do. We can form our own with the friends and family we trust."

I'd always expected to be part of a large coven, but the revelation of my affinity changed everything for me. Even if we could somehow convince the council not to murder me, I'd never fit into a regular coven. I did still have a lot to learn, though, and maybe Weatherstone was the best and only place to do that. Even if it would only ever be *part* of my power.

Logan brushed a few strands of hair off my cheek, tucking them gently behind my ear. "You don't have to decide today," he said, sensing my confusion. "Why don't we just go back for now, catch up with our friends, and then see how you feel after that? We should also start working out our game plan to garner support from powerful witches and warlocks in our community. Unless you want to suppress your magic again?"

I shook my head before he even finished speaking. "I can't. Not only does it impact our bond, but I also don't believe it's a sustainable long-term solution with how much power we share between us. Other reapers might have been able to lock themselves down for an eternity, but they didn't have you as their mate. We need a different path."

Dealing with the council and my affinity wasn't going to be easy, even if we did manage to gather enough support to make a stand. The fear of my affinity was ingrained deeply in our past, and unless I could offer them a deal they couldn't refuse, I would have to either fight or run.

Not just me, but Logan as well.

I didn't want that life for either of us. We might not be destined for covens, but we had bright futures waiting out there. Futures I would not let them steal.

CHAPTER 35

Logan and I walked through Weatherstone's front gates holding hands. It was the first time we'd been here with both unlocked magic and our mate bond visible to the world.

It was early on Wednesday, with most students still in their dorms, but there were enough around that we drew attention. Whispers followed us as we moved along the frozen path.

Seasonally we were past the depths of winter, but remnants lingered in the wind, along with icy snaps of rain sprinkling from the heavy clouds above. Anytime the skies opened up, Logan's power kept us warm and dry. "Feels weird to be back here," I admitted, looking around. "It's still beautiful and intimidating, and I'm glad I was chosen for this college, but I can't shake the sense of not belonging here now."

Logan released my hand to wrap an arm around my shoulders. Cradled against his heat and energy, I felt the full force of his love and protection. "You don't need Weatherstone," he reminded me. "Neither of us do. But until we decide what to do, I think it's best that we act as normal as possible."

"Do you need to be present at the company after Rafael's death?"

He shook his head. "Our lawyers left a message this

morning asking me to meet with them soon. I inherited the full shares in the company. Rafael never allowed it to be a publicly traded entity. He liked control too much."

"That's a lot of responsibility," I said as I tried to wrap my head around running a billion-dollar company. "How many employees do you have?"

"About thirty thousand across the world," Logan said as we reached the front steps of the main building. "Thankfully, Rafael had decent witches and warlocks running the upper levels, giving me breathing room before I have to step into the CEO position."

"That's good."

"Yeah, despite the shit Rafael pulled, his technologies have been instrumental in improving the human medical world. Robotics have increased the success rates in surgery and other fields tenfold. I don't want it all to fall apart just because he was an evil fuck. Some good should come from that warlock."

The urge to whisk Logan back to our bubble at the farmhouse thrummed strongly within me. "You're already the good out of his evil."

"For you, I'm good. But if anyone stands against us, I will be as evil as my father. Whatever it takes to keep you safe."

I probably shouldn't be so turned on by that statement—along with the feral look in his eyes—but here we were. There was no part of Logan that I didn't love. Even the darkness.

Often, I wondered if it was the darkness that drew me in the most.

"I will destroy anyone that tries to hurt you, Logan. Even if I have to call every monster in existence." I lowered my voice, but apparently not enough, as a shocked gasp drew our attention.

Belle stood at the top of the stairs, her face completely

drained of color. She swayed forward, and by instinct I reached out as if to steady her. Not that she was about to let us touch, wrenching herself backward to fall and hit the ground hard. The simmering anger I'd felt ever since she'd started ignoring my messages and calls over the winter break surged hotter. If there hadn't been so much going on in my life, I'd have confronted my former best friend weeks ago—I had no idea what she'd been going through, and she didn't know how close to death I'd come. We were virtually strangers.

I stepped through the doors of the college front hall, and Belle scrambled backward, the skirt of her uniform flying as she moved. She was fast, and when she hit the stone wall, she used it to hoist herself to her feet.

I halted my pursuit, giving her a second to compose herself. "Paisley," she choked out. "You're back?"

"I am," I replied, crossing my arms. "And you're still avoiding me. Why?"

Her tongue darted out to moisten her lips, and to her credit, she got her breathing under control fast. When she looked between Logan and me, I expected her to ignore my question, as she'd done most of my messages through the break, but then she let out a low sigh. "You know why. You're evil."

Logan's magic pulsated around us, his anger as hot as literal flames in the entrance hall. "You have no fucking idea what you're talking about," he said, and in a contrast to his power, his voice was filled with cold disdain. "Paisley is the best witch I've ever known, and you'll regret losing her friendship—when you finally pull your head out of your ass."

Logan's unwavering support of me eased the hurt I felt facing Belle. Deep in my essence, I'd worried that I was evil. But after Rafael, I understood the difference between making a mistake and making a conscious decision to hurt another. Reapers might not be accepted, but we weren't inherently evil.

Leveling my gaze on Belle, I let my sadness seep out in my words. "Not that I owe you any explanation, but an affinity doesn't make you evil. Your father is an elemental, and a horrible warlock. Because he fears me, he hates me, but you have known me for an entire year. We were friends, and yet you believe I would deliberately hurt someone. I'm not a bad witch."

Color blossomed in Belle's cheeks. "Tell that to Gerard Donovan. I'm sure the fact that you're *not a bad witch* will be a great comfort to his family after your monster tore him to pieces."

With that blow, she spun on her heels and hurried away from us, heading up the stairs. Darkness blurred the edges of my vision as I fought my own guilt. When Logan wrapped his arms around me, I slumped against his chest. "Donovan is not your fault," he said with a snap. "You almost died in that attack too. In truth, our world and the council let you down by not assuring you were properly trained in your affinity. By wiping out all the reaper witches, you couldn't join with your brethren to bloom as you should have done. There's a lot of blame to go around here, but there's never been any doubt that not even one speck of your magic is evil. Not a single speck."

A sob slipped through my tightly pressed lips, but I didn't let tears fall. I'd never fully move past my guilt over what happened to Gerard, but I also understood what Logan was saying. This wasn't all my fault. Outside of self-defense, I'd never deliberately hurt anyone.

"There has to be a point to all of this." My words were mumbled against Logan's chest. "To my affinity. Why would reapers exist without a reason for our magic?"

Every other affinity fulfilled some role in our magical world, and there was no reason to believe reapers were different. Logan held me tightly, keeping my broken pieces from shattering, and eventually I had myself together enough to continue into Weatherstone.

We didn't speak as we ended up in front of Logan's dorm. "I want you in here with me," he said, pressing his palm to the scanner. "Where I can protect you. I'll get your stuff from your room."

"Don't forget my babies," I said, hoping my herbs were still alive and well. I hadn't had a chance to reinforce my magical watering spell, but it had only been a few days.

Logan's lopsided smile did dangerous things to my body. "I'd never forget about your babies," he teased. "And I'll give you plenty more to love in the future, Precious. All the babies."

Fuck. Me.

"Are you talking about plants?" I rasped.

Logan snorted before shaking his head. "Sure, baby. Plants." He pushed the door open for me to enter. "Do you want your crystals?"

I shook my head, which still spun at his reference to babies. Not that I couldn't imagine a family with Logan, but definitely no time soon. "Leave my crystals there for now. With my powers unlocked, I need to be careful about boosting my magic."

"Soon I will figure out a way for you not to have to hide. I promise."

He left to grab my stuff, and I got to work unpacking

what I had in my overnight bag, thinking about my crystals and the hope that one day I could embrace my full affinity.

Already my reaper powers surged strongly inside, and if the council was searching, they'd find me easily enough. Find and destroy me with their misguided fear and hate.

After classes today, we had plans to meet up with our friends and figure out the next steps.

Rafael might be dead, but I was far from safe.

Belle's reaction had proved that, and she was only the tip of the iceberg.

CHAPTER 36

"Ms. Hallistar! I'm impressed. I expected to see more weakness after your days off sick, but here you are, showing the true skills of a spellcaster."

Professor Damone's normally unflappable features slackened as she watched me draw air around myself and funnel it up through the specially made glass tubes in her classroom. The rest of her was as put together as always, from the tight chignon in her blond hair, to the perfect eyeliner she always wore. But her expression . . . I'd stunned her.

The air wrapped me in its embrace as my magic flowed with the element and back into my center. It was hard to remember when I'd been locked down and working against my own powers. The icy strain of reaper magic wasn't present when I touched elements, keeping me safe from revealing my secret.

Professor Damone, like all my professors today, had presumed that my spellcaster side was finally blossoming. None of them looked any deeper than that, which would hopefully be the norm moving forward. I'd already spoken to Mom at lunchtime, and after she chastised me for not stopping by home before heading back to school, she'd offered to send a suppression potion with Dad. *That's my last resort*, I'd told her, and even though she sounded worried, she didn't argue with me. A suppression potion wasn't a long-term option. It couldn't be.

My magic whispered that hiding her nature had weakened Gran to the point that she hadn't survived childbirth. Our magic was innately part of our essence and strength, and I would have been surprised to find any suppressed reaper living to old age. Cutting off our magic long-term was destructive to our health and well-being.

Ever since I'd felt that connection to Gran at our family crypt, I'd had a closer link to my affinity. A part of her spirit remained within me, and I was sure it would help me learn to control the monsters and make reaper-related decisions moving forward.

By the time class was over, I all but bounced from the room, feeling stronger than I had in forever. The curse had been draining me for so long I'd forgotten what feeling good was like.

It was amazing.

Amusement washed through my newly cemented connection to Logan—who was in one of the few classes he couldn't miss—and with it came a fizzle of excitement in my stomach.

Sensing him the way I did now, a true connection, had never been described in the texts. I knew bonded *and married* magical pairs had a connection, but I could *feel* Logan in my essence. Our magic was freely linked, even over distance. It was almost as if his energy was there beneath my fingertips, ripe for the taking. Not that I'd be taking any to leave my mate weaker, but it was an interesting sensation all the same.

Sara met me at the door of the classroom; she'd been working with a few seniors today. "Your magic is on fucking fire," she said, slinging the arm not holding her school satchel around me. "You're going to kill it as a spellcaster."

I smirked as her voice rose, and when Marcus fell in on her other side, all amusement dried up. Rafael had never confirmed he was the other spellcaster waiting in the wings to curse me, but I wasn't taking any chances.

"Go away, Marcus," Sara snapped, snuggling me closer to create a gap between him and us. "Before her mate rips your fucking head off and uses it as a bowling ball."

When heat burned around Marcus, I tapped into my own magic.

I didn't need to call a monster to scare him away.

Reapers carried all the same magical ties as a spellcaster, with the addition of a beefed-up necromancy. "You don't speak for Paisley," he snapped, his energy crackling, which Sara wiped away with a wash of air. She was a strong elemental, made even stronger by her attitude of giving no fucks.

"In this case, Sara absolutely speaks for me," I told him coldly. "She's also not kidding about Logan. He's not particularly happy about what he heard from his father . . . you know, Rafael Kingston . . . regarding you. I'd watch my back, spellcaster."

I'd deliberately baited him to reveal his part in all of it, and sure enough, there was a subtle flinch when I mentioned Logan's dad. "I have no idea what you're talking about," he said stiffly, looking around the hall. "Never met the guy, and I heard he was dead anyway. Blew himself up with his own curse."

With that, he spun on the spot and hurried in the opposite direction. "Fucker," Sara seethed. "At least we know Noah and Toby's story is holding up."

That was a relief. We already had enough issues, without having to defend ourselves from a murder charge too. "I can't believe Marcus," I said. "He established a connection and then just lay in wait in case Logan didn't fulfill his side of it." Hence the weird hot-and-cold act he'd been throwing my way through last year.

"Logan is going to kill him," Sara said with a smirk. "And he deserves that and way worse."

"I might kill him," I said with a shrug. "I mean, don't get me wrong, I enjoy Logan blasting shitheads to pieces for me, but I also enjoy fighting my own battles." Now that my magic was free for such ventures.

Sara held up her hand for a high five, and I rolled my eyes but gave her what she wanted.

"Well, that was the last class for the day," she said, an extra pep in her step too. "Should we meet with Haley in the library and get our homework done?"

I was weirdly looking forward to our study session. "Yep, we have a couple of hours before dinner. The guys will find us, I'm sure."

"They always do," Sara said with a sigh, but she didn't sound too upset. Tobias hadn't fully won the witch over yet, but he was a Hel of a lot closer. I'd seen the two of them in many discussions lately, and there'd been hardly an insult or accidental blast of elemental magic involved.

Haley already had a large table staked out in the best section near the fireplace. Over the next hour this place would be full, so we spread out to save seats—our warlocks weren't exactly small.

I started on history first, delving further into the conception and evolution of Weatherstone College. We were researching the time when the two original witches—Writworth and Ancot—decided they couldn't just specialize in necromancy if they wanted to produce the strongest students and army.

"Professor Jones is being a hard-ass this year," Sara groaned, waving her hand and letting air hold her pen for a few minutes. "Who decides to assign a five-thousand-word essay that's due in the fourth week? That's cruel."

Haley snorted. "It wouldn't be so bad if you started three weeks ago like the rest of us." She'd had her assignment finished for days and had moved on to the next one. She was always two steps ahead, and I'd tried to stay that way as well, but this year hadn't exactly gone to plan.

"I'm with Sara," I said, letting my head bang on the table. "I need another thousand words, and I'm fairly sure the crux of my argument is ridiculously weak, and I fucked up some of the timeline." It would take hours to read through and fix it once I got my word count up.

Haley's expression was sympathetic. "Witch, you were literally dying from a curse. You have an excuse." She leaned forward with her hand out. "Let me read through what you've got and I'll see if I can help."

I hesitated, having never needed help with schoolwork before. Sara patted my arm. "Seriously, take the assist. You deserve it after everything you've been through."

"Feels like cheating," I admitted with a huff.

Haley grumbled out a laugh. "I'm not going to finish it for you. I'll just make notes, like an editor would."

I couldn't see an issue with that, so I handed the pages scrawled with my sloping handwriting to her. A few of our other professors had assignments and homework due, so I moved on to them while Haley read my history essay.

When I was halfway through research into protective spells that used angelica as the main binding agent, my magic vibrated softly, telling me Logan had entered the library. Our connection perked up, and I tried to remain focused on the spells, but it was almost impossible. As his energy closed in, I found myself staring at the exact spot I knew he was about to appear, my pulse thrumming like a trapped butterfly.

Green eyes pinned me in place, and my pen fell from my hand and rolled off the table. When Logan was in the room, he eclipsed everything else in existence.

Would it always be like this?

An all-consuming desperate need.

Two large warlocks followed Logan, and somewhere in my mind I knew it was Noah and Tobias, but again, there was only awareness of the spellcaster. He stalked forward, and when he reached my chair, he hauled me into his arms, burying his face against the side of my neck. A gust of air escaped him, tension releasing as he slowly drifted his nose along my skin, breathing me in.

He finished with a press of his lips just behind my ear, and I gasped, my lungs screaming at me. Logan had me so fucking discombobulated that I forgot to breathe.

"Mate," he growled against my skin. "I missed you."

We'd only been apart for a few hours, but in this newly blossomed bond, that was far too long for both of us. "I missed you too," I whispered, my throat tight, need fluttering in my core. "So fucking much."

He let loose another growl. "Precious, I'm two seconds from hauling you over my shoulder and heading for our room. If you still have schoolwork to finish, tell me now."

I couldn't imagine any class more important than being alone with Logan, and just as I was about to tell him that, Haley piped up. "She has a lot of work to finish, so drop her back into her chair, lover boy."

My bookish bestie didn't use her teacher tone around powerful warlocks much, but today she meant business. Logan groaned as he gently returned me to my seat. "You get her for another hour," he grumbled. "Then she's mine."

A shiver of anticipation raced down my spine and into my magic. Noah, already understanding what his best friend needed, reached out and dragged Haley's chair away from mine, making space for Logan at my side.

He pulled a chair up and sat close, leaving me breathing in ragged, awkward gasps. "Deep breaths, baby," he whispered, handing me my dropped pen. "You have fifty-eight minutes now to finish your homework."

"Paisley," Haley snapped, and I shook my head in the hopes of finding focus. "Here's your essay." She leaned around Logan to return it. "It's quite good, actually. You write in such an easy-to-read and engaging tone, but you're right about some of the timeline and facts being out of order. I've made notes of where you need to look, and I suggest you get to work."

I pressed my lips tighter to hide my smile. "Yes, ma'am," I chirped, dragging the papers toward me. "And thank you. I appreciate your help."

She blew me a kiss. "I'd do anything for you, Paisley Hallistar. You and Sara are my chosen sisters." Her eyes were glassy as she continued. "We almost lost you, and I'm eternally grateful that we're all together now."

Noah wrapped a beefy arm around her, his expression thunderous as he stared at the tear that spilled down her cheek. According to Haley, they hadn't had the conversation yet about what they were to each other, but it was clearly coming. Noah's possessiveness toward my friend reminded me of Logan, and there was only one path for a warlock with those feelings.

"I'm grateful too," Logan said, the tenor of his husky voice filling the air. "But the danger isn't over just yet. We still need to discuss our next steps. Not here, of course," he added, eyeing all the full tables around us, "but when we leave for our gig next weekend, we will talk about the future."

A tense silence descended over our group; even Tobias wore a composed expression.

Our moments here at Weatherstone were nothing more than a reprieve.

A reprieve from the next battle we had to face.

How to stop the council from destroying me.

CHAPTER 37

"Little Gem!" I heard Dad's call as I hurried toward the breakfast cart.

I'd gotten up early hoping to grab coffee and food for Logan before he woke up. He'd been working overtime to look after me and needed rest. For once, I wanted to be the one who took care of him.

"Hey, Dad," I said, shooting him a smile as I waited for him to catch up. "I didn't expect to see you here so early." Classes didn't start for at least an hour and Dad usually spent as much time as he could with Mom in the mornings.

When he didn't return my smile, dread slithered through my stomach, twisting it into knots. "What happened?" I asked, not sure I could handle the answer. "Is everyone okay? Mom and the twins?"

He wrapped his hand around mine. "They're all fine, honey. I'm sorry to scare you, but we need to talk, and quickly."

Anxiety was my new bestie as I followed Dad through Writworth and up two flights of stairs to his office. I hadn't had any reason to visit the row of faculty offices, and I was surprised to see dozens of doors open, professors already inside preparing lessons or meeting up with students. Apparently, Dad was one of the few not normally here early.

He was greeted warmly as we passed, his colleagues glancing my way as he all but dragged me along, but no one made any comment. When we reached his office, I was waved toward his spare chair; he shut the door firmly and pressed his palm against the frame. I felt a wash of magic as he murmured a spell to shield our voices from being overheard.

It was a familiar chant I'd learned in class last year.

"Dad," I said softly, not wanting to spook him in his current mood. He was liable to burn the school down if his energy grew any more out of control, and this time he would absolutely end up in prison for it. "You're freaking me the Hel out."

Dad took his time making his way to his chair on the other side of his desk. His office was sparsely furnished, the only personal item a framed family photo on the overflowing bookshelf—which was otherwise filled with his favorite texts on fire and general magic. "I've been keeping an ear out for council news," he said as he sank into his chair, eyes dark as they met mine. "It was unremarkable until this morning."

Leaning forward, I swallowed roughly and tried to keep the tendrils of panic from spiraling. At the other end of my bond, Logan's energy stirred, and I didn't want to wake him. At least not before I knew how serious this was.

"What happened this morning?"

"The full roster of elders are gathering," he said hoarsely. "Elder Monroe called them all in, and I can't remember the last time they gathered as a whole."

"Do you know why? Could it be about the spellcaster issue in Europe? I know it's somewhat died down, but I heard on the news that they're back to meeting with the council in regard to giving spellcasters more say in magical decisions."

Dad shook his head. "It's not that, Paisley. That's been

going on for months, and it hasn't required all the council to gather."

Right. *Crap.* "Elder Monroe being involved is a bad sign," I admitted as the hold on my magic wavered, sending my panic down my mate bond. "He's been quiet since Logan interfered with him attending your trial."

That slipped out before I remembered Dad hadn't been aware of it. Only, he showed no surprise as he rubbed a hand against his right temple. "Logan shouldn't have done that," he said with a huff. "He painted a larger target on us all, and I would have been fine either way."

"He did it for me," I said, feeling strangely soothed at the mere memory of his caring actions. "He knew how worried I was about the outcome."

Dad looked pained as he leaned closer to me. "I love you, Little Gem. You know I love you more than anything, and I can't imagine life without you, but I think you and Logan should disappear for a while. Just take off and lay low until Monroe finds a new target for his rage. He's been an asshole since his wife left him and made her base in India. He doesn't like to lose, and especially not when it's to do with his family. You befriended his daughter, and he won't let you have her. He'll do whatever it takes, and unfortunately, it won't be difficult for him to convince the council to investigate. They have the evidence from the monster attack here last year."

"I won't break in front of them," I promised him. "No matter what he does, I won't call the monsters again. I have complete control of my magic."

Not totally accurate, but I was confident that even if I accidentally called a beast, I could send them back fast enough that no one would notice. *Hopefully.*

"What if he threatened someone you cared about?" Dad

said as fire licked across his skin. I hadn't seen my dad lose control like this in a long time. "You're vulnerable because you have a lot of witches and warlocks you love. He will use them against you, Pais. He will take and hurt until he gets what he wants. I can't have that happen. You have to run."

My distress had called my mate; Logan's energy was getting closer. "Okay," I said with a rasp. "Okay, Dad. I'll leave today. How will I know when I can get in contact with anyone again?"

Logan's power grew stronger, until my magic swelled. Dad's flames expanded as he felt my magic. "We'll grab burner phones for contact. Here are a few months of suppression potions to get going." He reached into his bag on the floor and lifted out a small pouch. "From your mom. But you will need to contact us for more."

"Here's hoping Logan has some of his billions stashed in cash," I said, my laugh strangled and weird.

Speaking of, the spellcaster's energy crashed against the warded door, and Dad shot to his feet to remove his spell before Logan blasted it to pieces. Logan strode through in a cloud of darkness—not literally, but I could feel it in our bond. "Precious," he growled, eyes locked on me, before they ran over my face as if checking for injury. "Why are you panicking?"

I'd been so focused on the power that rode around him like an entourage that I missed the part where he was wearing black sweats and a soft gray shirt, his feet bare and hair mussed. He'd clearly rolled out of bed and grabbed the first clothes he could find to get to me fast.

Moon goddess, I had a hot mate. That was one upside to life on the run. There weren't many others.

A fraction of his tumultuous energy eased up as he noted

my general well-being and blatant perusal of him. His finger tipped up my chin. "Focus for me, baby," he chuckled, and I wondered how he smelled so good when he hadn't showered or brushed his teeth. Had he used magic to clean his teeth as he rushed here?

"She's less focused than usual," Logan said, raising his head to meet Dad's gaze. "Maybe you'd better fill me in."

Just as I found the will to shake off the thrall he held me under, Logan lifted me from the chair and settled in, pulling me onto his lap. Yep, okay. Thrall was back and much, *much* stronger.

Dad didn't react to the way I was plastered against Logan, but then again, I'd seen him like this with Mom more times than I could count. He understood the driving need to be close to your mate, especially after almost losing them. "You have to take Paisley and run," he said. "The council gathered today as a whole, which never happens. And it was called by Elder Monroe."

Logan's fingers, which had been gently tracing up my spine, stilled, and that darker energy returned. "What time were they called?"

The fact that my unflappable mate was taking this seriously had me forcing my focus back to the situation at hand. "Mom sent suppression potions for us both," I told him, my voice now as weird as my laugh had been before. "Do you have cash stashed to get us through the next few months of lying low?"

Logan's body was rigid beneath me. "I have plenty of cash, Precious, but we need to consider that Monroe won't ever give up. He's been making noise about me keeping him from the trial, even though he doesn't have any evidence that I was involved. This is personal on two fronts now. Unless we want to hide forever—" he shifted me so he could meet my gaze "—and I will if that's what you want. But if not, we need to think of another path."

"What path?" Dad's facade of cool was gone in a blaze of flames.

Logan didn't pull his gaze from mine. "We should petition the council and ask for a public hearing. The entire magical world needs to know what they did to reapers in the past, and what they plan on doing again. We're civilized in a way we never used to be, and I think a lot of magical families would be against outright executing a witch because she was born with an affinity they fear. Paisley has control now. She can show them that the creatures aren't a risk."

Dad looked like he'd rather take any suggestion over that one, but as we sat in silence, I could tell he had no better ideas. "What about the fact that a student died here last year because of her affinity? They're not going to let that slide."

Logan shook his head. "We have to convince them that she was let down by the magical community, shunned for her ability. That she has worked to control it, and that she deserves the same chance as any witch who loses control of their magic. It happens more than you'd think, that a witch or warlock from an elemental or necro family blooms as a spellcaster. They never anticipate how strong their magic will be, and when their energy blooms, it quite often destroys whoever is nearby. None of them are set for death . . . or even jail time. They all get another chance, and Paisley should be no different."

It took a few fortifying breaths, but eventually Dad was on board with this new plan. "Okay, I'll reach out to an elder I've been friends with for years. I'll see if I can get this moving forward before they track Paisley down and take our choices away."

Logan's entire body shook beneath me, his magic as

heated as Dad's. "Not even I can go up against the entire council, especially since they'll bring in spellcasters from the armed forces. We must make this work."

No matter what happened, I wouldn't let Logan get hurt to save me. I didn't care what it took, or how many monsters I had to release, he would walk away from this meeting with the elders.

If it was the last thing I ever did.

CHAPTER 38

The feeling of dread I'd had from the moment Dad had called me to his office didn't abate for the rest of the day. I could barely remember a word the professors said during class, and by the time I left Air Elemental 102 with Sara in the afternoon, I was on the edge of a panic attack. Through sheer force of will, I managed to block my loss of calm from Logan, but it was too late to save myself. "I can't do this," I huffed, my lungs constricting as I attempted to breathe deeper. "They're going to kill me. They've killed every other reaper."

"Pais!" Sara shouted my name as her hands wrapped around my biceps. She yanked me away from the curious bystanders in the hallway and got me into an empty classroom.

"You need to calm down, babe!" She sounded panicked now too. When I attempted to focus, two Saras stared back at me; flashing dots danced across my peripherals. "Breathe with me, Pais. In and out. Slow down. You're going to pass out."

As desperate as I was to make my way through this panic attack, I was equally as desperate not to lose it in case I accidentally called monsters. I'd grown accustomed to keeping my energy firmly here in the living plane, but I already knew it would be easy for it to slip.

Especially when *I was slipping.*

A firm slap of icy air in my face jolted me, startling me from the anxiety that had me trapped. Blinking, I rubbed my hand across what was no doubt a red welt and was relieved to breathe normally for the first time in minutes.

"Oh, thank the goddess," Sara choked out as she tilted her head back and uttered another prayer. "You scared the magic out of me, witch."

I opened my mouth to apologize, but she didn't let me, throwing her arms around me and holding on in the tightest of hugs. "I'm sorry," I said in a breathless whisper. "Thank you for helping me."

Sara just held me tighter. "Babe, you never have to apologize to me. Never! What you're going through would shake the strongest of witches, and as far as I'm concerned, you're handling it better than most. It would be odd if you didn't lose it every now and then."

I hadn't told her about the new plan yet. No one outside of Logan and my dad knew that we were trying to force a public acknowledgment of my affinity, to prevent a repeat of what happened to reaper witches in the past.

This shit had been allowed to go on for too long, but if there was one thing I knew about the magical community . . . they weren't great with change. They didn't mess with the status quo or question the rule of the council often. I'd been the same, but this was life or death for me, and I would not go quietly.

When we exited the classroom into the hallway, a lot of students were milling around. Most classes were done for the day, and they were catching up with friends, working out their plans for the evening. Their lives looked really simple from the outside. Free and without imminent destruction breathing down their necks.

I'd been like that when I first arrived at Weatherstone too. A legacy.

Not superpowerful, but still a Hallistar witch with an amazing family and a bright future.

"Are you okay, Pais?" Sara asked, squeezing my hand. I'd been so lost in thought I hadn't even noticed her grab it. "We won't let them hurt you. I don't care what it takes."

Tendrils of that panic tried to slither back through, but I fought them off. "I can't let any of you get hurt because of me," I said, keeping my voice small. I'd already been raving about reapers in the hallway before and had to hope no student had ever heard of my affinity. "I'm worried for myself, of course, but my greatest fear is that I'll get someone I love hurt. I'll behead my-freaking-self before that happens."

Sara rumbled, and it was cute rather than scary when coming from her tiny frame. "Don't even say that out loud, Paisley Hallistar. No one is losing their he—"

The air crackled with magic, and we ground to a halt as dark-robed witches and warlocks filled the hall in front of us. A glance over my shoulder indicated they were behind as well, surrounding us. "You were saying," I whispered, releasing my hold on Sara.

"Paisley Hallistar," a warlock elder said. He looked older than my parents, with just wisps of gray hair and dark, muddy brown eyes. His expression was hard, closed off, as he eyed me with distaste. "You've been requested to appear before the council."

I'd known who I faced the moment their energy registered within my magical essence. There was too much power here, including more than a few spellcasters. "What's this about?" I asked politely, sure that my dad's friend on the council couldn't have arranged this so quickly.

"Shut the Hel up, reaper," a familiar voice snarled. "We

don't speak with demon-witches." Belle's dad stepped forward, and unlike the other somber elders, he wore an expression of absolute delight. "I've waited a long time for your downfall, demon," he said, lowering his voice as he got closer to me, his rank breath washing over my face. "You'll never hurt me or my family again, and I'll take down your spellcaster as well. His days of manipulating our world are done."

My control wavered at that threat, but we were so vastly outnumbered, I knew I couldn't lose it yet. "Paisley cannot be taken without reason," Sara piped up. She didn't sound scared, despite the dozens of council members who surrounded us.

The first elder who spoke to me nudged Elder Monroe to the side. "We have reason to believe that Paisley Hallistar is in possession of an affinity that was outlawed decades ago. It's dangerous and has already caused the death of one student in this school. For that reason, she must stand before a tribunal of elders, who will decide her fate."

Decide my fate. Cute.

We already knew what their decision would be, considering they'd already mentioned my affinity was outlawed. There was no way to remove a witch's magic without the removal of her head.

Or heart. It wasn't a hard science.

"Where will this trial take place?" I asked, still struggling to remain calm. Logan's energy was hitting me through our connection. Despite my best efforts, he'd felt my panic from earlier and was on his way. The only reason he didn't already stand in this hallway was his class had been on the other side of the lake.

"In our main chambers, of course," the elder said, his expression a fraction less severe as he looked me over.

"Could I request that you test my affinity and conduct

your trial right here?" My voice wavered, but I kept it together. "Before the entire school. If you find me to be in possession of a dangerous affinity, as you claim, then a public trial is an excellent deterrent to any others out there."

Whatever softening I thought I'd seen was gone as soon as I gave him a suggestion. "You're in no position to bargain, Ms. Hal—"

"Great idea!" Elder Monroe interrupted, looking thrilled by the prospect. "This will be a lesson for them all to learn, and I will be asking for your senior position on the council, Jeffries, as a punishment for thinking I had lost my mind. I shouldn't have had to bring you proof via my Belle, and I will not let that slight go unpunished."

Jeffries wasn't impressed and looked like he was about to argue again, until other council members voiced their approval of this change of plans. By the time Jeffries's eyes met mine, I didn't imagine the sadness softening them, and I wondered if he was the one Dad had been going to contact. It'd make sense if he'd already tried to discredit Elder Monroe.

My lips tilted in a strained smile, and I tried to wordlessly thank him for what he'd done. With a shake of his head, he turned away and pushed through the robed elders. Once he was gone, I was left facing an elated Elder Monroe. "Come on, demon," he said, his smirk growing. "You're about to be the most important lesson we've ever taught the modern magical world."

Sara tried to stay with me, but she was pushed to the side by a strong blast of air. "It's okay," I called as they marched me away. "Just let Logan and my dad know what's happening. Tell them not to do anything rash, okay?"

I could only just see a flash of her tear-streaked face before air magic wrapped around me, locking my limbs as I was lifted from the ground. It felt like spellcaster energy, and I knew I could fight them, but now wasn't the time. Fighting was a last resort, after I'd pled my case to the magical world.

Acting against every instinct, I pushed my magic down and let them bind and carry me like a criminal through the halls of the classrooms and up the stairs to the assembly hall. The last time I was in here, Headmaster Gregor had stood on the raised stage and addressed the college. Today it was empty as the council members and spellcaster enforcers hoisted me up to the higher level.

"Call the rest of the school," Elder Monroe said to one of his lackeys. My head was locked in place, so all I could see were the thick timbers that lined the ceiling. "And figure out how we can broadcast this to the magical world."

My vision righted a beat later when they produced a chair for me to be magically strapped into. A spellcaster stepped in front of me, and when he waved his hand, the energy locking my face in place eased. Moistening my lips, I shot him a dark smile. "Usually, I'd require dinner and drinks before any kinky bondage, but I guess I can make an exception for you."

He was quite good-looking, if not ten years older than me. He had dark blue eyes, messy brunet hair, and brown skin. "This isn't the time to joke," he said with soft malice, eyeing me like I was a bomb about to explode on his watch. "You're in a lot of fucking trouble."

My annoyance slipped out as I rolled my eyes. "Real genius, aren't you? Imagine being in trouble without doing a single thing wrong, other than being born, of course."

He didn't bother to respond, crossing his arms and settling in on Paisley watch. His energy had my magic controlled to the point that I couldn't touch the elements, but the icy lick of power that connected me to my reaper side remained freely floating inside me. Spellcasters couldn't touch necro magic, and mine was the most beefed-up version of it they'd ever experienced.

The spellcaster's composure was rattled when a clap of thunder shattered the silence and the assembly hall walls started to shake. Logan's power crackled through our bond, smashing the hold the spellcaster had on me, and I'd have been thrilled if it was just those two going head-to-head. But there were dozens of powerful witches and warlocks here.

"Logan, no!" I shouted, jumping to my feet, only to be knocked down again by magic. I was freaking out too hard to see where it came from, my focus only on reaching Logan before he got himself killed.

Looking like he was carved from the gods, a furious Logan charged into the assembly hall, his magic visibly flaring around him in a storm of ice and lightning.

A few of the council's enforcers attempted to get in his way as he marched down the aisle, only to find themselves plastered against the far walls on either side.

Peering around the spellcaster still blocking me, I found Logan's gaze, and when he saw that I was *relatively* unharmed, his pace slowed. "What the fuck is the meaning of this?" His bellow knocked a few of the elders back, leaving them scrambling and red-faced.

To my surprise, the brunet spellcaster shot me a semi-amused glance. "Did he buy you dinner and drinks first?"

A snort of laughter left me, and I had officially lost my mind. "He bought me the fucking restaurant. I'd crawl over broken glass and through lava for Logan Kingston."

Logan heard me, and I felt the heat of his love wash through our bond. "Release my mate, Jacob," he said, close enough now that his magic sent striking sparks across my exposed skin. He was stronger than anyone here one on one, even five on one, but with dozens of elders and their lackeys present, we didn't have the numbers on our side today.

Jacob, the spellcaster holding me, lowered his crossed arms, his magic growing stronger until I swore I could smell the atmosphere they heated. "This is a council matter, Kingston. You don't have any jurisdiction here, not even as powerful and rich as you are."

Logan's laughter was a dark rasp, sending shivers down my spine. "You hold my bonded mate in a farce of a trial. You're breaking your own laws, and I don't think that's just or fair. How about you?"

Elder Monroe stepped forward. "Is the spell in place to record and broadcast the trial?" His loud question echoed around the room.

"Yes," Logan answered, not tearing his gaze from me. "I'm not letting you hurt Paisley. If I have to expose your corruption to the entire magical world, I'll do it."

Heat buffeted me, and I had no idea who it came from, but there was a fire elemental about to lose their shit nearby. Which all made sense when Dad popped into view, hurrying in from a side entrance. He was one of the first to arrive, and I had to assume his friend on the council had filled him in. His face was flushed, but he managed to reel his magic in when he saw I was alive and unharmed. For now.

Before he could say a word, students started to pour through the doorway of the hall. Confused faces flashed toward the stage as they filed in and took their seats much faster than I'd ever seen before.

Looked like this trial was about to get started.

The trial for my life.

CHAPTER 39

While Dad was held back from where I sat by spellcasters blocking his way, no one stopped Logan from joining me on the stage. When his hand landed on my shoulder, the magic holding me in place vanished completely, as if he'd cut through their ties.

"Baby," he rumbled, burying his hands in my hair and pulling me close. "I'm so sorry I wasn't here when they first arrived."

Letting myself fall against him, I breathed him in for a few seconds. "I love you," I whispered. I'd been scared that they would kill me before I had a chance to tell him that one more time.

"Don't you give up, Precious," he growled softly into my ear. "This is far from over."

I knew that. Neither of us were going to just sit here and let them kill me, but that didn't mean we'd win the battle. "I'll never give up," I promised him.

His kiss stole the air from my lungs as the council tittered around us, annoyed that no one could stop Logan. They knew he'd turn this hall into a battlefield, and apparently they were still hoping to murder me without a fuss. Apparently, they'd decided to let Logan remain at my side until judgment was passed.

The hall was almost full by now, and when Headmaster Gregor hurried in, most of the other professors joined him. Dad moved to follow his boss, finally able to get closer.

"Welcome, Council," Headmaster Gregor said, approaching the main group of robe-covered assholes. "To what do I owe the pleasure of you taking over my college?"

Elder Monroe, the spokes-warlock of the moment, stepped forward. "I hope you were unaware of what you housed, Gregor," he said with a snarl. "You didn't keep your students safe, and if you were aware of this abomination in your school, I'll make sure you pay as well."

The headmaster shot me a quick glance, and he looked very confused. He'd had no idea. "Are you referring to Ms. Hallistar? She's a fledgling spellcaster. Her magic has only registered with most of the professors in the last few days. I'd hardly call that anything to worry about."

Monroe studied him closely. "You're about to find out how wrong you are, Gregor. Take your seat."

The headmaster's expression tightened, but he didn't argue at the order, settling into a chair beside a professor I didn't know. Dad didn't follow this time, moving to the other side of me, his hand gently gripping my shoulder. He didn't say a word, but his support said everything.

My friends and family wouldn't leave me. They'd fight and die for me.

I couldn't let that happen.

"Step forward, demon." Elder Monroe had run out of patience.

"Who are you referring to?" I asked quietly. "Demons don't exist on this plane, and I'm clearly standing right here."

The warlock scowled at me and then waved me on. "You

know the abomination you are. And it's time for everyone else in our world to find out too."

Knowing that it was in my best interest to show the world how unthreatening I was, I didn't fight again, stepping forward. Dad and Logan remained near my back as I moved closer to the edge of the stage. Most of the elders and their hired muscle stood behind us, while Jacob and Elder Monroe stepped in on either side of me—they wanted me front and center, so no one could miss who was on trial here.

"Quiet, students," Elder Monroe shouted into the hall, magically amplifying his voice. "The High Council stands before you today, bringing a live and public trial to the magical community. You all will bear witness to this historic event, as for the first time in decades we're faced with the threat of an affinity that was destroyed decades ago."

I didn't know most of the students. There were hundreds across the four years of Weatherstone College, and I'd only met a small number. The most important of whom were in the front row, tense as they stared up at me.

I shook my head when Sara half rose to her feet; Tobias put a hand on her arm to keep her from drawing attention. He kept his gaze over my shoulder on Logan, no doubt waiting for the signal to make a move. Not that I knew what any of them could do, except die with me.

"Paisley Hallistar, a student here at Weatherstone—" my attention returned to Elder Monroe's theatrics "—is not a spellcaster as you all believed but is in fact . . . a night witch. Also known as a *reaper of Purgatory.*"

His voice lowered over my affinity, but he didn't quite get the reaction he must have expected. Most of the students— and professors—simply looked confused. I'd have enjoyed the frustration on the elder's face if I wasn't in such a fucked-up position. "Our education system needs a major overhaul," he groused, waving his hand. At first I thought he was performing magic, but he was indicating that he needed another of the elders. A small ancient-looking woman stepped forward with a black square device in her hand. Monroe turned to take it and used his energy to power the box as light filled the front of the stage.

In the light, images appeared.

The image wasn't solid, it flickered like an old, half-forgotten memory, but there was no mistaking what it showed. A massive field, blackened and burned, covered in what looked like multiple bodies. Two witches stood in the middle of the carnage, and they were soaked in blood, to the point that it dripped from them to pool on the ground.

"The last two recorded reapers," Elder Monroe said, his magically enhanced voice lowering ominously. "After their creatures tore apart a village. You can see what remains."

He sent more energy into the device, and the light expanded, bringing more of the scene into view. The students gasped as the monsters appeared, dozens of them, spanning out behind the two witches. I wasn't sure if the others could see the tethers binding the monsters to the reapers, but I saw their glow immediately.

These two hadn't lost control. Had they really massacred an entire village? Innocents and everything?

"Our ancestors called them demon-witches," Monroe continued in his eerie whisper. "No matter how they start out, they always lose control and destroy those around them. They have the power to call on demons from the Purgatory plane. They are beyond our necromancers, and even worse, they also have the power of a spellcaster. Without any control."

"How do you know that's what happened there?" Haley shouted, sounding fiercer than I'd ever heard. "You have one flickering image from the olden days with no context. Anything could have occurred that day."

Elder Monroe sneered at the audience, seemingly blinded by the light of his projection and unable to see Haley directly. "There's a reason our ancestors chose to destroy their kind and outlaw this affinity. We must protect ourselves." He swung around and pointed at me. "Paisley is a risk to everyone here."

"And yet you have her contained by a dozen council members and a few spellcasters," Logan drawled, seemingly more relaxed than his energy felt through our bond. "Her magic can't be much of a risk, and you can't just condemn and murder an innocent witch because of a past prejudice. We are better than that now. We know better."

"Innocent," Monroe snorted. "She called monsters to this school last year, and a student died. Where is the innocence in that?"

More gasps from the audience, and I let my head hang as guilt smashed into me. This was the judgment I'd expected every time I'd had to tell my story. My friends had remained loyal—most of them—but the other witches and warlocks in this room didn't feel the same way.

They had no idea I wasn't an evil person. As far as they were concerned, my magic had called a monster that killed a student, and it could happen again.

This was a trial of my peers, and I wasn't sure I could win.

"She had no idea of her affinity," my father said, speaking up for the first time. He stared into the eyes of the elder and then out into the hall. "There are many cases of spellcasters accidentally hurting or destroying innocents when their power bloomed. They were all given a second chance on the premise that there was no intent or malice in their actions, and that they were barely out of childhood, with much to learn. It is the responsibility of fully qualified witches and warlocks to guide our young and give them the tools necessary to keep themselves and others safe. In this, we failed Paisley. Our entire community failed her."

I took a shaking step forward until my shoes almost hung off the edge of the stage. The council reacted, lurching toward me, but strangely, Jacob didn't move. "I just wanted to say a few words," I said, but my voice was too soft to be heard over the hall.

Logan shared his magic with me, and my next words were louder. "I'm so sorry about what happened last year." A tear slipped free even as I fought to keep my voice steady. "I promise, I had no idea that I was the one calling the monsters. I'd never even heard of my affinity, and I've been locking my power down ever since I truly found out what magic I hold. But I'm not a bad person."

"A lot of you would remember that Paisley threw herself at the monster in the hallway," Logan added. "Her first instinct was to try to protect students, and she almost died in her attempt. Would an evil witch, as the council here would have you believe she is, risk her life for students she doesn't even know? Her affinity is no eviler than any other, especially spellcasters. The power we handle is immense, and when one of us turns to the darker magic, it's absolutely devastating to the magical community. My father is an example of that. But we don't just destroy an entire affinity because of a few bad eggs." Logan waved his hand toward the flickering projection Elder Monroe had left up for dramatic effect. "We don't know what happened here, but even if two reapers used their powers to hurt others, that shouldn't mean every other reaper is sentenced to death. We have a chance to change now. To stand for more and be better."

The students were quiet, and I couldn't see most of their expressions to know how they were reacting. "It's the council's decision," an elder said. I couldn't see her as she stood in the back of the crowd around me. "We need to test her affinity first and then rule on her fate."

Elder Monroe couldn't have looked happier if he tried. "You'll all see," he said as he turned his broad smile toward the crowd and the live broadcast stream. "You'll learn to fear her as you should."

Five spellcasters joined Jacob, and despite the small flicker of what appeared to be sympathy in his expression, he lifted his hands and released a burst of his power, joining in with the others. It was a stronger-than-expected attack, shuffling Dad and Logan away from me. Before they could recover, a group of elders cast a spelled circle around them, which would hold the two warlocks for only a few minutes. Which was apparently all the time the spellcasters needed.

"Brace yourself, little witch," a female spellcaster said. She was tiny, no more than five feet tall, but her power was like a blowtorch as she gave it everything she had. "You're about to be tested."

If our magic didn't bloom in the year after our twenty-second birthday, there was a way to force it from within. It was rarely used due to the barbaric and dangerous results, which apparently no one cared about today. Logan's rage reached me through the bond, and I felt his power smashing into the elders' spell, almost cracking it in one blow.

"Don't do this," I begged. "If you release my magic through force, I might lose control of the monsters."

Elder Monroe laughed, sounding unhinged. "Like you ever had control of them. Your kind knows nothing but death and destruction."

"No," I screamed, fighting the spellcasters' magic. "You're wrong, and you're risking everyone here. I can call the creatures without all of this. I can show you how I control them."

None of the witches and warlocks holding me cared to listen; they'd already made up their minds. I was the enemy, and all they had to do was prove it.

As I reached for the icy tendrils inside, I closed my eyes and sent one last prayer to Selene that I could stop them from reblooming my magic. An act that would normally be illegal, but clearly the council didn't give a single fuck in their bid to prove I was a demon-witch.

I couldn't let them win. I had to take control and call tethered monsters before it was too late and everything I'd fought for was lost.

CHAPTER 40

"Oh no you don't," the female spellcaster said—she must have felt the surge of my icy magic. "You're not in control here. We are."

The spellcasters hit me with everything they had, and it was so forceful that my own magic slipped beyond my reach. Energy swelled inside until there was an explosion of power, ricocheting across the room in an echoing boom. It sounded as if storms were rolling in, but it was just magic.

Out-of-control reaper magic.

A veil descended over my vision until the air was midnight ice, my breaths visible in front of my face as it turned to night. I'd called a lot of monsters by accident before, these *demons of Purgatory*, but this was more than even that.

The spellcasters' magic had merged our plane with Purgatory's, thinning the veil and colliding two worlds that should never meet.

"Shut it down!" Logan's roar shattered the hold most of the council and spellcasters had on me, but he couldn't take them all. Especially not when one half of his mate bond was spiraling out of control.

The spellcasters released me and turned to take on a now free Logan. Even when their energy stopped blasting me, it wasn't enough to return the planes to their normal separation. What they'd set in motion could not be undone.

My magic continued to drain, seeping from my essence, until I slumped forward, a sluggish pump of blood and power all that kept me alive.

I felt Noah and Dad nearby, fighting to keep the council from me, but one of them had slipped through their battle: Elder Monroe. He dropped down at my side, wedging his hands roughly under my arms to haul me up. He started to drag me across the stage right as screams rang out in the hall, and that was when I felt the monsters arrive.

Unlike the graveyard, they didn't pop in one at a time; they flooded through that thinning veil in the hundreds.

"Evil!" Elder Asshole screamed in my face. "Demon-witch. You did this, it's all your fault, and now you need to die!"

"Dad!" Belle was on the stage, stepping around the battle between the council and my friends. He paused his assault at her soft voice. "You guys forced her magic out and caused this. Paisley is the only one with a chance to fix the imbalance before the demons destroy everything. You have to let her go!"

"What do you mean?" he rasped. His steps slowed as he shook me like I was a rag doll and shouted, "Call your beasts off now!"

He released me as if I were diseased, but Belle caught me before I could face-plant onto the wooden stage. "You've drained all her magic," she said, releasing a distressed moan. "And you never even gave her a chance to show you her control. This isn't what we discussed. You're acting outside of our rules, and *you* brought these creatures by reblooming her magic. Your council needs to either figure out how to send them back or figure out how to give Paisley enough power to do it."

Panic wreathed his features as he squinted out into the chaos of the assembly hall. The screams were getting louder, and there was more magic blasting around than I'd ever felt as students and professors battled the creatures. "We can't send them back! Only a reaper calls the demons of Purgatory."

Belle tightened her arms around me. "If you don't figure it out and fast, we're all going to die. You took out our one chance to deal with them."

Drawing on the flickers of magic left in my center, I tried to reach out for the creatures, but there were just too many. It would require more magic than I'd ever held, even before they had drained me within an inch of my life. "Kill her!" a council-witch shouted. "Rid us of this scum, and the demons will leave."

"That's not a good idea," Belle said, sounding panicked. "If she's our one chance to control them, maybe we should—"

I was yanked out of her hold, and Elder Monroe had me once more. "You'll thank me for this one day, sweetheart." He started to mutter random jumbles of words, before adding, "You'll thank me for the sacrifices I've made to keep you safe."

Amazing sentiment. I loved when killers justified their evil actions by claiming they were to keep others safe.

Belle screamed as he wrenched me across the stage and slammed my head against a hard object. I was too drained to put up any fight, barely keeping my eyes open. "Remove her head," a witch said. "Byron will call fire so there's no mistakes. Slice right through."

A surge of energy sent a shock into my limbs as fight or flight kicked in, but it wasn't enough.

"Paisley!" Logan bellowed his rage, and I felt the brush of his power through our bond.

But we were both too drained.

What they'd done to my magic had impacted Logan's as well, and he'd been fighting dozens of spellcasters and council members from the moment they struck me with their power.

Flames caressed my cheeks, and as I sank into myself, I prayed that my execution would end all of this at least. It would be comforting to know my death would save lives, but a part of me was pretty sure that wasn't going to be the case.

There was an excellent chance that with my demise, the joining of the planes would be a permanent fixture, and the magical world would find out what a life without *any* reaper witches was really like.

The fire increased, and as the witch gave the order to strike, I sent my magic deeper into my essence than I'd ever been. I had no idea what I was searching for in the empty depths of my magical well, but in my last seconds I held on to that feeling of familial magic I'd experienced in the crypt with Gran. If there had been more reapers here today, we could have dealt with the council. A united affinity.

Come on, Gran. I really need your help.

The tiniest spark of blue flame surged in my chest, and I wrapped my essence around it.

Right as the fire-wielding warlock sliced through my neck to remove my head, those flames engulfed me, and everything went dark.

CHAPTER 41

LOGAN

Spellcasters poured onto the stage as I fought to get to Paisley. These assholes had this well planned, knowing I'd destroy any witch or warlock who stood between me and my mate.

There were multiple spellcasters waiting in the wings to take me down. Marcus, Connor, and Sergei approached me from the right, leaving Danielle and another guy I didn't know circling from the left.

"You might be the most powerful," Marcus said, his energy arcing between his hands in small bolts of lightning, "but we have the numbers. She's not worth dying for, bro. No pussy is worth dying for."

This arrogant asshole was the one who was going to die today. I'd been wanting to take him down ever since he put his hands on my girl. *Mine.* My. Fucking. Girl.

The other spellcasters had Paisley, which meant I couldn't drag out this fight; I'd waited what felt like a lifetime to claim my mate, and no one was taking her from me today.

Smashing through the first row of spellcasters, I pushed

more and more power with each blast, while also strengthening my shielding. I let free a crack of lightning focused on Marcus.

Two warlocks had to die today no matter what else happened: Marcus and Monroe.

No mercy.

My magical attack scattered the other spellcasters, but they used air to shoot themselves to their feet almost instantly. Marcus didn't get up, and I ripped through him with a blast of fire, muttering a short spell to ensure that it would burn for at least the next twenty minutes with no chance of quenching.

I left the spellcaster screaming on the floor—there was no time to confirm he was dead, but even if he wasn't, he would suffer greatly.

Darkness split my vision as Paisley's power spilled from her. The monsters had filled the assembly hall, students screamed and started racing through the aisles to try to escape. Using Earth energy, I ruptured the ground and sucked all remaining spellcasters into the abyss before they could offer a counterattack. The stage was restructured above them in another whispered spell, and even though they'd free themselves in a few minutes, I had enough time to get to Paisley.

More spellcasters entered the assembly hall, late-arriving backup. I recognized many from the wars in Europe. Apparently, the meeting with the council had gone so well that they were now working for them.

Racing across the stage, witches and warlocks got in my way. To their own pain.

A burst of power knocked everyone back, and I glanced over the assembly hall to see even more monsters spilling into the room.

Fuck. This day was going from bad to death.

Students screamed, but my focus was internal on the ragged nature of Paisley's magic. She was there, but no more than a wisp, like the time she almost faded in my arms. The air practically glittered with magic as professors and students tried to fight the creatures, but they weren't powerful enough to do much more than hold them back before dying.

We needed Paisley. *I needed her.* My existence was tied irrevocably to the beautiful reaper. I was nothing without her, and my singular focus was getting between her and this fucking council.

Spellcasters circled me, another new group, and as I readied myself to blast them, Elder Florence shouted, *"Kill her!"*

I remembered nothing else as my magic detonated, slamming everyone in near vicinity to the ground. If I'd been at full strength, that would have crushed their skulls, but today, all I could manage was a nasty concussion.

Calling on air to wrap around me, in both shielding and transport, I lifted myself over the crowd, while using earth to fracture the stage again and send more of them below. Utilizing multiple elements at the same time was one of my strengths, and even with waning energy, I was faster and more skilled than most here.

I'd had to be to survive Rafael and be strong enough for my girl.

Paisley deserved the strongest partner, and I would not let her down.

I caught sight of her from across the stage as Monroe dragged her limp body, slamming her head against the edge of a chair. Sending lightning toward their backs, I tried to shield her through our bond, but I was running on fucking dregs of power.

Air faltered beneath me, but I pushed on, determined to place myself between the council and Paisley.

If one of us had to die here today, it sure as Hel wasn't going to be her.

A powerful fire elemental stepped up behind her as I closed in. My winds swept others out of the way, but I hit a wall when I got near him. The council was shielding the fire elemental with everything they had.

Through our bonded link, Paisley was so weak I could barely feel her. Where her icy magic usually resided, there was a blue flame. It clouded my mind as I landed just in time to fall between the fire elemental and Paisley.

Right as he released a blade of burning metal. My weak blast of water diffused the fire as intended, but the edge remained sharp and true as it crashed into Paisley.

I was too late.

The blade sliced through her neck, and I grabbed her in time to see the light fade in her perfect face. A thunderous roar filled the room, and it wasn't until every window shattered, filling the hall with glass, that I realized it came from me.

No. No, please goddess. Fucking NO!

Not Precious. The fucking reason I got up every morning and survived the torturous years with my unhinged father. Not the one piece of good in this fucked-up life.

As I held her to my chest, covered in her blood and my tears, an unnatural calm descended over me. This was followed by the eeriest silence as my power sent such a shockwave through the room that even the monsters were calm—the remnants of the bond which hadn't quite died in my chest yet allowed me to stand with her body against mine.

I already knew I'd be following her into the next existence—there was nothing here for me now—but before I went, everyone here was going to pay.

I would take the entire magical world with me.

Purgatory monsters had nothing on a spellcaster without his bonded mate.

As I tilted my head back, my rage rose until conscious thought was gone and I was a living, breathing force of wrath. The cries from students grew louder as I drew on the energy of the world, of the universe, in a way we were forbidden as spellcasters.

To end it all.

PAISLEY

It was dark in my place of death. A drifting of the tides of time, moving from my birth and subsequent life-journey, toward the end, which came far sooner than I'd ever expected. I had no substance, a soul without a body, as mine had been destroyed.

Without a body, I didn't feel the cold, but as I drifted, I sensed that my surroundings were beyond icy.

Why am I drifting?

Was this the normal pathway to the Eternal Lands? Or was I judged evil, to never find peace within the final plane? The living world remained close to my soul as I dwelled on the mess left behind, and I was surprised to find that I hadn't quite cut my ties with my former life.

Logan. Pain bloomed like newly released magic in my soul. It burned in a way I wished I could die from all over again.

The urge to return to him crushed me in its grasp, and if there were an ability to make noise here, I'd have been screaming.

When a stream of fiery ice appeared before me in blue waves, surrounding whatever remained of the darkness, it drew me closer until I was bathed in its illumination. My magic thrummed to life with me even in death, and I was once again soundlessly screaming in the vacuum.

I could feel other magic around me.

Other reapers.

Paisley . . .

I heard the call as loudly as if it were shouted into my ears, which was impossible because I no longer had those.

Our sister.

It was a chorus of voices, nearly deafening in its intensity.

We are reapers. Your sisters. Our power is a collective.

Their words were a concerto of layered voices, combined with a magic that called strongly to my own.

We drew forth the beasts to devour dark magic. We kept the planes from colliding in a cataclysm of power. We had an important role to play in the magical world and they destroyed that. You are the last of our kind. We cannot let you fall, or everything falls.

The blue flashed, and with it, a scene appeared in the flames. I recognized the buildings immediately . . . I was looking at Weatherstone College. Only, it wasn't the prestigious college I was used to seeing. Instead, its decaying walls dripped with a pulsing darkness that appeared to be devouring the very material used to build the grounds.

This is how the school looks beneath the veil. That darkness of the planes colliding. It's been happening for so many years now that all the worlds are on the brink of collapse. We need your power, Paisley. We need the reapers. You must return.

The pitch and cadence of their layered speech grew until it crashed against me. The blue fire caressed my skin, sinking deeper into my essence, and I felt it tugging at my soul.

I didn't fight it.

I'd always known there had to be a reason for our affinity, and it turned out I was right. The fear of the past was almost the magical world's entire undoing. We were on the brink of destruction, with the five planes merging to annihilate the natural world.

I was all that stood between them and the end.

The voices of my ancestors, sister-witches, the other reapers . . . filled me as thoroughly as the blue fire, and it was only when every cell in my body flooded with power that I realized what the icy fire had been all along.

My connection to the collective magic of reapers. We were never supposed to work alone. We didn't call the monsters and control them without the help of our sisters.

Darkness trembled around us, and with this, a new unease filtered through to me.

Go! they chanted at me. *Your mate is unraveling the existence of the world. You must stop him, and then together, you will save them all.*

Logan!

They filled me with their communal power, the equivalent of hundreds of reaper witches; I'd take this part of them with me to the plane of the living.

My bond to Logan was drawing me back home.

To finish what the council had started.

CHAPTER 42

I jerked to life with a gasp.

Lurching to my feet, I glanced down at the coat that had been covering me, the scent of mint and evergreen embracing me.

Logan.

He'd covered me with his jacket near the edge of the stage, and as I ran my hands over my unmarked throat—memories of that blade slicing into my neck flashed in my mind—I couldn't believe I was alive and whole.

Power thrummed in my center, and as I glanced around the room, it was to find that I was the only one standing. A blanket of magic had the entire room locked down, students, council, and professors alike pummeled into the ground. The foundation of the school was shaking, just as it had been when I'd drifted in the darkness.

Following the flickers of our bond, I glanced up and my world stopped turning.

"Logan!" I shouted, using magic to force my way through his power.

His body floated in the middle of the room, a visible expulsion of energy seeping from him. He'd moved into the darkness of a spellcaster, tapping into the essence of the Earth itself. The power he'd called in his grief was enough to level not just Weatherstone, but half the world.

Magic tingled in my fingertips as my well of energy all but overflowed from the shared power. It took zero effort to use air currents to fly myself up to Logan, where I could see his eyes were closed, dark strands of hair floating around his face. The closer I got to him, the harder it was to penetrate his magical field.

Logan! I shouted through our bond, and for a moment I felt a response. *Mate. I'm only going to say this once. Stop destroying the world.*

Another flicker of awareness. Another sliver of *my* Logan returning to me.

Come on, baby, I coaxed. *I love that you're annihilating everything for me. It's very villain of you. But I still want to live here, so let's save it for later.*

This time the flicker was a lightning bolt, and I gasped as a heavy weight slammed against me. Logan sent us into what remained of the far wall of the assembly hall, turning just before we hit so his back was the one to crack against the wood panels.

His hold on me was so tight . . . so complete . . . that there wasn't a sliver of space between us. As his lips crashed against mine, I was consumed, forgetting the world was ending momentarily.

"Precious," he growled against my swollen, bruised lips. "You fucking died. Don't ever do that to me again."

My laughter was soft, and I felt him shudder in my hold as he tightened his arms until it was painful. Not that I cared. "I'm sorry, love," I said in a breathless whisper. "I was momentarily removed from this plane, but I found support from my sister-witches in another. They showed me the way."

His piercing green gaze focused on me, and I squirmed

under his intensity, even as I soaked up the love that I had almost lost. "Your power . . . baby," he said slowly. "What happened?"

His magic tentatively probed where we were bound.

"Reapers were never supposed to work alone," I told him again, my voice breaking as I recalled floating in the darkness with my sister-witches. "We're guardians. Protectors of the magical world. We were all who stood between the living place and dark energy from the other planes. I know you can't see it, Logan, but our magical world is covered in darkness from the other planes. It's eating away at Earth's energy, and soon there'll be nothing left. Purgatory will filter through every plane, including the Eternal Lands."

Logan kissed me again, as if he couldn't help himself, and I heard him whisper, "Even as a child, you were extraordinary, but as an adult, you are beyond belief."

I wished I could stay wrapped in his arms forever, but our battle wasn't over yet. After placing another kiss against his soft lips, I pulled back. "Can you release the school now, best friend?" It was no longer a phrase used to create distance, but one of shared memories. "We need to show the world that we're too powerful to fuck with—oh, and that we're kind of the only magic preventing the utter destruction of everything."

Logan's face darkened as he took in the room, and the witches, warlocks, and monsters held down by his magic. With his release of the apex elemental energy he'd been channeling, the shaking of the building had eased. "I'm going to destroy the council," he told me, no inflection in his tone as his fingers flexed against my skin. "There's nothing that can save them now. We will rebuild the magical world with those more worthy."

Capturing his chin, I held him still so I could glare into his face. "Logan Kingston. You will *not* murder dozens of witches and warlocks. That's not the way forward."

The slightest smirk played around his lips. "There's a few less than there was already," he admitted. "Belle no longer has a father, and the witch who ordered your death . . . she's in a million pieces. Marcus got fried, though he might still be alive and wishing he was dead."

I examined his expression to determine if he was kidding or not—*definitely not*. "Are you angry about that?" he asked with little more than curiosity in his tone. "Do you wish I'd acted less savagely?"

It took me about one heartbeat to decide how I felt. "I'm not angry at all. If they'd hurt you, I'd have let my demons tear them and this entire world to pieces."

I'd finally accepted that my monsters were demons from Purgatory.

Logan's smile was feral, and when we kissed this time, I felt him drawing his magic out of the hall and back into our bond. I already thrummed with a hundred times more power than I'd ever contained before, and when we added in the spellcaster energy, we were an atomic bomb about to explode. This amount of power couldn't remain within us, and thanks to my sister-witches, I had a very good idea of what we needed to do next.

We landed in the middle of the chaos. Logan's power had kept everyone as living statues, aware of what he was about to bring down on them, but without the means to break his energy and stop him. Now they were free, the battle between demons and students resumed, but they were all very aware of Logan and me nearby.

We were as dangerous as the monsters and they knew it.

Without thought, I tethered all of the dark creatures.

One moment they raged in mindless pursuit of blood, and the next I had them in my grasp, moving them toward me. "Can we broadcast this again?" I asked Logan, searching for my friends and family in the crowd. There were a lot of witches and warlocks here I loved, and I needed to know they were all okay.

"It never stopped," he said to me, looking through the crowd as well.

Excellent. That meant whatever I did now would be broadcast to the world.

As the students grasped that they were no longer fighting for their lives, I sent almost all of the demons back to Purgatory. Five remained standing behind Logan and me, silently observing the confused students.

"Pais!" Sara burst out of the crowd, looking a right mess. Her dark hair was everywhere, and she had a nasty cut on her cheek, but she was alive. Haley pounced on us a few moments later, and I wasn't surprised to see Noah and Tobias right behind her. When Noah reached us, he leaned over and murmured a few words to Logan that I couldn't hear, but I would guess they were something along the lines of *Thanks for not actually destroying us all in your rage, bro.*

"Bring the council here," I said to Logan, drawing my demons closer. They were a mixed group including a bear, a centipede, and a spider, and as they towered over us, I knew we painted a terrifying picture. My aim, before they partially removed my fucking head, had been to present myself as harmless and sweet. A complete nonthreat.

That was no longer the plan.

My friends glanced up at the demons but didn't move away, demonstrating once again their complete and utter trust in me.

"Little Gem! You're alive!"

At Dad's call, the first tears pricked my eyes, but it wasn't time to fall apart. *Not yet.*

He crashed against me, and I fell into his familiar warmth and ashy scent. "Trevor and J?" I asked as I pulled away.

"They're fine," he told me, brushing his hand over my cheek, pushing my hair behind my ear. "How are you okay though? I saw them use fire magic against you. I saw you fall . . ." He wore a look of anguish that I hoped to never see again. It shattered my hold over my emotions, and a few of the tears slipped free.

"The power of the other reapers saved me." This was an explanation for the world, so I wasn't surprised when my magic swelled, and my voice amplified to fill the hall. "Reapers are a guardian affinity. We're supposed to be a collective, the only affinity who can truly join their powers to keep this world safe. We stopped the five planes of existence from colliding and collapsing into one, which would have the darkness of the realms devouring Earth's natural light and energy. But the Council of Fools, through the years, murdered us all. We're lucky that the fallen reapers lent me their powers, and now I have the means to make it right."

The dark veil that had appeared when they rebloomed my energy was no longer present; it had been healed with my return and the banishing of the demons. But that was only the tip of the problems the magical world faced.

It was time to show them what they'd wrought with their ignorant actions.

Icy energy flowed from me, and my eyesight tilted for a breath. When it rightened itself, the darkness I'd seen in the vision from the reaper witches coated everything—the walls and floors where students sat and lay, *everything.*

"This is dark energy," I said harshly. "It's from Purgatory, and it's the main food source of my demons."

Tugging on the tethers of the five that remained, I sent them out to do what they did best: devour the darkness. They raced forward, and students started screaming again, but they shut the fuck up when they realized that nothing was attacking them.

The demons were fast. Starting in one corner, within minutes they had eaten through a decent chunk of inky energy.

"I've seen them do this before," I said, my voice no longer amplified. "I thought they were chomping on air because I didn't look deeply enough into the magic around us."

Half a dozen cloaked members of the council were all that remained. Logan's magic was wrapped around them as he dragged them down to kneel before me.

It was a nice, but unnecessary, touch.

I didn't make him release them though.

"You need me," I said coldly. "You almost destroyed the world when you murdered me without trial. I'm the last reaper, and therefore the only one who can bring the demons here and ask them *very nicely* to eat up the darkness that's throwing the balance of our world out of order." I angrily jabbed my finger at the walls. "*That* covers our magical world. It'll take me decades to clean up your mess."

Okay, it wasn't exactly their mess, since most reapers were destroyed long ago. It also wouldn't take decades with the power of hundreds of reapers at my disposal. But there were points to be made, and I wanted them really drilled home.

"You're one reaper. Can you control enough of the demons to truly save our world?" The council member lifted his head to reveal a surprising youthfulness. He couldn't be older than his late thirties, and considering members were generally fifty at the youngest, he must be quite powerful.

"I'm the only hope you've got, so you better pray to Selene and every other goddess that I'm enough. And you better be grateful that I'm even willing to save this world—and your sorry ass with it." I was done with their shit, and I was done with the magical world as it stood, but I wouldn't let them all die. They were lucky I loved my family, friends, and Logan fucking Kingston. Otherwise, they'd be screwed.

"I'm finished with college," I said, more to myself than anyone else. "I already have an important role in the magical world."

"We will pay you," another council member piped up, a woman who looked like she was a few years from death, her pale skin thin and wrinkled. "A fortune. You can name your price."

"She doesn't want your blood money," Logan snarled. "I take care of my mate."

My lips twitched, but I managed not to laugh. I gave them one last warning: "You won't ever control us, not with your money or your magic. Pray that I don't stop caring at some point, because who is left to take my place?"

With that, I wrapped my arms around Logan and breathed him in, the last of my panic and pain fading under his touch. "I'll keep you safe while you keep the world safe," he whispered. "I love you, Precious."

"I love you too," I said on a sob. "You brought me back from the deathly planes, Logan. Our bond led me to the light."

The mention of my death had him grumbling as magic

blazed between us, but he didn't lose it again. He just held me, which was exactly what I needed.

When I lifted my head to check on my demons, I noticed a small witch standing near the edge of the aisle between overturned chairs. Belle met my eyes, and the sadness there was overwhelming, but she didn't come any closer.

We kept eye contact for several long seconds, before she nodded and turned to leave the room. I wasn't sure we'd ever recover our friendship after what happened, but in the end she'd tried to reason with her father *for me* before he went too far.

That was important, especially if it went further with Trevor and her. She might be my sister-in-law one day, and if that happened, I would find forgiveness. Eventually.

EPILOGUE

"Who's ready to rock this fucking stadium! Here's who you've all been waiting for . . . Caaaasterrrrrs!"

The autotuned voice rang out and the crowd screamed to near deafening levels as the band ran onto the stage. Noah settled in behind his drums, while Logan and Tobias took their places near the front of the stage, guitars strapped over their shoulders.

Their magical masks were in place, but we knew what they had planned for tonight. This was the moment the world would realize whom they'd been worshipping.

"I'm so excited and nervous I could vomit," Haley said, running her hands through her tousled brown curls for the twentieth time. She was dressed in a short, light blue baby doll dress, the skirt floating around her waist and hips while the bodice hugged her slim frame. "I can't believe they're going to face reveal tonight."

The guys had had many discussions over the past few days about this moment. They knew it might cost them fans; some of the appeal in their music was the mystery that surrounded their identities. But they were done hiding from the world.

Logan needed music almost as much as he needed me—it was a part of his soul. He wanted to engage more with his fans, and to do so, he had to step into the light.

"They're so fucking hot, as if this won't increase their popularity by a million percent," Sara scoffed. She was in the tightest dress I'd ever seen that wasn't actually body paint. It was black, short, and had her tits on full display. Add in five-inch stilettos and she was going to give Tobias spank bank material for years. Those two weren't as loved up as Logan and me, or Haley and Noah, but they'd almost found their way there.

Tugging my crystal necklaces with my hands, I let their energy race through me, drawing up the reaper powers in my center. The last few months had been a whirlwind of work and drama. The extra power of my ancestors had come in handy as I sent demons across the world to right the imbalance of darkness from the planes, and as the energy of my sister-witches waned, I used crystals to boost my own.

Over the months, the balance between the five planes had begun to restore slowly. My work would never be done, but I was no longer destined to lose my head. If anything, the council now treated me as a precious commodity, and if one more person asked me if I was planning on popping out a few extra reapers anytime soon, I'd probably transport them straight to Purgatory.

Logan and I were enjoying the freedom to explore our relationship, and even when we were ready for kids, there were absolutely no guarantees that I'd pass the gene on.

Though, I had a feeling that with the need for my kind, fate might step in to repopulate our bloodline.

The crowd's screams pulled me back to the present, and I realized I'd missed the band's introduction. They were already into their opening song: "Burn Them All Down."

Casters' music was as familiar to me as my own heartbeat now. I'd know the soothing sounds anywhere. Logan's power thrummed in my chest, his love for me filtering through each strum of his guitar and the delicious rasp of his voice as he sang about destroying the ones who tried to keep love apart. He dedicated that one to Rafael Kingston. May he rest in Hel.

"I want to have his babies," Haley said with a sigh, and I jerked around to find her staring dreamily at Noah from where we stood backstage. "He's honestly more than I ever imagined I'd find in a warlock. Like . . . am I dreaming? Did I stumble into a fantasy novel? It's too much."

She fanned her face with her hand, a flush slowly rising in her cheeks. Girl was going to combust if she kept drooling over her boyfriend.

Noah had been planning on leaving Weatherstone with Logan and me, but then he couldn't part from Haley. They shared a dorm room now and, according to my bestie, missed most of their morning classes. My nerdy friend had discovered her horny side, and she was exploring it to its full extent.

"I'm happy for you," I said, throwing my arm around her shoulders and pulling her into my side. I did the same with Sara on the other side, the three of us swaying together as our boys played their music.

"Belle asked about you yesterday before we left," Sara said when we were about ten songs deep into the band's set. "She also told me that everything has been awkward with Trevor, and she's not sure they're going to make it."

I didn't react. I'd shed more than a few tears over Belle, and even though we'd never found our way back to friendship, I didn't feel any bad will toward her these days. I wasn't surprised that she and Trevor had issues though. He was finding it difficult to forget the part she played in his sister losing her head. Problem was, he loved her . . . a lot.

I didn't want either of them miserable, so I kept my opinions to myself. They'd either work it out or not, and I'd support Trevor no matter what he decided.

Keeping my focus on the stage, my heart started to race when the music eased. Logan softly strummed his guitar in one of his favorite chord sequences, the lilting melody intricately woven in and around itself. A soothing yet tantalizing sound. "We're so grateful for your years of support," he said into the mic, that delicious rasp of his deep voice sending trills down my spine. "You followed us without ever knowing what lay behind our masks, and as a reward, we were wondering if . . . you'd like to know?"

The crowd lost their fucking minds. They jumped and screamed, and there was the sense that a riot would break out any second. Logan's laughter had me unconsciously taking a step toward him, our bond urging me closer. "Well, if you insist."

Logan walked toward Noah, who stood from his kit, Tobias joining them from the side. They huddled together as Logan removed the magic that hid their faces, while they mimed the actions of removing a mask. Flutters of energy caressed my skin, but humans would never notice, and when the guys turned around, all that was left were their devastatingly handsome faces, there for the world to see.

"I'm Logan Kingston," he called to the audience, stepping forward. "And these are my brothers, Noah and Tobias." The three of them remained on the edge of the stage as the screams of twenty thousand of their fans nearly lifted the ceiling on the indoor stadium. "We're Casters."

"We're going to be fighting off the ladies now," Sara said with a sigh, but the smallest of smiles played around her lips. With magic, it would never be an issue for us. We could cast a spell that would make us unnoticeable when we walked down the street. Or to confuse whomever we wanted, even other witches and warlocks. Not that Logan and I weren't already quite famous in our world after our battle was broadcast across the entire magical community.

Famous and feared, which allowed us to remain unaccosted wherever we went.

It was nice.

The crowd screamed for so long I wondered how they still had voices, but eventually they let the band return to their instruments and finish their set. When they walked off-stage, the audience called for an encore for a solid twenty minutes. To no avail.

Backstage, Logan scooped me into his arms. Unlike the girls, I was dressed in tight black jeans, a red corset top, and Logan's leather jacket, so I flashed no one when I wrapped my legs around his waist. He was sweaty, but I didn't care. I hugged his hard body as close as I could get. "You were incredible," I said, pressing kisses all over his face before I found his lips.

A rumble rocked his chest, and I found myself slammed against a nearby wall as he demanded entry to my mouth. When I parted my lips, his tongue swept across mine, and he controlled and dominated the kiss until I was panting and arching, needing relief.

"I love you so fucking much, mate," he growled, his adrenaline high enough that I could feel his power zapping through our bond. "I need to be inside you. Right. Fucking. Now."

My moan wasn't as soft as I thought, but no one was paying attention to us. Our best friends were all wrapped up in each other, and the crew was busy clearing the stage. "Let's get out of here," I rasped, all the moisture in my body flooding lower, leaving my mouth dry. The desire I felt for Logan was borderline unbearable. I was going to lose control if he didn't sate this need soon.

"We're out," he called to the others, his piercing gaze never leaving my face.

Our friends catcalled after us. "We'll be at the farmhouse tomorrow for breakfast," Tobias shouted. "Nice and early."

Logan sent him flying into the wall with a well-placed zap of energy, moving so fast there was no chance of Tobias countering. "Okay, lunchtime," he groaned as Logan took us into a back room. "Stay safe, kids."

Anything else he had to say was cut off by the door closing. Logan's grip on my thighs tightened as he pulled me flush against his hard length. "You're the greatest magic I've ever known," he whispered against my cheek, his energy flooding me until I temporarily forgot the English language.

"Mine. Forever," I mumbled against his mouth, and he had me in such a daze I missed our transport magic arriving and the journey through to our home.

The lavender farm had felt like home from the first time I'd stepped through these gates.

Tonight, Misti, our massive guard cat, padded down to us from where she'd been waiting on the front porch, and I'd never felt such comfort.

Logan had given me so much. Everything, really.

Tonight, we would christen every room in our house. Again.

If this was how I got to live the rest of my life, I'd gladly die over and over.

I'd die for one more second with my mate.

Just like this.

★　★　★　★　★

ACKNOWLEDGMENTS

Wow. I'm sitting here staring at that last word, wondering how I can ever let Paisley and Logan go. Not only them, but the rest of this world and the supporting characters. I love them all. I dream about them so often that I wonder if maybe they did leave a little of their magic in these pages.

Thank you to everyone who shared and loved on this series during the past twelve-plus months. All of the bloggers, readers, influencers, and anyone else in the amazing book community. You made my day every time I saw your posts and reels and beautiful smiling faces. I wouldn't be here without your amazing support, and I need you to know just how grateful I am.

Thank you to my incredible publishing team at MIRA and HarperCollins. Especially Cat Clyne, who honestly has shown so much faith and belief in my work. She picked this series up from a synopsis and three chapters. *THREE CHAPTERS*. She never really knew how this would play out in full, and since I handed her books one and two at the same time (written back to back), she just had to trust that I wouldn't screw up the story, HAH! Her faith in me means everything. You're the best, Cat, and I hope to have many more years working with you.

Thank you to my agents, Flavia Viotti and Meire Dias, at Bookcase Literary Agency. You're always in my corner, and I wouldn't have been able to make Weatherstone College happen without your support.

Thank you to the amazing editors, proofers, art director Mary Luna and cover artist Franziska Stern, Ambur Hostyn of the marketing team, publicists, and the many others who work tirelessly behind the scenes to bring these books to life. The deluxe editions are some of my favorites, and I'm in awe of your talents. An extra special thanks to my PA, Jane Catherine, who was such an enthusiastic supporter of this book and world.

Thank you to my husband, as always, for loving me unconditionally, supporting me in every way he can, and keeping me from spiraling when everything gets to be too much. I couldn't do this without you. I love you eternally. Thank you to my two daughters, who are the magic in my world. Your mum loves you more than life, and I would destroy worlds for you.

Until next time, which hopefully won't be too long, sending you all the hugs and sexy book boyfriends.

Love,
Jaymin